Placing his finger beneath her chin, Ewen tipped her face up to his.

'Would you care to tell me what the Countess was referring to when she said you were already skating on thin ice? You told me you were betrothed and that when you walked away it caused a scandal. Is there anything else you want to tell me?'

Shrugging his finger away, she shook her head. 'No.'

'There must have been something in your past to warrant her remark.'

'There's nothing, I tell you—except that suddenly and painfully I learned that when one breaks with convention one can never crawl back to its comforting shell again. I became cut off from the past and all its connections. At the time the realisation was both chilling and daunting, but I will not— cannot—go back.'

AUTHOR NOTE

CAUGHT IN SCANDAL'S STORM is the sequel to A TRAITOR'S TOUCH. Characters that appeared in A TRAITOR'S TOUCH are mentioned, and appear in the final pages of CAUGHT IN SCANDAL'S STORM, which can be read as a stand-alone book.

Ewen Tremain is the younger brother of Simon Tremain, the hero of A TRAITOR'S TOUCH, who, as a fugitive, was forced to flee Scotland following the Battle of Culloden. CAUGHT IN SCANDAL'S STORM picks up twenty years after the battle.

After eight years as a slave in North Africa, Ewen Tremain returns to civilisation to forge a new life for himself—but he is haunted by the betrayal of a beautiful woman and the terrible sufferings he endured at the hands of his captors. Only when he meets Alice Frobisher does he begin to feel that happiness is within his reach. But Alice, who is trying to come to terms with a disastrous betrothal which forced her to leave Paris to avoid further scandal, has issues of her own to deal with.

Both Ewen and Alice are beset with emotional conflicts that must be resolved before they can emerge victorious in the battle for their love.

CAUGHT IN
SCANDAL'S STORM

Helen Dickson

First published in Great Britain 2015
by Mills & Boon, an imprint of Harlequin (UK) Limited,
Large Print edition 2015
Harlequin (UK) Limited, Eton House, 18-24 Paradise Road,
Richmond, Surrey TW9 1SR

© 2015 Helen Dickson

ISBN: 978-0-263-25545-4

Harlequin (UK) Limited's policy is to use papers that are natural,
renewable and recyclable products and made from wood grown in
sustainable forests. The logging and manufacturing processes conform
to the legal environmental regulations of the country of origin.

Printed and bound in Great Britain
by CPI Antony Rowe, Chippenham, Wiltshire

Helen Dickson was born and lives in South Yorkshire, with her retired farm manager husband. Having moved out of the busy farmhouse where she raised their two sons, she has more time to indulge in her favourite pastimes. She enjoys being outdoors, travelling, reading and music. An incurable romantic, she writes for pleasure. It was a love of history that drove her to writing historical fiction.

Previous novels by Helen Dickson:

THE DEFIANT DEBUTANTE
ROGUE'S WIDOW, GENTLEMAN'S WIFE
TRAITOR OR TEMPTRESS
WICKED PLEASURES
  (part of *Christmas by Candlelight*)
A SCOUNDREL OF CONSEQUENCE
FORBIDDEN LORD
SCANDALOUS SECRET, DEFIANT BRIDE
FROM GOVERNESS TO SOCIETY BRIDE
MISTRESS BELOW DECK
THE BRIDE WORE SCANDAL
SEDUCING MISS LOCKWOOD
DESTITUTE ON HIS DOORSTEP
MARRYING MISS MONKTON
DIAMONDS, DECEPTION AND THE DEBUTANTE
BEAUTY IN BREECHES
MISS CAMERON'S FALL FROM GRACE
THE HOUSEMAID'S SCANDALOUS SECRET*
WHEN MARRYING A DUKE…
THE DEVIL CLAIMS A WIFE
THE MASTER OF STONEGRAVE HALL
MISHAP MARRIAGE
A TRAITOR'S TOUCH

Castonbury Park Regency mini-series

And in Mills & Boon® Historical *Undone!* eBooks:
ONE RECKLESS NIGHT

Did you know that some of these novels are also available as eBooks? Visit www.millsandboon.co.uk

Prologue

1746—after the Battle of Culloden

Prince Charles Edward Stuart had come to Scotland to reclaim his father's throne and restore the Stuart monarchy. This handsome young man's head was full of great revolutionary ideas, ideas that had driven him to associate with those who would turn a revolution into a bloodbath on Culloden Field.

He had defeated the Government army at Prestonpans, but the Jacobite troops were cut to pieces on Culloden Moor. Prince Charles had become a fugitive fleeing for his life, leaving those who had supported him to face the brutal retribution of his enemies.

Government repression was brutal. Homes were raided in the search for Jacobites. Some were driven into the hills and those captured were swiftly put either to the bayonet, the hangman's rope, or burnt alive in their homes. Women, children and the old were no exception. No quarter was given.

At Rosslea, the ancestral home of Iain Frobisher in the borderlands, the servants, fearing for their families and their lives, fled. Mary Frobisher was left alone with her twelve-year-old son William and her month-old baby daughter Alice. Two of her sons had been killed on Culloden Field; her husband, Iain Frobisher, was a prisoner of the English.

The house stood high upon a promontory overlooking the village below. When dusk came there was a stirring in the valley. Scarlet-coated men moved among the cottages. They came with their torches to burn and to kill. Mary heard musket fire, then screams. They would soon set their sights on Rosslea.

Mary was prepared. Gathering what was left of her family and the few possessions she could carry, her money and jewels sewn into the seams of her cloak and gown, she was quickly away to the cover of the trees.

When darkness shrouded the land, the glow of fire from Rosslea lit up the sky. It was a blazing inferno, feeding greedily on the precious treasures it housed, the flames penetrating high into the night sky. Biting back her tears, Mary turned away. Now was not the time to show weakness.

Numb with shock and driven by fear, carrying Alice wrapped in a plaid and urging William on, familiar with the terrain having lived in these parts all of her life, she followed the drovers' roads over the border. She managed to reach the west coast and cross to Ireland. From there she took ship for France, joining others who had fled persecution after Culloden.

It was in Paris where she learned of the death of her husband. Mourning three members of her beloved family, Mary managed to make a life for those who were left.

Ten years later—
somewhere off the coast of North Africa

Lieutenant Ewen Tremain could not be sure whether it was the scratching of a rat—a faint, irregular rasping, made audible only by the intense, muffled silence of the night, coming from somewhere between the oak bulwark that divided the cabins and narrow passageways of his Majesty's ship the *Defiance*—or another soft, furtive sound that had awakened him.

It was scarcely more than a gentle lapping of water against the hull—or could it be the splash of oars? Surely not. It must have been the rat that had awakened him, he thought, relaxing with a small sigh. It was absurd that such a small thing should have dragged him out of sleep and into such tense and absolute wakefulness. His nerves must be getting the better of him. Or perhaps it was the ship, becalmed for four days, that had something to do with it.

He tossed and turned restlessly, but he was unable to go back to sleep—that faint rasping sound frayed at his nerves. Slowly, very slowly, a peculiar sense of unease stole into the small cabin—a feeling of urgency and disquiet that was almost a tangible thing. It seemed to creep nearer and to stand at the side of him, whispering, prompting, prodding his tired brain into wakefulness.

Rolling off his bunk, he shrugged himself into his clothes and went up on to the deck, deserted except for the man keeping lookout for any corsair vessels. Standing by the rail, he gazed into the darkness. A sea mist hung low in the air, veiling the ship in a damp, diaphanous shroud. The night and the brooding silence seemed to take a stealthy step closer and breathe a lurking menace about the isolated ship. There was something out there that clamoured with a wordless persistence for attention. Ewen's tired brain shrugged off its lethargy and was all at once alert and clear.

Suddenly, for the first time in days, there was a breeze, a faint uneasy breath of wind that sighed and whispered among the rigging and ruffled the canvas.

A bleary-eyed Captain Milton appeared beside him, rubbing his stubbled chin. 'The wind's getting up, Mr Tremain. Come dawn we'll be underway.'

Ewen remained silent, straining his ears. The splash of oars became more distinct. Suddenly, out of the mist a dark, sinister shape emerged, closely followed by another two ships, the oars manned by galley slaves. When the flag on the mainmasts became clear—a human skull on a dark background—it became apparent that the mysterious ships had not come in friendship. Ewen stared, held in the grip of a sudden, sickening premonition of disaster as he considered the evil fate which, in the shape of two great white-winged ships, had come out of the mist to menace them.

Unless some unexpected turn of events occurred, their chance of escaping seemed slender. To be captured by Islamic Barbary corsairs, who treated their captives with ruthless savagery, or to die in circumstances too horrible to contemplate, was a terrifying thing indeed.

Returning to Britain from West Africa, it was the summer of 1756, when Ewen Tremain, along with Captain Milton and the crew of the *Defiance*, was captured by Barbary corsairs and taken in chains to the great slave market in Sale in Morocco. Poked and prodded and put through his paces, he was sold at auction to the highest bidder, a tyrannical brother of the Sultan.

Resourceful, resilient and quick-thinking, Ewen was soon selected for special treatment. As a personal slave of his master, while dreaming of his home, his family and freedom, he witnessed at first hand the barbaric splendour of the Moroccan Court, as well as experiencing daily terror.

When his master was absent from the palace for six weeks, his circumstances changed for the worse when his eyes lighted on a Moorish girl named Etta. Cruel, savage, passionate and beautiful, with tigerish green-and-gold eyes, decked in gold and pearls, she was his master's favourite concubine. It was whispered that more than one handsome, well-muscled slave had entered her apartment by night through a secret door to satisfy her sexual appetite, their corpses later found washed up on the shore.

Handsome, haughty and virile, and unable to see any way out of his prison, except for the grave, Ewen was unable to resist Etta. Twining her slender arms about his neck and using all her witchery to captivate him, she made him her pliant, willing slave. Their clandestine meetings were made with great risk and their lovemaking did not lack passion. She was a bright and beautiful beacon in Ewen's dark and miserable world. He found a kind of happiness when he was in the arms of this infidel concubine who seemed to have cast a spell on him and in whose body he found the forgetfulness he craved.

A chivalrous and honest man, who would later deplore the fact that he had kept such a large streak of naiveté in his make-up, Ewen found it hard to grasp the guile behind the soft smiles, or fond words, especially when they came from the mouth of this exotic concubine.

He believed Etta loved him, but how purring and persuasive and soothing that voice of hers could be. He could not have guessed for a moment what weight of treachery it concealed. When his master returned to the palace and summoned Etta, she went to him willingly, happy that her position as number one concubine would resume. Since Ewen did not appeal to her heart or her feelings, she felt strong. The smile and caressing voice she bestowed on him when passing could not cancel out the hard, calculating expression of her eyes, or her betrayal when she denounced him to her master, accusing him of lusting after her even after she had spurned him.

Ewen saw what she did, heard her denounce him. He hung there, his eyes blinded by a scalding rush of tears. When he straightened at last, the tears were gone. What had come to take their place was rage at his own weakness.

And so she condemned him.

He was to be given one hundred lashes, and, if he survived, he would be consigned to the galleys and chained to an oar for the remainder of his life.

Ewen had thought himself indestructible. But what man of flesh and blood could hope to prevail against these barbarians? At first he had hoped against all hope and reason that he would emerge from his servitude miraculously safe and sound.

But now he realised that there would be no miracle—until the galley was sunk by a British man-of-war off the coast of Spain.

Ewen could not believe his good fortune when the oar he had been chained to for two miserable years snapped and he was eventually washed ashore. There was one other survivor—the youth Amir who had worked on the same oar every day for the past year. He lay close by on the sand. His body was hunched, the knees drawn up to his chin, arms bent, in the position babies are supposed to have within a mother's womb. He looked small, vulnerable, helpless. A feeling of pity for the sad, lonely youth overwhelmed Ewen. His heart went out to him as it had many times. He wanted to hold him as he had never held a child. It was a totally new feeling for him.

Lying there with the wet sand beneath him, Ewen closed his eyes and prayed to God with all the fervour of his being that they would both survive. Slowly, strength began to flow into him. It surged within him, bringing the peace of determination. Picking himself up, he went to Amir. The youth stirred, and, supporting each other, they made their way inland.

After many days, as they toiled over the steep,

difficult terrain, Ewen's thoughts were not on his present discomfort. He kept imagining that he saw the face of Etta stepping out of the mist, with her treacherous smile and cat-like eyes, which held nothing but betrayal. His throat became tight with pain and anger and he had to close his eyes against the wetness. Dragged down with weariness, for a moment he suffered so cruelly that he was tempted to lay himself down and wait for death. Only Amir and the instinct of self-preservation—a force greater than his pain and suffering—urged him to keep going.

His hope of seeing his family again was powerful enough to have carried him through so many trials. The journey from Morocco to the towering peaks of the Spanish hills and the refuge of the monastery a traveller had directed them to was a Calvary for Ewen.

When Amir stumbled and fell, Ewen raised him to his feet and held him. 'Come, Amir. Be strong,' he urged while his own strength was failing. 'The monastery can't be far now.'

Just then, as if to lend weight to his words, the faint sound of a single bell reached him through the air and he gave a sigh of relief.

'The bell for lost travellers! We are on the right path!'

At last they came in sight of the monastery, where the man had told them men of all faiths and creeds were given sanctuary. The moon shone clear of cloud and its cold light streamed down on the low-roofed buildings with thick walls huddled at the foot of a narrow pass. A square tower stood over them and the road passed under a stone archway into the ancient monastery.

From somewhere within those walls came the faint sound of religious chanting. It was so unexpected and so unfamiliar that Ewen stopped to listen. A faint hope awakened in him. He found himself believing that the old chant must be God's answer to his fervent prayer. He had reached the limit of his strength. Incapable of taking another step, he collapsed on to his knees. He saw the dim glow of lanterns passing to and fro, carried by human hands. To the weary man, these lights signified life and warmth and hope.

Chapter One

1766

The swirling snow encircled the young woman, freezing her body and mind with a numbness that blocked her senses, but could do nothing to alleviate the pain in her heart. As she stumbled through the park she clutched her cloak tightly beneath her chin, the wide hood covering her hair. Blinded with snowflakes and buffeted by wind, she was unaware of the intense cold which numbed her hands and feet and turned her cheeks to ice. Her gait was that of a person in pain, but her pain was not physical. Her body was strong and youthful and healthy with the benefits of good living.

The whirling white flakes were coming down so thickly that she could not see more than a yard in front. She thought of her father, a man she could not remember, and was surprised to feel tears pricking her eyes. It had been so long. Since she had left Philippe, she had not been able to cry. She feared that if she gave way for a moment, she would shatter into a thousand pieces and never stop. So she kept her emotions wrapped tightly inside her. But now, the thought that her father was alive when she had thought him dead, that she would see him, pierced the barrier of her emotions and her cheeks were flooded with her tears.

Suddenly a dark form loomed up through the driving snow immediately ahead of her. She swerved wildly, but she was too late and cannoned into something solid. She would have fallen but for a hand that gripped her arm and held her upright. Panic struck her and she tried to wrench herself away, but the grip on her arm might have been a vice. A man's voice said curtly, 'What the devil are you doing out in this?'

Alice opened her mouth, but she was unable to speak. Her throat, along with the rest of her, seemed frozen and the wind drove thick snowflakes into her eyes, blinding her.

'What's the matter?' the man demanded, his voice deep and rough. 'Lost your voice?'

Her captor raised his gloved hand and brushed the snow roughly from her face, peering down at her in the hazy light. She had a fleeting impression, blurred by the driving snow, of height, and a pair of eyes, hard and flint grey and very angry, before her own were blinded with snow once more. The man muttered a low curse under his breath. She did not recognise the voice and she was suddenly very afraid.

The grip on her arm relaxed and in that moment, with a strength born of fear, she wrenched her arm free and fled as fast as she was able. Thankfully the ground beneath the trees was in her favour, being sheltered and only thinly covered with snow, and she was able to widen the gap between them. She heard him call out to her, but he did not follow as she vanished into a seemingly solid wall of snow.

Fifteen minutes later, blinded by snow and buffeted by wind, breathless and shaken by her encounter with the stranger, Alice reached Hislop House in the heart of Piccadilly. Hislop House was the grand residence of Lady Margaret Hislop, Countess of Marchington. At present it was all abustle as servants busied themselves preparing for the grand occasion Lady Marchington was hosting that very night, to announce the betrothal of her niece Roberta to Viscount Pemberton, the Earl of Winterworth's eldest son. Alice barely had time to compose herself before Roberta came hurrying to her across the hall.

'I'm relieved to see you back, Alice. Although why you had to go off like that with a blizzard screaming outside escapes me.'

'You know why, Roberta,' she replied, managing with a supreme effort of will to keep her emotions well hidden. 'I can't bear being cooped up all the time. It's so stuffy in the house. I need to breathe the fresh air.'

'I know and I'm not complaining, but you know Aunt Margaret doesn't like you to go out on your own. You should have taken one of the servants.'

Alice heaved a rueful sigh. 'I hoped she wouldn't notice.'

Alice had ignored the stricture which required that she take someone with her, after receiving a letter the day before from a person by the name of Duncan Forbes. Forbes had informed her that he had information regarding her father, whom she had believed deceased these past twenty years. Deeply troubled and anxious to find out more, Alice had fled to nearby Green Park without a chaperone to meet him at the designated time and place.

'Aunt Margaret misses nothing. She knows everyone's secrets and nothing is hidden from her. You should know that by now.' Roberta gave Alice a speculative look. 'Did the letter you received yesterday have anything to do with you going out?'

Alice shook her head. There had been few secrets between them since Alice had come to live at Hislop House two months ago. She had confided in Roberta about her reason for not marrying Philippe—though not all of it, for some of the things she had done with Philippe were too sordid for Roberta's gentle sensitivities. Roberta was aware of the scandal that had shamed her and that, with her reputation in tatters, Alice had been forced to flee Paris. Alice would keep her meeting with Duncan Forbes to herself for the time being.

Duncan Forbes had told her that after the Battle of Culloden, back in '46, her father, Iain Frobisher, had been captured and taken south to stand trial for high treason. He'd been held on the hulks in the Thames. Justice for traitors was swift and he had been stripped of his possessions and estate. When the guards had come to take him to Kennington Common for his execution, he had leapt into the murky waters of the Thames in a reckless bid for freedom. Although he was shot and the river searched, his body was never found. He was presumed dead.

Duncan Forbes had told her that he himself had been a common soldier at the time of Culloden and had been on the hulk with her father. He was one of many who had been released under the Act of Indemnity which was passed in '47.

What Duncan Forbes hadn't told Alice was that he had fallen on hard times. He had given little thought to Iain Frobisher since the day he'd jumped into the Thames, until he'd met a man in London recently who bore an uncanny resemblance to his companion on the hulk. His suspicions were proved correct, and after spending a short time reminiscing, the two men had gone their separate ways. But on reading a small clip in the papers about Alice Frobisher's fall from grace in Paris, and learning that she had come to London to reside with Lady Marchington, he realised the information he had acquired could be turned to his advantage. He had sent a note to Marchington House addressed to Alice Frobisher, stating that he had information concerning her father she might find interesting.

Having whetted her appetite and seeing that

she was desperate to know more, he had told her to meet him at the same time and place the following day. Alice had agreed, by which time she would have acquired the money to pay him what he asked for the information.

'No, of course not,' Alice lied in answer to Roberta's question. She handed her snow-clad cloak to a waiting footman, who was not at all pleased to have water dripping all over his buckled shoes. 'I'll go to Lady Marchington as soon as I've changed my gown. The hem is quite sodden. See,' she said, kicking a booted foot out in front of her to prove her point.

'I think she wants to see you now.'

Alice threw Roberta an exasperated look. 'Really, Roberta, unlike you I do not feel that I always have to do your aunt's bidding. If I were you, I'd stand up for myself. No one would blame you.'

Roberta smiled tolerantly. She did not possess a strong will of her own and often allowed herself to be browbeaten into compliance by her Aunt Margaret. It was easier that way. 'Aunt Margaret has been very good to me—to both of us, Alice. If it hadn't been for her, I would have been sent to live with strangers. I could not have borne that. Aunt Margaret has done a lot for me.'

Roberta had the misfortune to be an orphan, but it was fortunate for her that she possessed as her sole relative and guardian the Countess of Marchington, Lady Margaret Hislop, a widow these ten years past and without offspring. Roberta had long ago become submerged in the strong waters of her aunt's personality, for Lady Marchington was an autocratic, domineering woman who employed outspokenness to the point of rudeness as a form of social power and was feared and deferred to in consequence.

She had an eye that could bore holes through granite and a tongue that could flay the hide off a rhinoceros. It was pretty unnerving to those who found themselves in close proximity to the formidable lady. Roberta submitted herself to Lady Marchington's authority without complaint. Strong men withered before her and women ran for cover. She was a highly colourful character, tall and slender with iron-grey hair and a face wrinkled with age, but it was said she used to be a raving beauty when she was a girl.

Alice was not afraid of her, but then she always took care to avoid her. 'Oh well,' she said, heading for the stairs with Roberta following on behind her, 'as long as you feel like that about it. What do you suppose the party will be like tonight? The whole of London is anticipating the announcement of your betrothal. Indeed, they can talk of little else. I doubt the bad weather will prevent those invited from attending.'

'I sincerely hope not, but we will just have to wait and see.'

'I am certain the evening will be a tremendous success.' Alice cast Roberta an amused, knowing glance. 'Knowing how enamoured he is of you, Roberta, you can be assured of Hugh's company all night. The manner in which you become quite flustered when you are with him tells me that his attentions are not unwelcome. Come, do not deny it. It is forever Hugh this and Hugh that,' she gently teased her friend, who had turned as red as a poppy when Alice pointed out this slowly growing obsession.

Roberta's china-blue eyes never left Alice's face, the soft brown ringlets demurely hiding her rosy dimpled cheeks. She was quite tall and slender and cast in a gentler mould than Alice. It was not just that, Alice mused bitterly. What she lacked and what Roberta had in abundance was a tender innocence to add to her sweet beauty.

'You're quite right, Alice,' Roberta said, warming to her subject despite her strongest wish to be sensible. 'It's an exciting feeling. When I see Hugh I always feel so happy. I—I do love him, Alice.'

Alice smiled at her. She did not begrudge Roberta her happiness, but she did envy her and wished with all her heart that she could have found the same kind of happiness in her betrothal to Philippe. '*That* you cannot deny and very soon you will be his wife.' When Roberta and Hugh were together, mostly they talked. Occasionally they touched each other's hands, tentatively, the lightest of movements before making a shy retreat. Marriage would be a steady arrangement which Roberta would be content with and Hugh would have an absolute single-minded devotion for her. How Alice envied her friend these feelings. Let her not be disappointed as she had been.

'I confess that I cannot wait,' Roberta softly replied.

'Although what will happen when Hugh discovers you were once betrothed to another—may still be betrothed to him since the engagement was never broken—is anyone's guess.'

The light vanished from Roberta's eyes at Alice's mention of Ewen Tremain. 'Aunt Margaret says Lord Tremain no longer counts. He pledged his troth to me in Paris. But where is he now? He left over a year ago after being summoned to his brother's home in Bordeaux on a family matter and there has been no word from him since. Living close to Paris, did you never meet Lord Tremain?'

Alice shook her head. 'I know of him. His brother Simon fought alongside my father and brothers at Culloden.'

'I recall you telling me that your brothers did not survive the battle.'

'Sadly, no. Two of them were killed. William was too young to fight. I have no memories of my older brothers. I was just a baby at the time. My mother died soon after we went to live in France. Now there is just William—and me, of course.'

'Aunt Margaret has written to Lord Tremain on numerous occasions, without the slightest result. He could not have done more to earn her displeasure. He is deserving of her contempt, and mine. It would seem I've been fortunate to escape marriage with a man who is unworthy. In fact, I think Lord Tremain is the only man who has ever snubbed Aunt Margaret firmly—and, she says, with intention. I have to say that it's a salutary experience for her. Which is why she has relegated Lord Tremain to the past.'

And which was why, Alice mused, Lady Marchington was giving a ball tonight to display Roberta like a costly gem to be admired, a diamond to be destined for a coronet, no less. Lady Marchington was the matchmaker, the woman who would marry her niece to the most eligible bachelor in London. She had thought of nothing else since Lord Tremain had left Roberta in Paris. Lady Marchington was fearfully strong willed and quite ruthless about getting her own way.

'I do recall you saying how relieved you were when he left Paris. You had an aversion to him, I believe.'

'Not an aversion exactly,' Roberta answered, raising her skirts and having to hurry to keep up with Alice as she climbed the stairs.

'Does he still trouble you?'

'On occasion. We were not well acquainted, but on the few times we met he was always polite and considerate towards me. He was a man to stir a female's heart—quite dashing—handsome, too. But he was a mysterious man—secretive—sinister even, I often thought.'

Alice had become very fond of Roberta. She

was angry at the treatment her friend had received from Lord Tremain and was persuaded that he was unworthy of Roberta's devotion. She was determined to remain just as sensitive to Lady Marchington's motives of ridding Roberta of that erstwhile suitor, yet if Lord Tremain was as handsome as Roberta would have her believe, then one would assume he had made quite an impression on her. The loss of such a magnificent suitor would have made any woman resentful of an aunt who was determined on his removal from her life. Alice was of the opinion that, if for no other purpose than to make Roberta happy, Lady Marchington had been justified.

'But what of you?' Roberta asked. 'I would not ask, Alice, but I fear I must. I'm so glad your brother sent you to live with my aunt and me, but you must miss Paris.'

Alice drew up her slender shoulders in a small, distressed shrug, not wishing to recall the events that had made her leave her brother's house, the shame she had brought on William's good name. Now that she was in England, she was keenly aware that her memory of those weeks was best put behind her for the sake of her own peace and well-being. 'It wasn't Paris I had an aversion to, Roberta, only the man I was supposed to marry.'

'You jilted him. But if you did not love him, then you have nothing to reproach yourself for.'

Despite Roberta's charitable words, Alice realised she was still feeling the effects of the nightmare of what she had done. A fleeting frown touched her smooth visage as a memory stirred in her mind of the self-satisfied smirk Philippe had worn that first time he had taken her to bed. It was almost as if she had become a possession he could flaunt to lord it over others. The day had come when she had told him she would not marry him and walked away. She had never loved him and had soon come to despise him, so she knew he could not break her heart.

William's wrath had been terrible at first. *'How could you?'* he had berated. *'Have you no shame? No remorse? You're a disgrace to this family and especially to the memory of our dear mother.'*

Alice had closed her ears at that point. She wished he hadn't mentioned their mother. That had been unfair of him. Alice couldn't really remember her—she had been just four years old when she died of a weakness of the lungs. All she knew of her was what she had gleaned from William and she had taken his memories to herself. She might not have known her mother long, but she felt sure she would have listened to Alice, that she would have understood and taken her side.

But when William's wrath had subsided, for the first time Alice had seen sadness rather than anger. *'What happened to you would be shocking and tragic even if no one in the world knew of it but me,'* he had said. Alice saw that her brother was sincere in this and the realisation had thrown her off balance. It was true that William's pride was wounded, but that was not all. He genuinely feared for her welfare. Alice was sorry she had hurt him, which had added to her disgrace.

And then London. She was sent to London to live with Lady Marchington and to learn some wifely skills and, presumably, the sense that her brother set such store by. She had told herself it was for the best. She had to trust William to have her best interests at heart. On saying farewell, he had looked mortally wounded. Alice had felt regret like a sudden pain. It gave her no satisfaction to see her brother's distress. But then his expression had changed. *'Don't worry,'* he had said. *'The matter will be dealt with. I'll take care of everything.'* There had been a hardness in his voice that had made her uneasy. But, encased in her own misery, she had thought no more about it.

It was when she had been in London for two weeks and received a letter from William's wife that she realised there was a side to William she did not know. She shuddered, not wishing to dwell on the contents of that letter just now—of how her brother, defending her honour, had fought a duel to the death with Philippe. She kept the guilt and shame locked away, and there it would remain until, coward that she was, she could face what had happened.

'I suppose there are many who would say running away never solved anything,' Roberta said, breaking into Alice's reverie.

'It is a fresh start, Roberta.'

'A happy one, I hope. Whatever people say I, for one, am glad you're here. So now I insist that you forget all about him and begin by enjoying my betrothal party.'

Alice no longer lived in dread of seeing Philippe again, but nor was she able to relax. She was suspended in a past for which she felt a deep shame and hated to think about, and a future she could not bear to contemplate.

Although she had not been raped by Philippe

it had still been an assault—she had been so young and innocent, and what he had done had had life-changing repercussions. She was no longer the happy, carefree girl she once was and she mourned the loss of her innocence. Her heart had been badly damaged and she felt so tainted that she had lost her faith in love. Romantic love was just a silly dream. Feeling insecure in herself, she did not feel capable of having a successful relationship after all that she had endured, nor did she imagine that she could ever be truly happy again, or make someone else happy.

With Roberta hard on her heels Alice hurried along the landing and passed through her chamber doors. She began to unfasten her dress. 'I'm surprised Lady Marchington agreed to allow me across her threshold—although I suppose William's wife being the daughter of her closest friend had something to do with that.' What she said was perfectly true. Lady Marchington had taken her in as a favour to William's wife, Anne, but also to act as companion to Roberta. Alice was in no doubt that as soon as Roberta wed Viscount Pemberton, Lady Marchington would lose no time in securing a match for her. Although, she thought bitterly, she could not hope for as fine a catch as Roberta. Anyone would do as long as Lady Marchington got her off her hands.

Seeing her fingers struggling with the buttons, Roberta went to her. 'Here, let me.' After a moment she asked, 'What was he like—Philippe? Was he handsome?'

Alice's gaze hardened as her heart had hardened when she had decided not to marry him. 'Oh, yes, he was handsome. It was a matter of fact rather than opinion. But it was his handsome looks that annoyed me. They added to his air of arrogance and his self-belief. Confidence was not lacking in that particular male either. It never occurred to him that he would not get what he wanted.'

Roberta helped her off with her gown and draped it over a chair for Alice's maid to attend to later. 'But he must have attracted you for you to agree to marry him.'

'Perhaps a little—in the beginning. Philippe Duplay, the Comte de St Antoine, was the kind of man women dream of—a man to whisper words like little pearls into their ear. Weak men would give their souls to be like him, to be as tall and fair as him, to possess those laughing blue eyes— witty and gay—and to ride and dance like him. But strip away those pretty words and fine titles, and what is left? Arrogance, a blackguard—a roué, a gamester.' She spoke with such bitterness that Roberta looked at her with a questioning eye.

'You speak of him as if he were dead, Alice.'

Alice stiffened and looked at her hard. 'He is, Roberta. Philippe *is* dead. And now, if you don't mind, I do not wish to discuss him further.'

Turning away from the shocked expression her revelation had caused, Alice moved to the window and watched the snowflakes flutter down. Roberta disappeared into her dressing room to compose her thoughts and to select a suitable gown to wear for her meeting with Lady Marchington.

Alice thought of William, with whom she had lived for most of her life in a village close to Paris. When she had reached eighteen, William had only one ambition and that was for his sister to marry—and to marry well. William was wealthy in his own right and would offer a substantial dowry. Suitors came and went, leaving Alice feeling like an animal at the local market. It was finally decided that she would wed Philippe Duplay, Comte de St Antoine, who had long been enamoured of her.

But from the start Alice had felt out of her depth. The scale of the Duplay family's power and wealth intimidated her, reflected as it was in their grand chateaux and vast estates and the value of everything with which they surrounded themselves. The treasures that filled the Châteaux Duplay were all manifestations of the Duplays' significance.

'What you did,' Roberta said, emerging from the dressing room with a plain blue day gown over her arms, 'deciding not to marry him—knowing a scandal would ensue—was a brave thing for you to do, Alice.' Much as she would have liked to ask how Philippe had died, not wishing to distress Alice, she refrained from doing so.

Alice was normally a mistress of restraint. She hated being the subject of gossip and speculation. Generally she kept her thoughts and opinions to herself, observing the outbursts of emotion and the careless talk of others with disdain. With Philippe, she had learned to control her feelings better than ever. In this way she kept up the appearance of being a perfect fiancée. Sometimes, however, when provoked too far, she would allow herself the luxury of a spontaneous outburst. When it came, it had the impact of a summer storm, which was the case when she told Philippe she would not be his wife.

She had not been prepared for his vicious retaliation or how she would afterwards be ostracised by society. To cover his embarrassment on being jilted, Philippe had let it be known that she had the morals of a harlot.

This piece of slander was repeated all over Paris and with much embellishment. At first Alice was hurt, then she was angry. With strength and determination, she made herself come to grips with what she had done and faced the painful knowledge that her former life was permanently over. She learned how to cry lonely, private tears for all she had lost, then put on a brave face and her brightest smile. But unable to avoid the publicity and the very unsavoury scandal, she left Paris for good.

'I would not have been happy married to Philippe. When I thought of him I could not see him as my husband. He gave me so much grief when we were together I could not bear it. I decided to weather the scandal of walking away rather than live the rest of my life with a man for whom I felt neither love nor respect.'

Roberta looked at Alice's still figure and sighed. 'We have both experienced a broken engagement, Alice, so in that we are alike. I can only hope that in the future you find yourself with someone who will make you as happy as I am with Hugh.'

Alice very much doubted she ever would, and at this present time, when bitterness continued to gnaw at her heart, the very last thing she wanted was another man in her life. She supposed she would marry eventually. A good man. One who would treat her with the respect and tenderness due his wife. *Please God*, she thought, *let such a man exist.*

Roberta moved to stand behind her, her face flushed with disquiet. 'I—I'm sorry, Alice. I hope I didn't sound insensitive—I didn't mean to.'

Smiling reassuringly, Alice turned and patted Roberta's hand. 'You were not insensitive, Roberta. I was merely thinking.'

'But you had such a melancholy look about you,' Roberta said plaintively.

'These are melancholy days,' Alice said softly. 'Now I'd best go and see Lady Marchington before she comes looking for me. No matter how agreeable I always try to be, I will never find favour with her.'

Leaving Roberta to go to her own room to begin preparing for the evening's festivities, Alice went in search of Lady Marchington. Her astringent tones could be heard uplifted in comment and criticism from the ballroom as the footmen and servants rushed about to do her bidding. Alice cringed as she descended the curving staircase and braced herself to receive the force of her wrath. Lady Marchington emerged from the ballroom with the unshakeable confidence and regal bearing that came from living a thoroughly privileged life. She regarded Alice with an attentive, critical expression in her eyes.

'Ah, Alice, there you are. I was looking for you earlier. Well?' Her voice was as cold as her face. 'If it's not too much trouble, perhaps you would explain yourself. Where have you been?'

'I merely stepped outside for some air, Lady Marchington.'

'Stepped outside? Really! How dare you disobey me? How dare you leave the house without a maid to accompany you—and in this weather?'

'Lady Marchington—I am sorry…'

'It is most unseemly that you should embarrass me in this way.'

'That was not my intention. I did not mean to upset you in any way—'

'Hold your tongue, Alice,' the formidable lady snapped. 'Your unacceptable behaviour is why you left Paris in disgrace. I will not have it. I am most displeased with you, most displeased. Now run along and get ready for the ball. I'm sure Roberta could do with some help. I trust you will be on your best behaviour tonight. I want you to remember that this is Roberta's night. I want nothing to spoil it.'

She turned away to speak to Simpson, the butler, who was requiring her attention, but it was evident she continued to seethe at Alice's disobedience. Lady Marchington had opened her house and her purse to help Roberta on the demise of her parents, Roberta's mother being her stepsister, her father being Lady Marchington's brother-in-law by marriage, she wanted nothing to jeopardise Roberta's marriage to Viscount Pemberton. Just four weeks ago she had extended her hospitality to Alice Frobisher, the sister-in-law of the daughter of an old and valued friend.

Alice's circumstances had necessitated her flight from her family in Paris. Her brother had sent her to London to join the Marriage Mart, and the man she married would become the recipient of a dowry generous enough to elevate his status considerably. Lady Marchington had agreed to take charge of her and opened her door to the girl in the hope that a suitable husband could be found.

Unfortunately the scandal of jilting her betrothed on the eve of marriage had followed Alice to London and given her a certain notoriety that was unsavoury and most unwelcome. Ever since she had made her appearance at her first society event, she had become the focus of everyone's scrutiny, male and female. The admiring looks of eager young males followed her wherever she went, and with so many posturing about hoping to gain an introduction, she could have the pick of the bunch. But Alice seemed to have ideas of her own. She showed no interest in the rich, titled and handsome men she met—in fact, she scorned them all, much to Lady Marchington's annoyance, for she was eager for her to make a good marriage and be off her hands.

Relieved that the moment had passed, Alice returned to her room.

As she dressed for the ball she couldn't stop thinking about her meeting with Duncan Forbes. What did he have to tell her? If her father was still alive, then where was he? It was twenty years since he had leapt into the Thames. Why had he not contacted William? It was a mystery to be certain. She was impatient for tomorrow when she handed over the money and Duncan Forbes would reveal all.

Her nerves were strung tight and she was in no mood for socialising. She could not wait for the night to be over.

Alice was right. The weather did not deter the guests from arriving. An unending line of carriages filled the circular drive and overflowed through the double gates into the neighbouring streets, lined with big private houses. To be invited to the Countess of Marchington's ball was an honour, a true mark of distinction.

The grooming and dressing preparations for her engagement ball took Roberta, her maid and Alice three hours. Adorned in a chiffon gown with an overskirt dusted with shimmering silver spangles, her hair brushed until it shone and arranged in soft brown curls high on her head, she resembled a fairy princess.

Alice stood back to survey their handiwork and smiled. 'There! All done. You're looking as radiant and as beautiful as the bride you will be in just a few weeks!'

Lady Marchington swept into the room, wearing

an elegant russet-and-gold satin gown trimmed in cream lace. 'Nearly everyone has arrived,' she announced as Roberta's maid finished putting the last touches to her *coiffure*. 'It's time to make your grand entrance, Roberta.'

Roberta faced her aunt obediently, but her knees were trembling. 'I would much rather have stood in the receiving line with you, Aunt Margaret, so I could meet the guests separately. It would have been less nerve-racking.'

'But not nearly so effective. Come along—you, too, Alice,' she said, casting a critical eye over the young woman standing by the vanity, her shining black hair caught up at the crown in a mass of thick, glossy curls entwined with ropes of tiny pearls. Roberta was lovely, but Alice was the acknowledged beauty of the two. Tonight no one would have eyes for anyone but her.

Footmen dressed in formal, claret-velvet livery trimmed with gold braid stood to attention in the hall, which resembled a flower garden and smelled just as sweet, with tall silver stands holding urns of freshly delivered flowers and exotic pots of airy ferns. So as not to take the shine off Roberta's entrance as she walked beside Lady Marchington, stiff with pride, Alice followed in her wake. Simpson stood at the entrance to the ballroom and announced her name in stentorian tones.

A lightning bolt of anticipation seemed to shoot through the crowd, breaking off conversations as three hundred guests turned in unison to look at the girl who, it was rumoured, had stolen the heart of Viscount Pemberton. But the majority looked beyond the pretty brown-haired girl with her shining eyes focused on the young man striding to her side, to feast their eyes on the exotic, raven-haired goddess beside her, a young woman who had fled Paris to escape a scandal of her own making according to the gossips. Alice was dressed in a shimmering gown of sapphire watered silk decorated with serpentine ruched robings on the stomacher, the sleeve ruffles in matching lace fabric. The fashionable style was elegant, the colour matching her lustrous deep-blue eyes.

Indeed tonight she was breathtakingly beautiful. The slender rope of diamonds that adorned her throat flashed with white fire as she stepped into the glittering light of the ballroom, rousing an answering flash of envy in the eyes of every woman present and of their male escorts, too. But the gentlemen's desires were bent as much on the wearer and the perfection of her smooth features as on her diamond necklace. And yet if one troubled to look harder, they would see something at once remote and detached in the attitude of this dazzling creature, an indifference to her surroundings that was almost melancholy.

When everyone was present, Simpson stepped towards the Countess and called for attention. Conversations broke off and guests slowly turned to their hostess.

'Ladies and gentlemen,' she said in an unsurprisingly carrying voice, 'I have the very great honour of announcing the betrothal tonight of my niece, Roberta Hislop, to Viscount Pemberton. I ask you to raise your glasses to the happy couple. I will ask them to do us the honour of performing their first formal duty as future husband and wife by officially opening our ball.'

Simpson signalled to the musicians in the gallery with a nod of his head to start the music. It was a happy crowd that watched the handsome Viscount Pemberton take Roberta's hand and lead her on to the dance floor to begin the dancing. Scrupulously polished mirrors around the opulent ballroom reflected the dazzling couple as they danced before some of London's richest and most influential people.

Alice watched them, moved by the happiness she saw shining from Roberta's eyes as she up-turned her face to that of her betrothed, which only emphasised her own miserable state. She was seized by a longing to run away. It was a primitive urge, a legacy perhaps from some long-dead ancestor. It was not cowardice—she was not afraid to face her troubles—but rather a need to hide her feelings from prying eyes and seek her own cure in silence and solitude.

The betrothal banquet was excellent. Only the very finest food was served, with many of the dishes so elaborately dressed that they were viewed and commented on before they were finally tasted. Huge ice sculptures of peacocks and swans formed centrepieces for the tables.

'Magnificent!' exclaimed one of the guests. 'A spread fit for royalty.'

'And suitable for the betrothal of the Countess of Marchington's niece to the grand Viscount Pemberton,' another murmured.

Above the ballroom Italian-crystal chandeliers twinkled and turned, their lights reflected in fancy glassware, ice sculptures and glittering jewellery. With extravagance the order of the night and with an army of servants dancing attendance on the guests, the hours of wining and dining succeeded in their objective of producing a truly unforgettable night.

Alice smiled and laughed, drank some wine and chatted with a group of ladies. She danced with several dashing young men who asked her and made polite conversation, sat through supper with an admirer and danced some more and listened to her partners' words of admiration. She even managed to keep smiling when one ardent gentleman who had consumed too much wine whispered lewd suggestions in her ear.

He was not the only man present who did not look at her for her wealth, who stared with a lustfulness that sickened her to her soul. She saw with a feeling of horror men who skulked about the edges of the room, now moving in on her like rats after the only morsel of food. As a result of the damage Philippe had done to her reputation, were these the only type of men she could attract now, men who would flaunt her at their sides like a trophy for all to view and envy?

When she could stand it no longer, seeking out

Lady Marchington and pleading a headache, she quietly left the ballroom and went upstairs to her room where she could close her eyes and let the darkness hide her.

She felt suddenly very tired. The nervous tension she had lived under since her meeting with Duncan Forbes had left her feeling drained, longing for nothing but the peace and sanctuary of her own room. Closing the door behind her, she crossed to one of the two French windows opening on to balconies with wrought-iron balustrades overlooking the garden. She pulled back the long curtains.

It had stopped snowing. The sky was still and bright with stars, the fountain and stone statues in the shrouded garden etched with a silvery glow. It was a night made for lovers and Alice sighed at the persistent twists of fate by which she, whom so many men desired, seemed doomed to everlasting loneliness because of her disastrous affair with Philippe, which had made her unwilling to become close to any other man.

Abruptly she turned her back on the night. She snuffed out the candles on the mantelpiece, leaving the room with no other light than the soft glow shed by the small lamps placed at the bedside. The room, with its dim, mysterious light and the soft, inviting bed, had the power to attract her. She had made up her mind to sell some of her jewellery in the morning with which to pay Duncan Forbes the hundred pounds he had requested for information about her father, whatever the consequences might be should Lady Marchington find out. She knew she would never rest until she had the truth and then she must write to William. But first she must undress.

Removing the pins from her hair, she shook it out with both hands so that it tumbled like a thick black mantle down to the small of her back. The dress was more difficult to manage and for a moment, driven to distraction by the innumerable hooks, she was tempted to summon her maid, but then she remembered that Philippe had admired her in the dress and with a sudden spurt of anger she tugged and tore the fragile material away from its fastenings and tossed it into a chair. Attired in just her shift, she sat on the bed and removed her shoes. About to stand up, she froze. She had the strange feeling that she wasn't alone, that someone was watching her. As she looked up her throat tightened and fear jabbed her in the chest.

A man was standing as still as a statue at the

window, holding the curtains apart to watch her, looking dark and severe in the shadows. His manner of dress told her he had not been invited to the ball. He wore a tightly cut coat of black cloth and a white cravat. His narrow hips and muscular thighs were encased in black breeches and his gleaming black boots came to his knees. His long hair was tied back in a somewhat unruly style which, she suspected, was the result of carelessness rather than deliberate design. It was a dark shade of brown and in its depths were several strands of glittering grey.

He took a menacing step forward, edging into view with a cynical twist to his lips, allowing the shifting light of the lamps to illuminate his features. The eyes seemed to bore through her, and the gaze was so bold and forward that Alice's eyes slowly widened and for a brief moment she held her breath, frozen by his steely gaze.

'You!' she uttered, struggling against that aching, mesmerising stare. It was him! The man in the park! She had not seen his face properly, but it was him. When he spoke, she was certain.

The intruder saw the wary look of a trapped but defiant young cat enter her transparent eyes, eyes of the deepest blue. 'Please do not be alarmed. Forgive my intrusion.'

'I do not, sir! If you lay one finger on my person, I swear I will scream.' With a cry of indignation and in fearful panic she sprang off the bed and made for the door.

'For God's sake, I am not going to hurt you,' he ground out, and as quick as a panther he moved after her. With no other thought than to stop her raising the alarm prematurely, he grasped her shift from behind and pulled her back, ripping the soft fabric.

Before Alice knew what was happening her foot became tangled in the loose folds of material about her legs. Her arms floundered wildly before she fell to the floor, dragging her assailant with her. She gasped with pain and tears of helpless fury filled her eyes. Her thick hair was trapped beneath the man's arm and she was unable to move her head. With this small measure of discomfort, something exploded inside her. Suddenly she ceased to care how much he hurt her, but she would not let him do the vile things to her that Philippe had done. His entire being was of finely tempered steel as he leaned over her, his head so close to her own that his warm breath fanned her face.

Fear pricked her consciousness that he would demean her and abuse her, and the surety that he would was beginning to loom monstrously large in her mind. Her mind tumbled over in a frenzy. *Please God, don't let it all be about to happen again.* Had she not suffered enough at Philippe's hands, when he had commanded and she had obeyed, when she had submitted to his pawing? She had wondered what evil she had done that he should abuse her most cruelly, while he pleasured himself at his leisure, telling her that soon she would come to enjoy what he did to her—but for the present she must learn to accept her lot.

Her already depleted strength would little deter this intruder's assault. But it was best not to dwell on the degradations that would precede the final one and Alice fought the despair that threatened to reduce her to a whimpering wretch.

A new strength surged into her. Like a baited wildcat that turns on its tormentors, she jerked her hair free and hit out at him. Managing to wriggle out from underneath him, in desperation she sank her teeth into his hand. With a string of oaths the man sprang to his feet.

'You little hellcat!' he bit out, taking her arm and hoisting her to her feet. 'Be still, damn you! I'm not going to hurt you.'

She struggled, but he held her easily, letting her wear herself out until she was still. Resolutely she detached her mind from what was happening, the grip of his hand, and thought with savage concentration of how she would punish him when she escaped to tell the constables how she had been treated.

With her breath coming rapidly from between her parted lips, she glared into the cold silver-grey eyes. There was no denying that this man was handsome, physically magnificent. Before Philippe had spoiled her for all men, she might have even dreamed of such a man. But never in those innocent dreams of romance did she imagine that her love would fly to her on the wings of violence.

'Take your vile hands off my person,' she hissed. 'I will scream, so help me I will. I don't know who you are, but I hate you! I loathe you! I despise you. I don't want you to touch me.'

'I promise you that nothing was further from my mind until you threatened to scream the house down,' he replied coldly.

Ewen Tremain's manner was almost calm as he looked at her. A more observant woman than Alice might have noticed the distinct hardening of his lean features, the tightening of his jaw, the coldness of his gaze—and taken warning.

Chapter Two

'Draw your claws in, lady.'

Alice shrank from him and a shudder of revulsion passed through her as his gaze went deliberately down her body, boldly, rudely evaluating every angle of her scantily covered assets.

'Despite what you think I am not here to ravish you. As lovely as you are, you're very tempting, but I have neither the time nor the inclination for such dalliance. I wish you no harm, believe me,' he said. 'If I release you, do you promise to be still?'

Alice saw no passion, no desire in his eyes, only his dark brows gathered together and the silvergrey eyes smouldering in well-kindled rage. After a moment of indecision, she nodded.

He looked at her hard for a moment before releasing her arm. Immediately Alice snatched her robe draped over a chair. Wrapping it around her as if it were a suit of armour, feeling less exposed, she lifted her chin and faced the intruder. She flung her long hair back from her face, sending it spilling down her back.

'You've got some explaining to do—prowling about my room at this hour.'

His face was in shadow, but his silver-grey eyes gave his angular face with its high-planed cheekbones a harsh expression. She glared into his eyes. They were as cold as ice behind the black fringe of lashes. Slowly his gaze descended, sweeping boldly down the length of her, bringing a blush to her cheeks as his appraising eye paused momentarily upon her heaving bosom. When he looked into her face again, one corner of his lips quirked in obvious approval.

'Who are you?' the stranger asked.

'Is that relevant?'

The man's interest quickened. Her expression was wary. Most females were nervous in his presence, but there was a watchfulness in this woman's eyes that suggested something more guarded.

'Don't be obstructive. I like to know who I'm speaking to.'

'You were not invited into my bedchamber so

I do not feel obliged to give you my name. Who are you?'

'Ewen Tremain,' he replied with an arrogantly raised brow.

The name struck Alice like a heavy blow. Why, it was Roberta's betrothed come to terrifying, throbbing life. Dear Lord! What was he doing here? The band of light slanted across his hard, chiselled face. His eyes were pale and fierce, like a predator. Frightening, powerful and fatally attractive, he looked like a warrior about to go into battle.

The room dimmed as dizziness seized her. She almost sank down on to the bed, but then braced herself. She would show him no weakness and despite her state of undress she refused to be intimidated by him. She swept him with a look of haughty disdain. 'So, the erstwhile Lord Tremain has at last deemed to grace Roberta with his presence. Tell me, Lord Tremain, do you make a habit of entering a lady's bedchamber or have you lost your way?'

'Both.'

Ewen moved slowly towards her. He saw a young woman with a sculptured face of incredible beauty. She had high, delicately moulded cheekbones, a perfect nose, generous lips and a tiny, intriguing little cleft in the centre of her chin. Beneath her dark brows her eyes continued to blaze with defiance.

'When you have finished scrutinising my face, sir,' she clipped out suddenly with a fine, cultured accent like frosted glass, 'I would appreciate it if you would explain what you are doing in my bedchamber.'

'I recognised you as the woman I met in the park earlier when I saw you looking out of the window.'

'You were in the garden?'

He nodded. 'It was easy enough to hoist myself up to your balcony window. If you wish to discourage intruders, you should instruct your maid to close it when the room is unoccupied.'

'Never mind that. What do you want?'

Ewen looked down at her face upturned to his, well aware that she was probably scared out of her wits behind her show of bravado. 'What has the dress done to you to make you treat it so?'

Alice cast her torn gown a sidelong glance. 'That is my concern, not yours.'

'When I saw you in the park, you were weeping. Clearly you were upset about something.'

'I wasn't crying. It was merely the melted snow on my face.'

He shook his head slowly. 'Deny it all you like. I know what I saw.'

'You have yet to tell me what you are doing here. Why now of all times?' she asked him outright. 'I know who you are and I sincerely hope you have not come to make trouble.'

'I have not seen my betrothed for some time. I thought it was about time I did.'

'In my bedchamber?'

He shrugged. 'I did not want to alarm Roberta by showing myself too soon. I wish to know how the land lies before I present myself. I assume you are Roberta's friend. Who better to ask?'

'Haven't you caused her enough sorrow and heartache?' Alice accused irately. She was incensed that this man could come here at this time and work his mischief. 'Must you mar the eve of Roberta's betrothal with more pain?'

The silver-grey eyes took on a steely hardness as they settled on her. 'How can she possibly become betrothed to another while she is still betrothed to me? What would you have me do? Ignore the insult and leave without a fight?' His low, sardonic laugh belied the possibility. 'Watch me, lady, and see if I will.'

'Why, what will you do? Go down to the ballroom and put an end to it? Make a show of Roberta and shame and humiliate her? If you have any heart at all, you will refrain from doing anything so cruel.'

'Then be so good as to summon the Countess.'

'I will do no such thing. I think you should leave this minute and come back tomorrow if you wish to speak to her—although she may not wish to speak to you. And please use the front door next time.' She pointed across the room. 'There is the window. Please—just go, will you?' The furious look on the intruder's face made Alice want to laugh so much that she forgot her fear for the moment. She could almost swear she heard him growl.

His eyes slashed hers like razors. Slowly he leaned forward, his hand reaching out and grasping her chin so that she was forced to look into the eyes that blazed white fire just inches from her own. 'Lady, let me assure you that it is unwise to cross or disobey me,' he declared through gritted teeth. 'I am not here to play games. I've already played them all and you wouldn't enjoy them even if you knew how to play. Now, if you will not go yourself then send one of the servants to summon her ladyship.'

'You dare to order me about?'

'I do dare.' His eyes were two slits of hard, unyielding steel. Alice tried turning her head, but the strength in his fingers held her chin firm. 'Do as I ask, otherwise the whole house will know you are entertaining a man in your room, which would prove highly embarrassing for you. So if you care for your reputation you will do as I say before I get tired of waiting and go myself.'

Insulted to the core of her being, Alice shot him an angry, indignant glare. She did care. She had no intention of causing another scandal for herself and running the risk of ruining her reputation even further. 'You seem to forget that this is *my* bedroom and it was you who insinuated yourself into it.'

Releasing his hold on her chin, he stepped back. 'Do it.'

Alice's heart skipped a beat as she gazed up at the powerful, dynamic man looking down at her. Masculine pride and granite determination was sculpted into every angle and plane of his swarthy face and cynicism had etched lines at the corners of his eyes and mouth. Relenting, knowing she would get no peace unless she did, she turned to the door to do his bidding.

They awaited Lady Marchington's arrival in silence. From beneath dark brows, Lord Tremain observed Alice with close attention, and with quiet patience he waited for Lady Margaret Hislop, like a cat before a mouse hole.

With arms folded, Alice slowly paced the carpet, aware that the brooding Lord Tremain's gaze was fixed on her, holding her in its silvery depths. Suddenly she was the captive of those fathomless eyes, but she gave his attention the lack of regard it deserved. Yet she found it hard to be at ease with his gaze following her with an intensity and vibrancy to which she was not accustomed. And if his staring were not unsettling enough, he seemed to possess some mysterious power over her traitorous gaze, as now and then she could not prevent it straying in his direction. It was as if his keen appraisal were tangible—she could feel the heat and weight of it, as surely and distractingly as if he were trailing the tips of his fingers over her flesh.

Feeling a flush bloom in her cheeks, she looked

away when the door opened and Lady Marchington walked into the room.

Lady Marchington's eyes honed in on the man who stood by the fire. When he turned his head and she saw his familiar features her face blanched and her hand lifted to her throat. Her mouth tightened itself into a hard, unattractive line. Confusion, then belligerence, clouded her obdurate features and her narrow face became etched with bitter scorn.

The bow he gave her was sufficiently formal to send a chill through her, but at the same time acted as spur to her determination to keep him away from Roberta. Lady Marchington had recently learned of Lord Tremain's past, a past he had tried to keep secret, of how he had been captured and held as a slave in North Africa. She had been totally ignorant of this dark past a year ago when she had agreed to a betrothal between him and Roberta. Had it been made known to her then, she would never have given her consent.

Since that day he had become a malignant presence in her mind—a man tainted by what had been done to him, frightful, barbarous things she could not begin to imagine and had no wish to, since to do so was utterly repellent to her. No man could emerge from eight years of slavery in North Africa and not be affected by it. From the moment she had learned of his past, even though it was not of his doing, she had decided that should he return and try to resume his betrothal to Roberta, she would not allow it. The thought of someone as naive and gentle as Roberta being joined in matrimony to such a man was inconceivable. Besides, his pedigree was way below that of Viscount Pemberton.

She assessed this new situation and chose her strategy on the instant. This dramatic and what could have been a very public invasion of the evening's event displayed that supreme arrogance only achieved through the acquisition of power. Her instincts warned her that she was under threat, but she could not, must not, allow herself to be disadvantaged on her own territory and within sight and hearing of her guests. At all costs her machinations to remove Roberta from her association with Ewen Tremain must be prevented from raising its dangerous head before so many witnesses waiting to receive the latest society scandal.

When she had ended her visit to Paris with Roberta and returned to promenade her in London society in search of a worthier suitor, she had avoided any association with the lower-ranked gentlemen as one might avoid physical contact with the plague. It was fortunate that as soon as he laid eyes on Roberta, Viscount Pemberton was completely enamoured—a sure sign that Providence was supporting her ambition for her niece. Indeed, Lady Marchington was prepared to concede that Fate's method of bringing Roberta within proposing distance of the Viscount was more ingenious than anything she might have engineered. And now here was Lord Tremain, in London from wherever he had spent the last twelve months since he had left, ready to take up where he had left off.

Her face was hostile, her heart cold as she faced Ewen Tremain. 'Surely, sir, you are a little late in the day showing your face?'

'You are perfectly correct, Countess.' Lord Tremain's voice was clipped. 'I was obliged to delay my return for family reasons. I must ask you to excuse me, but you must remember, at the same time, that it does not interfere with my betrothal to your niece.'

'You are mistaken. There was nothing in writing. You have no claim on my niece—*no claim at all.* How dare you force your way into my home! And why are you here—in Miss Frobisher's bedchamber? It is most inappropriate.'

Lord Tremain glanced at the young woman clutching her robe about her person. Frobisher! The name seemed familiar, but he could not place it just then. 'I apologise for any embarrassment I may have caused. It was not my intention. I imagine Miss Frobisher will explain how I come to be here later. I wrote informing you I would be back next month. However, as things turned out, I found I was able to return sooner—and just in time, it would seem. I believe the festivities taking place as we speak are to celebrate the betrothal of Roberta to Viscount Pemberton.'

'Roberta is no longer betrothed to you, Lord Tremain. You are correct. Tonight she has become betrothed to Viscount Pemberton, the Earl of Winterworth's eldest son.'

Ewen's lips formed a grim smile. 'I see you have been busy in my absence, Lady Marchington. I expected to be treated with all the welcome of a rabid dog. You do not disappoint me.'

'Then I have achieved something after all. I did not expect you to come here.'

His mildly amused smile did not waver as his

gaze settled on the face of the woman whom he considered had tricked him. 'And why is that? You must have known I would not stay away forever.'

'The longer you stayed away, the more I hoped you would. My trust in you was misplaced.'

Alice stepped into the shadows to observe the bitter altercation between these two, her eyes drawn more and more to Lord Tremain. The candlelight touched on his face and for a split second she was halted by the cold, stark features. He was Satan to her. Handsome. Ruthless. Evil? She had no way of knowing, but at that moment she had an overwhelming desire to flee the room and leave them alone.

His long, finely boned hands testified that he was indeed a gentleman, except that some of his fingers bore faint scars—almost as if he'd once been forced to perform heavy labour. His prominent cheekbones slanted attractively and there were tiny lines at the corners of his eyes, fine lines as if he had spent too much time squinting into the sun. His mouth with its attractive straight lips hinted of disapproval and she felt laughing, much like smiling, was alien to him. She was intrigued, for she felt that he had not always been so, that he had once been a merrier soul, but that something had driven the joy from his life.

When Lord Tremain caught her looking at him, Alice dropped her eyes. Gazing at her directly, he glimpsed a soft, slightly parted mouth and eyes so deep a shade of blue they stirred his imagination no small amount.

He didn't raise his voice, but when he responded to Lady Marchington's remark, the authority in it was clear all the same. 'As far as I am concerned the promises I made to Roberta before I went away are binding. I always carry out what I promise. When both you and Roberta failed to reply to my letters, you forced my hand, which is why I am here now.'

Alice stared at Lady Marchington, whose expression had not changed. She was suddenly confused, which deepened as she uttered an enquiry. 'But, Lady Marchington, I was led to understand there had been no word of Lord Tremain since he left Roberta in Paris.'

Lady Marchington glanced at Alice, feeling a stab of unreasonable irritation against the girl. Making no comment, she faced Lord Tremain. She had been caught out in her deception, but it did not concern her. So great had been her determination to keep him away from Roberta, that she had kept his letters from her and burned all his correspondence without a qualm. Yet she felt the crawling prickle upon her nape as the full weight of Lord Tremain's accusing gaze fell on her.

'I had Roberta's best interest at heart. Yes, I kept the letters from her, Lord Tremain. I admit it and have no conscience for having done so. I know what happened to you before I became acquainted with you in Paris. How could you possibly expect me to consider you a fit suitor for my niece after hearing that?'

Lord Tremain's expression froze. Apart from his close family and his fellow sailors who had shared his incarceration, the world at large knew nothing of the years he had spent in captivity—although it came as no surprise that the truth had surfaced now. 'And that would have made a difference?'

'Of course it would. You were less than honest with me. My main concern was how Roberta would react to such knowledge. I wanted to protect her.' A sudden flame leapt in Lord Tremain's eyes and she sensed the murderous anger behind his stare. 'Indeed, what happened to you left me wondering if your experiences at the hands of your captors had affected you in ways I could not begin to imagine. Roberta is of a gentle nature. By agreeing to her becoming the wife of a man with such a dark and troubled past was a risk I was not prepared to take.'

Ewen's eyes narrowed into glittering slits and he stared back at her as if she had struck him a physical blow. A thousand memories of his suffering rushed through his mind and coursed like poison through his veins, when the shadow of death had darkened the days that slipped by and fear had tortured his soul.

He leaned forward slightly, his eyes intense. 'Madam, your words are of the vilest nature! You may hide behind your title and your wealth, but beneath all your fine airs and graces you have the manners of a shrew. Were you a man I'd demand satisfaction for what you have just said.'

Lady Marchington's expression was one of scorn and contempt. 'I do not doubt it. I expect you learned that kind of brutality at the hands of your captors.'

The words Ewen would have uttered turned to ashes in his throat. His pride refused to let him divulge the torment that still bled in the core of his heart after all this time.

Watching him closely, Alice saw Lord Tremain

was wearing the same grim expression she had seen when she had become aware of him in her room. He looked strained with the intensity of his emotions, but slowly, little by little, he was getting a grip on himself. His shoulders were squared, his jaw set and rigid with implacable determination, and even in this pensive pose he seemed to emanate restrained power and unyielding authority.

'I hope I have made my feelings clear.'

'As crystal, Countess, so that even a misfit like myself can understand.' Her cold, insulting slight had brought him rudely to his senses, a cutting reminder of the impossibility of any further association between Roberta and himself.

'Roberta is to wed Viscount Pemberton. No woman in her right mind would give up the like of his title and wealth for a man who has lived as you have lived.'

'As a slave,' Ewen stated with sharp icy clarity, 'and not of my choosing, I assure you. I did not go to the villains of my own free will.'

'I do not imagine you did. But you cannot escape the fact that the taint of slavery still hangs over you. You shall probably never shake free of its degrading grip. I feel I should also remind you that you are also a Roman Catholic and a defender of the Jacobites.'

'I do not need reminding of my faith. I am a defender of my family.'

'With a brother who was involved in plans to bring James Stuart back to the throne—a brother who fought at Culloden—and afterwards his whole family were held to be traitors.'

'It is my brother Simon you speak of,' Lord Tremain replied, his voice thick with unsuppressed wrath. 'Whatever he has done in the past, he has suffered at the hands of those people who wish harm to the Catholic church.'

'If he were my brother, I should have become a Protestant long ago. All your troubles might then have been avoided.'

'I do not think my brother ought to be censured for doing what he believed was right. Had I been of an age, he would have had my full and active support.'

Ewen felt a perverse pleasure in seeing the Countess's face blanch at his carefully flung remark. He was surprised also by how angry her attack had made him. He had certainly never considered himself a defender of the Jacobites, not even of his own religion, but the Countess had forced from him a loyalty that he had not known before. After all, Simon had been stripped of his right to property and position. It was easy enough to forget now that twenty years had elapsed since the battle that had blighted his family and the Scots loyal to King James.

'Nevertheless, it is one of the reasons why I cannot countenance a marriage between you and my niece.' A mild-mannered woman might have quaked beneath the murderous contempt Lord Tremain directed at her, but Lady Marchington had never known anything but wealth and power. Her imperious disposition had been carefully nurtured by a demanding father, who had instilled in her the importance of aristocratic breeding and the family's pre-eminent ranking above worthier nobles than Lord Tremain. 'It is done.'

'Is it?' With those two words hanging in the air he turned away. Halfway across the room he turned and looked back. 'Have a care, Countess,' he warned. 'Have a care, for I would not hesitate to expose your most intimate family linen to the scrutiny of the illustrious company partaking of your hospitality below.'

Lady Marchington paled. 'You wouldn't dare.'

'Oh, no? Try me,' he challenged. 'We both know

there is one member of your own family whose connections to the Jacobites could not withstand the most scrupulous examination. I believe you know what I am talking about.'

He had hit a nerve. His words made Lady Marchington recoil. Her voice was barely audible. 'How dare you?'

'But I do dare. Where is he now, Countess? Or perhaps you have no idea since you quietly disowned him after he, too, fought at Culloden. You may not wish to know, but I will tell you anyway. He is in Italy, and on occasion in France, with Charles Edward Stuart, the Bonnie Prince. Although after all the years the Prince has spent in idleness and good living, he is not quite so bonnie these days.'

Lady Marchington stared at him in horrified silence as she weighed up his words. Should it come out that her only brother was a Jacobite who had once taken up arms against the King, it would be the society scandal of the year. There were many who would like to see the proud and mighty Countess of Marchington brought low. She would not allow that to happen.

'Whatever else you claim to be, sir, you are not a gentleman.'

His lips curled scornfully. 'Did you expect to find one from the slave pens of Morocco?'

'What are you trying to do? Destroy Roberta?'

'Destroy Roberta?' Lord Tremain echoed with a twisted smile on his firm lips. 'Oh, no. I am not here to harm Roberta. I intend to marry her. As God is my witness, Countess,' he grated out, 'I shall see our bargain carried through.'

Lady Marchington must have been aware of Lord Tremain's anger, for whatever she saw in his eyes made her let the matter rest without further discussion.

The moment caused a peculiar unease and Alice felt a little chilled when she looked at Lady Marchington and saw her staring at Lord Tremain. She could not begin to recognise the depth of Lady Marchington's fury, but she saw the taut rage emanating from every line of her body. There was a look of such cold calculation in her eyes as they rested on Lord Tremain that Alice felt the cold hand of fear race up her own spine.

Lord Tremain turned sharply on his heel and headed for the door.

Alice took a step forward, wondering if he would acknowledge her, but he was encased in his anger and resentment and either did not or would not see her. She watched him go with a feeling that Lord Tremain was a man with no room for forgiveness or emotion. Dismissing her without a glance, he strode to the door and went out, letting it swing shut behind him with a bang that echoed in the very depths of her heart.

Bringing herself erect, Lady Marchington cast a steely eye on Alice. 'What you have heard in this room tonight you will never speak of. Do you understand me, Alice? Roberta must not know of this.'

'Yes—yes, of course,' she murmured.

Without another word Lady Marchington walked out of the room.

A while later, lying in bed with her eyes wide open, Alice reflected on the strange occurrence that had taken place in her chamber and the man who had disrupted the events of the evening. What had happened to him to make him so objectionable? She suspected there was more to it than his broken engagement to Roberta. What Lady Marchington had disclosed about his past disturbed her. He had been a slave, she had said. How could that be? Alice wondered. There was something indestructible about Lord Tremain, something fear-provoking that made her shiver.

Ewen left the house with a firestorm of humiliated fury erupting from his heart, burning its way through every nerve, every vein and every artery. His pulse pounded out a primal drumbeat as he strode through the snow to where Amir was waiting with a horse.

With Roberta Hislop by his side, he had been looking forward to beginning a life as near normal as was possible for him. So he had been taken aback to find Lady Marchington had betrothed her to someone else—a Viscount, no less. He clenched his mouth in a grim line in roiling anger and persistent shame of himself, of the monster he had become.

The pain was back again. Not the crippling pain he had felt from the wounds inflicted on him by the whip, but the other, the bad, the unthinkable hurt that was inside him. It had no definite location, but filled the whole of him. It was inside and out, expanding until it tore through his veins.

During his years in captivity, where torture, deprivation and helplessness—compounded by Etta's treachery—had driven him to the brink of madness, he had struggled to retain his grip on sanity. He had sustained himself by focusing his mind on escaping his torturers and returning to the world as he had known it to pursue a normal life.

In his mood of dismal self-loathing, his eyes were often fierce. They were wild sometimes—with pain, with passion. Sometimes when he was alone, they were deep and dark and brooding—haunted, as he had been when he'd gone to live with his brother in Bordeaux after his captivity. His family had worried about him. They could not conceal it. He could not wipe out what had been done to him.

'Ewen,' his brother had said, 'you will either be destroyed by it—or you will change it. There won't be any compromises.'

His brother had been right. He would not let what had happened to him destroy him. But he was a changed man, no longer the light-hearted youth who had loved life and lived it to the full.

That honest part of his mind, that he had no control over, whispered, *You would give your soul to be like him again, wouldn't you, Ewen?* To laugh as he had once laughed, to be witty and gay, to dance and whisper words like pearls into a woman's ear.

On meeting Roberta—sweet, innocent Roberta—he'd believed he had been given a second chance at an untainted life. He would not allow Lady Marchington to rob him of that. He was Lord Ewen Tremain, master of Barradine, a man of honour. Having lost his dignity and self-respect for eight years of his life, it was important for him to assert his place in the world and fulfil past obligations.

A voice inside his head told him he should forget Roberta. To hell with her and her sweet and gentle face, her refined manners and her fine friends and her brilliant Viscount. He didn't need her. He didn't need anyone, but he could not, would not, leave Lady Marchington with the upper hand. She did not deserve to get off the hook so easily. It was intolerable to his pride and he would not let it rest.

He almost had the old woman, but not quite. He had to play his last card.

Taking a sealed letter from his pocket and a small purse of coin, he handed them to Amir. 'Take these, Amir. Find one of the servants who will deliver the letter to Miss Hislop. Bribe them if you must, but instruct them to be discreet.'

* * *

After Ewen returned to his lodgings, his mind remained occupied with the evening's events and the indomitable Countess of Marchington. But the last thing he thought of before he went to sleep was the young woman whose teeth had punctured his flesh when she had fought to defend herself from him, of the gentle fragrance of her perfume and the warmth and feel of her body when he had held her close.

Their meeting had affected him. As they had waited for Lady Marchington, he recalled how intrigued he had been at the way her hair had seemed to twine of its own free will about her shoulders. As his eyes had passed over her face, he was rather amazed to find the shape and delicate structure appealed to his senses. Her slender nose had the sauciest tilt, her eyelids the longest, darkest lashes, her brows were wide-sweeping above eyes that had seemed the bluest blue he had ever seen.

The following morning while the house was being set to rights following the ball, with Roberta and Lady Marchington still abed, Alice ordered the carriage and left the house to obtain sufficient funds with which to pay Duncan Forbes for information about her father. She hated having to sell some of her jewellery, but William had made her Lady Marchington's ward until she either reached twenty-one or married, and she did not have direct access to the money William had placed at her disposal.

A pawnbroker in Drury Lane bought her jewels for a fraction of their value, but it was enough to pay Mr Forbes when she kept their appointment later in the afternoon.

When Alice returned to the house, Roberta followed her into her room. There was a wild, almost desperate look about her. Alice looked at her with concern.

'Why, Roberta, what on earth is the matter? What has happened to make you look so anxious?'

'Alice, I am beset by a grave problem,' she murmured dismally. 'Something quite dreadful has occurred and I need your help desperately. There is no one else I can ask.'

Alice stared at her, wondering what on earth could have happened. 'I cannot help until I know the nature of the problem. What troubles you, Roberta? Why do you say such a thing?'

'A letter has been delivered to me from Lord Tremain. It was given to my maid. It would appear he is in London. Oh, Alice, what am I to do?'

Alice looked at her sharply. 'Lord Tremain? But—what did the letter say and why did he not come to the house?'

'He did. This morning. But according to my maid, Aunt Margaret told Simpson to say she wasn't at home to him. He wants to meet me. But how can I? After all this time? Where has he been since he pledged his troth to me?'

'When does he suggest you meet? Where?'

'This afternoon at four o'clock—in the park. But of course I couldn't possibly. Aunt Margaret would have a seizure. It's quite out of the question.'

'Yes—yes, of course it is.' Alice's brow puckered in a thoughtful frown. It was clear to her that Lady Marchington had said nothing to her niece about Lord Tremain's visit the night before and did not intend to. Alice would not betray her confidence, even though she felt like a traitor for not doing so.

'I do not want my association with Lord Tremain to jeopardise my betrothal to Hugh.' Tears welled up in her eyes. 'Oh, Alice, I couldn't bear it. Will you help me? Will you go to Lord Tremain and explain why I cannot see him, that under the circumstances it would not be appropriate?'

There was such anguish in her eyes that Alice was deeply moved by it. She was sensitive to Roberta's uncertainty and understood only too well the troubling disquiet Lord Tremain could rouse in a newly betrothed's breast. 'I'll do what I can,' she promised. 'Where can I find him?'

'He said he would be looking out for me. Please don't tell Aunt Margaret, Alice. When you explain to Lord Tremain that I am betrothed to someone else, I am certain he will understand and not trouble us again.'

Extremely uneasy about her meeting with Lord Tremain, Alice waited until she had to leave in a state of nervous tension. She had arranged to meet Mr Forbes half an hour after her rendezvous with Lord Tremain. When it was time, she left the house by a back entrance.

Slipping into the park, she covered her head with the hood of her warm cloak. Low leaden clouds dulled the light and deepened the gloom beneath the trees. Spitting snow stung her face and the wind wailed a mournful lament as it swept over the park. Thankfully the awful weather had kept most people indoors so it was relatively quiet, but there was a group of people hurrying by that she recognised, neighbours and acquaintances of Lady Marchington. They passed her, but by their curious looks Alice was certain they had recognised her.

Looking to her right, she could see a coach drawn by two horses with a lighted lantern waiting a little off. A driver sat huddled in a greatcoat holding the reins, his breath steaming before him in the cold air. It looked empty and the air was so bitterly cold that she shivered and hurried on. A sudden eerie feeling slithered down her spine and compelled her to turn her head and look back. There against the snow she saw her silhouette cast, but creeping stealthily towards her shadow from either side were a pair of other shapes, large and threatening shapes of men dressed in full capes and broad-brimmed hats.

'That's her! It must be,' a muffled voice said. 'Stop, miss,' the voice shouted. 'We would have a word with you if you don't mind.'

Alice breathed deeply in an attempt to quell the

trembling that had suddenly taken hold of her. The park, which suddenly seemed quite unrecognisable, seemed to be full of phantoms. They moved without a sound and this silence only added to the nightmare situation of the scene.

'Damn it!' one of the men uttered. 'This is not the kind of night to be hangin' about. She's gettin' away. Get somethin' to tether her with, Taff. You saw how eager 'e was to 'ave her. Our lives won't be worth tuppence if we go back empty-handed.'

Sprightly and spirited, Alice did not hesitate another moment. She dashed in the direction of the place where she had arranged to meet Duncan Forbes, her feet, though hampered by the snow, racing in time to her swiftly beating heart.

Before she had covered half the distance, the two men had quickly overtaken her. A long arm stretched out and closed tightly about her waist, snatching her from her feet and pulling her back against a solid and unyielding unknown chest. Appalled at this rude handling of her person, Alice struggled and kicked her heels against the man's shins. Only the sound of heavy breathing told her she had not been spirited away by ghosts.

'Get your hands off me, you—you swine.'

'Not a chance, love. You're comin' with us. Docile as a lamb, he said,' one of the voices grumbled. 'More like a she-cat if you ask me.'

Alice opened her mouth to scream, but the sound died away on her lips, stifled, not by that strange paralysis which follows a particularly terrifying dream, but by a large and unmistakably solid hand which had been clapped over her mouth. Now she was being wrapped in a large sheet of some kind, one end of which was flung over her head.

'Make it a little quicker, Hicks,' a muffled voice said.

'I'm doing me best.'

Terrified, Alice found herself in total suffocating darkness as ropes were wrapped round to secure her. She fought desperately against imminent suffocation and driving panic.

'Be still, lady,' one of the men ordered. 'We don't want you to suffer unnecessarily.'

'You brutes!' Alice cried. 'How dare you do this?'

Hicks could not find words to soothe the girl's ire. She had much cause to feel offended and he could not blame her for resenting them. Perhaps all would be well when she saw the master.

'We've been charged with your safety. We have to get you to the master in one piece.'

Alice stilled. The master! Who was the master? Who were these men and what did they want? She heard hushed voices, voices she did not recognise, and then felt herself being carried along. She couldn't scream because her mouth was muffled by the heavy sheet. After a short time she was put down—not roughly, but with some care, which she thought odd. It was as though they did not wish to hurt her. She must be on the floor of a coach because the driver of the conveyance—probably the coach she had seen loitering on entering the park—urged the horses on almost at once. The pace was slow, almost deliberate, and Alice's spirits plummeted as she found little hope of rescue.

After several minutes the carriage picked up pace. In her suffocating confinement she did not know that it was leaving Piccadilly behind and was now rattling along the road to the north. Her blood congealed with terror. This hideous adventure was like a nightmare from which there would be no awakening. She was like a trapped bird flinging herself against the bars of her cage, but only succeeding in hurting herself.

The cord-bound sheet restricted her movements and held her arms pinned to her sides. As the horses' hooves threw up splatterings of muddied snow with each step, Alice wriggled in her dark retreat, trying to loosen the choking folds of cloth, but there was no room to move. Her mind ranged far and wide, conjuring up a thousand evil deeds which might be done to her. She realised then that she was being kidnapped. But by whom? And why would anyone want to? For what reason? What was their intent? These terrible apprehensions dragging out the unknown played on her nerves so that the rattling of the wheels over the rutted road was as nothing compared to the wild beating of her heart.

Neither of her companions had spoken for some time. She might have panicked and struggled and kicked against her bonds, but aware of the presence of her abductors and not knowing who they were or what they were capable of, realising that all resistance would be useless, she was persuaded to hold herself still and hope she would soon be released of her bonds.

Yet she did wonder if these men had captured her for their pleasure? A cold, agonising dread congealed within her, but she finally and firmly settled the matter in her mind that if this was indeed so, then she would at least give them a fight worthy of her strength. She had been well tutored by Philippe, and though she had the body of a feeble woman, she had the temperament and determination of a brawler.

'Bit still, don't you think?' a man's voice said.

'I think she's fainted,' his companion answered.

'Better for us if she has.'

The journey dragged on and the longer she was confined, the more her discomfort increased. She grimaced as the carriage lurched around a bend. The bumps and jolts were making themselves painfully felt along every inch of her body. With her back and hips pressed to the floor, with no padding to cushion her, she began to suffer aches and pains in areas of her body she didn't know existed and, as illogical as the idea seemed, she began to wonder if she would emerge from her torture alive. Unable to guess how long the journey would take, gradually she grew more weary and numb and her mind, seeking relief from her distress, began to wander. In the stuffy confines her eyes closed and she drifted into some semblance of sleep.

The coach had passed through heavy iron gates and along a tree-lined avenue leading up to a house. The gravel sweep and smooth lawns were hidden beneath deep drifts of snow.

Suddenly the carriage came to a halt, bringing Alice immediately alert. A cold, agonising dread congealed within her and left her heart thudding heavily in her breast. One of the men spoke in muted tones and there was the sound of the door opening. Then she was being hauled out of the coach. The cloth became loose about her head and a gap appeared close to her mouth. Swaying and breathing in the cold night air, she felt life begin to flow back into her body. A helpless, plaintive cry escaped her lips before a hand was clamped over her mouth and she was lifted off her feet. Against her struggles to escape, she was carried up some steps.

Her tormentor cursed suddenly and snatched his hand away from the sharp teeth that tested the flesh of his palm. He set the slender form on her feet and then jerked back abruptly as her small foot came free of the cloth and kicked out with vicious intent, hitting her target and eliciting a satisfying yelp. She was pushed on to a sofa where she sprawled in a heap.

Struggling to toss back the restricting cloth and glancing up, she saw two men bending over her, looking stupidly down at her, one of them rubbing his sore hand. Focusing her eyes, to her surprise she saw these men didn't appear to be unduly awful and dangerous. The man she would come to know as Hicks was quite tall and of strong build with light brown hair and kindly brown eyes. The other man, Taff, was short and stout with unruly dark hair and twinkling pale blue eyes. Neither looked capable of doing the evil deed they had been charged with.

But this was ridiculous. How could she feel this softening towards them after suffering their rough treatment? Anger was now beginning to overcome her fear, reviving her instinct for self-preservation.

'You—you idiots!' she cried, still struggling with the cloth. 'Halfwits! Why have you done this? Why have you brought me here? Who ordered you to abduct me?'

A masterful voice rang out. 'What the hell have we here? Remove the cover and hurry up about it.'

The two men jumped in sudden alarm when they turned and saw a tall, cloaked figure sweep into the hall as if blown in by the blizzard raging outside. White flurries whirled about him in a frenzy. Slamming the door shut on the howling curtain of snow that was threatening to invade the hall, he strode towards them, removing his heavy cloak and tossing it over a chair.

The fretting Hicks was the first to relent. ''Tis the young mistress, m'lord,' he said, sounding as if he had a blockage in his throat. Then he cleared it and said, 'We've brought her as you instructed.'

'Unharmed, I hope. I *instructed* you to be responsible about her safety and comfort should she agree to come and see me.'

'Aye, m'lord, and so we were—although she's a bit put out, that's all.'

'Imbeciles!' Alice managed to gasp, incensed with fury. 'I can't breathe. For heaven's sake, will you get this thing off me? I'll see you swing for this, you, you—ignorant oafs!'

Ewen moved forward, impatient to explain and placate and soften the shock of the young woman's abduction with an explanation. He glanced at the untidy bundle and recalled the delicately formed brown-haired beauty. The possibility that such a display of temper could come from the sweet Roberta he had known was hard to believe. A frown of concern touched his face. 'Be still,' he ordered in the same commanding voice as a figure began to emerge from the cloth. Wildly tangled torrents of black hair masked the girl's face, but Ewen had no need to see the creamy visage to be crushingly aware that his ploy had failed.

Chapter Three

'So—it is you!'

Alice flinched before the exasperation in his voice. Flinging back the remaining cloth, she glared into the ice-grey eyes that fairly sparked with anger. For a moment she thought she must be going mad. Nothing seemed real—the time, the place.

'Lord Tremain! I might have guessed you'd be behind this. *Now* I understand.'

'Where is Roberta?' he demanded, looking beyond Alice, as if he expected Roberta to materialise from the shadows.

'In London—with Viscount Pemberton, where a newly betrothed young woman should be. Or are you about to argue that she is still betrothed to you?'

The door of Ewen's understanding burst wide,

igniting the fires of his rage. Feeling cheated, he said, 'I will not argue the point with you, Miss Frobisher.'

'I would not want you to,' she snarled the words venomously. 'So, you bade these imbeciles to fetch Roberta and they caught me instead.' Her eyes swept to her two abductors, whose glances passed from her to his lordship, noting the absence of the blissful smiles of lovers and beginning to understand their blunder. Her lips curled with contempt as she continued. 'How disappointed you must be. And you expected to find her here awaiting your pleasure like some love-smitten maid? If you truly believed that, then you're as dim-witted as your lackeys, Lord Tremain.'

The deep blue eyes fairly flashed with sparks of indignation. Ewen stared into them with a modicum of confusion and fury before he rounded on the two men who had failed miserably in the task he had set them. One was anxiously wringing his hands and the other was retreating slowly, clumsily overturning a chair as he backed away, unable to meet his master's sharply probing grey eyes in the face of his wrath. 'I could have your guts for this folly, so help me— And why are you nursing your hand, Hicks? What's wrong with it?'

'My—my hand, m'lord?' The man called Hicks looked down at his hand, as if somewhat surprised to see the tiny marks slowly oozing blood. He rolled his eyes towards his companion-in-crime in wary confusion, as if reluctant to speak on the matter of their charge. His lordship was genuinely enraged, there was no doubt. Those silver eyes fairly burned with rage, while the muscles twitched tensely in his lean cheeks. By long association both he and Taff knew that small movement boded ill for all concerned. ''Tis nothing—merely—'

'I think that might be down to me,' Alice retorted sharply. 'I bit him.'

'Aye,' Hicks grumbled. 'Never seen such a bloodthirsty wench.'

Ewen's eyes narrowed dangerously. 'I quite agree, Hicks.' He smiled ruefully as he rubbed the spot on his own hand that still bore the marks of her assault. 'You have a propensity for using your teeth as a form of defence, Miss Frobisher—as I have found to my cost.'

With sheepish looks at each other, Hicks and Taff quickly directed their attention elsewhere, one to brush the snow from his breeches and the other to fiddle with his battered hat.

'Who—who might the lady be?' Taff asked, gulping on the question.

'I am Alice Frobisher,' Alice provided coldly, 'ward of the Countess of Marchington.'

The two men's jaws went slack and they stared at her as if they were loath to believe they had abducted the wrong girl. His lordship was justified in his wrath.

'We didn't know,' Hicks whispered.

'So you do realise what you've done?' Ewen snapped, his tone slicing through the air in the vaulted hall. 'Your incompetence will cost the two of you—and me—dearly. I didn't tell you to truss her like a fowl and force her into the carriage. You had absolutely no right to bring her here without her consent. Why the hell didn't you make sure it was the right woman before you took her?'

'She was where you said she'd be. We were sure she was the one. Brown hair, you said.'

'Aye, brown—not black. Are you blind?'

'It was near dark, your lordship—seein' was difficult. It was an easy mistake to make,' Taff uttered squeamishly, afraid of testing his lordship's patience further.

'A mistake that should never have happened. You were supposed to bring me Miss Roberta

Hislop—if she was willing, I said—and instead you have saddled me with this maddening chit.'
Ewen prided himself on his own infallibility and he would not tolerate it in others, but he should have known to expect nothing less from these two incompetents. Losing patience with them altogether, Ewen waved them away. 'Leave us. I will speak to you later.'

The two men didn't need telling twice. Falling over each other in their haste, they scuttled across the hall and disappeared as if they had the devil on their tail.

Combing his fingers through his hair, after a moment Ewen turned back to the young woman. She had risen to her feet and stood glaring at him, her eyes shooting sparks and her chest heaving with outrage, having already decided that Ewen Tremain was more devil than man.

Of a sudden, Alice understood the two men's apprehension about provoking Lord Tremain. By his mere presence he dominated a room and now, in a towering rage, he was indeed fearsome.

Ewen studied her face. Her skin was creamy white, the creamy white of buttermilk, satin smooth and fine. It was completely unblemished, except for a small indent in her cheek, just near the corner of her mouth, which appeared when she smiled. She wasn't smiling now. She had the tense look of a hunted animal. As though she were poised for flight.

Looking at her, a smile of pure self-mockery twisted his mouth. *Consider well*, he taunted himself, *how your actions have affected this young woman*. Thinking back on his own experience of being taken captive, the fear of the unknown, he knew just how afraid she must have been. He cursed his rash decision to abduct Roberta, loathing himself with a bottomless loathing.

'Unfortunately what has happened cannot be undone.' He gestured towards the hearth. 'Please, come over to the fire and warm yourself. You must be tired after the long journey.'

For a moment it seemed to Alice that her eyes and ears must be deceiving her, but it was not long before she knew that this was no evil dream. He had said they'd saddled him with a maddening chit. Well, she would demonstrate just how maddening she could be. She found all her courage and fighting spirit come flooding back.

As always with her, the imminent prospect of danger galvanised her and restored her equilibrium— which waiting and uncertainty invariably drained away. She knew, could feel, with an almost animal instinct she had, that this man's machinations had very likely lost any attempt she had of finding her father. Everything in her rebelled. A sound of rage left her mouth and before Lord Tremain could react she kicked the final remnant of the sheet aside and launched herself at her abductor.

The force of her attack took Ewen by surprise, but it only took a split second for him to react. As she was about to deliver a blow to his head, he stepped back, at the same time swooping an arm about her waist and lifting her up against him, crushing her brutally against his body.

With a strangled gasp of outrage and pain, feeling the terrifying strength of his lean, hard body and her own helplessness, Alice struggled, horrified that he could be so familiar with her person. Her ribs creaked beneath the strain and breathing seemed futile. Though she mustered every bit of her energy, she could not escape his iron hold.

'God damn you!' Ewen bit out savagely, his glittering eyes alive with rage. 'Stronger men have tried to best me and failed.' The vivid memories of some of the vicious and bloody fights he'd been drawn into in the slave pens of Morocco—some resulting in his opponent's death in his desperation to stay alive—were seared into his mind. Without further ado he pushed her down into a chair, where she sat glowering up at him, her chest rising and falling in sharp, shallow breaths, appalled that she should have behaved with such violence.

'Do you forget your own captors, my lord, when you were a slave?' Alice needled.

He leaned forward so that his face was on a level with hers. Cupping her chin in his hand, he forced it up until she stared into those savage silver eyes. His face was rigid and his words snapped into her like bolts from a crossbow. 'I do not forget, Miss Frobisher, and I do not need reminding by you. So far you have survived our encounters.' His tongue gave his words added venom. 'But your luck is about to run out. I'll see this matter to my advantage.'

Ewen stood back. Reaching for a decanter, he poured a draught of sherry into a glass. 'Settle yourself,' he bit out when she made a move to stand up. 'Perhaps a little libation will calm your nerves.' The words were spoken with a sardonic twist of his sensual mouth and a lifting of his dark eyebrows.

'My nerves are not the issue. It is your nerve that must be reckoned with.'

She took the glass he held towards her and drank the fortifying liquor straight down. She was glad of its heartening glow, but well aware that she must hoard her strength and keep her wits about her if she was to escape unharmed from this new and frightening situation—and the insufferable Lord Tremain. How right Lady Marchington had been to distance Roberta from him. Alice could not guess what feelings could have driven him to such mad, desperate actions. He did not love Roberta, otherwise he would not have left her for so long.

She put the glass on to a table next to her none too gently. 'Of that, my lord, you have no short supply.'

She was suddenly acutely aware of her dishevelled appearance. She brushed at the dust on her cloak and ran an ineffectual hand through her hair, hanging down her back in a shining, tangled cascade. 'It was no wish of mine to come here, Lord Tremain, I assure you,' she said in a passable imitation of Lady Marchington's high-nosed tones. 'I was on my way to an important appointment when I was set upon by the simple pair of dolts you paid to kidnap Roberta and who used me quite abominably. It was painful and unnecessary. If Roberta is so important to you, then why did you not meet her yourself instead of sending two incompetents?'

'It was my intention, but I was unavoidably caught up on another mission.'

Ewen had been escorting his mother, stepfather and his uncle to Dover for the Channel crossing to Calais. Weather permitting, they would go on to Bordeaux after a short stay in Paris. He worried about them. All three were in their seventies and unfit to be travelling far in such atrocious weather. He had thought he had plenty of time to get back to London and meet Roberta, but he had not bargained on the heavy snow, which had made his return journey arduous.

He had instructed Hicks and Taff to meet Roberta should he be delayed and convey her to Mercotte Hall. Despite her betrothal to Lord Pemberton, he had been confident that she still had feelings for him and would not resist the opportunity to be with him. It was unfortunate that Miss Frobisher had been the one to keep the appointment—although he had not expected Hicks and Taff to manhandle her into the coach. He could well imagine her fury and how she must have fought them. No matter how one looked at the situation, he must take full responsibility. How could he have done this to her? Hating himself with a virulence that nearly strangled his breathing, Ewen looked at the angry young woman, knowing it would be no easy matter placating her.

'I demand that you convey me back to London immediately,' Alice ordered haughtily, confirming Ewen's fears.

Ewen's eyes narrowed. 'You are in no position to make demands, Miss Frobisher. It is out of the question that you return now. It may have escaped your notice, but the snow has set in for the night. The roads are hazardous. Even a seasoned traveller would not venture forth in this. I will, however, send a man to London, as soon as it is possible for a horse and rider, to inform the Countess that you are here and that you have come to no harm.'

A natural resilience began to assert itself in Alice. She stood up and stepped towards him, hair tumbling and eyes flashing blue fire. She had been abused and felt a need to slap Lord Tremain's insolent smile away. Anger ruled where good sense trembled in fear. She stood before him, feet spread and arms akimbo.

'No harm? It is my opinion that to be set upon by two ruffians and forcibly bundled into a carriage with no care for my person is indeed harmful. I have been pushed, shoved and prodded in the most degrading manner—on your orders. You are a loathsome, despicable beast for having put me in this predicament.'

A moment earlier Ewen had begun to soften towards her, but her verbal abuse and her stubborn refusal to look at the situation sensibly hardened him. The eyes he turned on her were as cold as ice. Being encased in steel could not have made him more impregnable. During his years of captivity, he had grown lean and strong. He was unrecognisable from the young lieutenant who had seen action at sea. He was not about to be moved by a chit of a girl.

He lifted his broad shoulders in a slight shrug. 'You abuse me, Miss Frobisher, but no matter. I've borne the hatred of fiercer foes than you.'

Her eyelids dipped to convey her acceptance of his statement. 'Until I can find a more appropriate description of my opinion of you, my statement will have to suffice.'

Ewen gave a nod of acquiescence. 'As you wish. It is evident that neither of us have any great love for the other, but I fear we are both caught in a situation which cannot be easily resolved. I cannot send you back to London and you are not of a mind to remain here with me. Therefore I suggest we call a truce.'

'The only way I will make a truce with you is when you send me back.'

Ewen looked at her hard. 'Impossible. 'Tis a pity you are not of the same temperament as your friend.'

'Roberta and I are not in the least alike—but we are close and share most things. Can you not get it into your head that she is to wed Lord Pemberton?'

'I do not dispute that. However, I know my wants and seek them out.'

'You do not look to me like some love-smitten swain. You should have approached her at the house. Have you so little honour that you have to stoop to trying to lure her away with secret missives?'

Ewen was angry, particularly since he now regretted his hasty decision to abduct Roberta. He had intended to return her to the Countess, who would undoubtedly keep the incident quiet until she knew for certain what had befallen her niece.

He'd not bargained on Miss Frobisher keeping the assignation in her stead.

'Honour? Aye, I have it.' He tossed his head and stared at her, his silver-grey eyes brittle. 'I take it the Countess kept my visit from Roberta?'

'Can you blame her? I am of the opinion that she was right not to tell Roberta.'

Alice took a moment to peruse her surroundings. The hall was warm, with an immense stone fireplace and a fire blazing in the hearth. It was panelled in golden oak, with plaster designs moulded into intricate geometric shapes above. Brought to an unknown destination, she was at this man's mercy. She had no idea where this hideout was situated—only that it was about an hour's distance from London. The likelihood of anyone tracing her route would be slight.

'Your cohorts snatched me from the park and brought me to God knows where.' She fell silent, looking about her. 'Is this your family home?' she asked, finding it difficult to imagine the ill-tempered Lord Tremain living in this house, for, despite his presence, it had a lovely atmosphere of calm and security. This house reminded her of her home in France. It had the same kind of charm. 'Where is this place?'

'It's Mercotte Hall. It belongs to my uncle, Sir John Tremain. At this present time he is with my mother and her husband, Matthew Brody, in Dover, where they will take ship to France. They will then journey to Bordeaux to spend some time with my brother Simon and his wife, Henrietta. Mercotte Hall, as you see, is a fine house.'

'I am not here to admire the architecture. Don't tell me you have brought me all this way to—'

'Don't be flippant,' Ewen snapped back. 'Since you wish to know where the house is situated, it is just north of London.'

'Where I insist on returning at once.'

Ewen stared at her, irritated by her repeated request. 'Believe me, Miss Frobisher, nothing would give me greater pleasure than to have you taken back post haste, but I have already told you it is out of the question. Surely you have more sense than to consider venturing out in this weather. You must remain here for the present.'

In desperation Alice's mind flitted about, trying to find a way to make him comply. Her one thought was to find Mr Forbes and obtain the information about her father. 'I hope you realise that Lady Marchington will see you hanged for this— but,' she said, softening her manner, thinking that if she could not best him by argument, wit and feminine wiles might, 'if you were to supply me with a horse, I am sure I could find my own way back in the snow.'

She stepped closer, a wry and twisted smile curving her soft lips. Ewen read her face and knew full well that mischief was brewing in her beautiful head. For the sake of caution he took a step back.

'I won't tell Lady Marchington what you have done,' she continued, 'that you abducted me if that's what you're afraid of. I—could say I had no idea who snatched me and that I managed to escape. I swear I won't tell anyone. No one would be any the wiser.'

Ewen looked at her good and hard as he digested what she had said. She feigned a warmth that was capable of stripping away a man's defences, but for Ewen, who was still bound by betrothal vows, her attempt to cajole him failed. His lips curled with scorn.

'Please don't look at me like that,' Alice retorted crossly, disappointed that her offer had not had the desired effect. 'Can you not see that I am offering you a way out?'

'That's an absurd promise. Admit it.'

Alice stared at him in furious silence, knowing he was right about the promise being ridiculous, but refusing to admit it.

'You can't really expect me to believe that you would let me get away with kidnapping you, then be so grateful to me for doing so that you would keep a promise to me you made under extreme duress? Doesn't that seem a little insane to you?'

'Do you expect me to debate my thinking when my very life could be at stake!' she burst out.

'Miss Frobisher,' Ewen uttered with strained patience, knowing full well the depth of their precarious situation, 'don't make this any harder on yourself than it needs to be. I realise you're afraid, but your life is not at stake, unless you put it there. You have my word that you are not in any danger unless you create it.'

'Your word!' she scoffed, tossing her head with defiance. 'Your word means nothing to me.'

'Nevertheless you have it,' he said, his voice edged with sarcasm. 'I have killed and been accused of appalling deeds. I doubt abducting a young lady and spiriting her away to my lair will besmirch my character more than it has been already. Consider also that the Countess of Marchington has no authority here, so I am quite safe from the hangman's noose.'

Alice thrust herself out of the chair in frustration. 'But you *have* to let me go. I *must* return to London. You must understand that I…' She fell silent, reluctant to reveal too much about herself and the real reason that had taken her to the park that day.

Ewen heard the note of desperation in her voice, saw it in her eyes. His curiosity stirred. 'I suspect it is something other than the Countess's wrath you fear. Tell me.'

'There—there is someone I have to meet.'

His brow arched upward in curious question. 'Was that the reason you were in the park?'

'That and to see you. Your note sent Roberta into a frenzy. She didn't want to see you. She couldn't, so she asked me to meet you instead and explain the situation. I—I had arranged to meet someone in the park a little later so I agreed to her request.'

Ewen looked at her, an inexplicable, lazy smile sweeping over his face as he surveyed her from head to foot. Alice had the staggering, and impossible, impression that he actually liked what he saw. 'Now I'm beginning to understand. You had a clandestine meeting with a beau perhaps. My apologies if I ruined your tête-à-tête with your lover.'

Alice stared at him aghast, her cheeks aflame. 'I was not…' she spluttered. 'I don't… Oh! You couldn't be further from the truth.'

Ewen gazed down at her with sardonic amusement and a scornful smile. There grew within Alice a strong desire to rake her fingernails across those handsome features.

'Your men forcibly took hold of me, bound me and dragged me into a carriage where I suffered such wretched torment I thought I would not endure it.'

'For which you have my sincere apologies, but I think you have survived very well.'

'Be quiet,' she cried. 'I did not know what they intended to do with me. For all I knew they could have been abusers of women, murderers or both.'

The amusement died from Ewen's eyes and his expression was sombre. Despite the stubborn lift of her chin and her rebellious tone, there was a tiny quaver of fear in her voice. When Ewen heard it, his annoyance with her evaporated. She'd shown much courage, such indefatigable spirit since she had been taken—she'd hit out at him so relentlessly that he'd actually believed she wasn't afraid. Now, however, as he looked at her upturned face, he saw that the ordeal he'd put her through had left faint blue shadows beneath her lovely eyes and her smooth skin was decidedly pale.

'You are quite right. I accept my actions towards you were—what I put you through—were inexcusable and unpardonable. Lord knows I endured much at the hands of others when I was a captive. The last thing I would wish to do is inflict the like on another human being. I am profoundly sorry if my actions have caused you pain. Truly.'

'Your half-hearted apology is not enough for all I have been through.' He looked and sounded sincere, but Alice was in no mood to be mollified.

'I am sorry you see it that way, but you must see that at present you have no choice but to accept my hospitality. You have my word that your every comfort will be considered.'

Alice clenched her teeth at his blunt refusal to comply with her wishes, her eyes flashing with ire. She would never find her father now. There followed a terrible silence in which her thoughts ran riot. She had the impression of living through some dreadful, unbearable nightmare from which it was impossible to wake. All of a sudden she felt like screaming, crying aloud to relieve the agonising sting of a colossal disappointment and frustration. She controlled herself with difficulty, burying her hands in the folds of her cloak.

With a mocking smile she leaned towards her captor so that her face was just three feet from his. 'I would consider very carefully if you insist on keeping me here against my will. I warn you, Lord Tremain, that I will make such a nuisance of myself and give you not one moment's peace that you will rue the day you brought me here. I am not Roberta, who would have expired within minutes from the rough treatment I received at the hands of your cohorts.'

Ewen responded with a dubious laugh. 'I cannot believe that. You are much too fragile to give your threats substance. Had my men taken Roberta, I'm sure she would have been satisfied to stay.'

'How could you possibly know that? Did you ask her?'

The simple question set Ewen to glowering. 'I intended to. I meant to ask her last night. I'm sure I could have soothed her fears at being taken from Pemberton.'

'That is the kind of arrogant assumption I would have expected from you.'

He watched her face flush red with her ire and laid a gentle, consoling hand on her shoulder. 'Calm yourself, Miss Frobisher, and say no more. It would be foolish of me to defend myself from a woman of your tender years.'

'Be that as it may, my lord,' she flared, shrugging his hand away, 'but I promise you that I will torment you until the day you let me go.'

Realising that she was perfectly serious about her threat, Ewen could only marvel at her tenacity. 'If you fail to be reasonable, I will have you locked in your room and stand guard outside the door if necessary. I am determined to return you to the Countess in one piece.'

'Will you want me to serve supper in the dining room, my lord?' An oldish woman had appeared, dressed from head to toe in black and with a smile of welcome on her face.

'Whatever is more convenient, Mrs Mullen. I am sure Miss Frobisher won't mind.'

Alice glared at him. 'If you expect me to dine with you, *my lord,* I would rather dine with the devil. Since I must eat to survive this ordeal, I will do so in the room you've had prepared for Roberta—alone.'

Supressing a grin, Ewen said, 'As you wish'. He

looked at Mrs Mullen. 'I think we can take that as a no, Mrs Mullen.'

'Very well, my lord,' she said, going back to the kitchen.

As she turned away, Alice thought she heard him say, 'Coward', but she couldn't be sure so she ignored it. She looked towards the stairs where a young man of medium height with dusky skin stood waiting. He had appeared as silent as a shadow.

'Meet Amir,' Ewen said. 'He will escort you to the quarters I had prepared for Roberta. You will find everything you need.'

Alice looked at Amir with curiosity. His dark eyes glowed at her through their strange metallic glaze, inscrutable and withdrawn. His noble, regular features were immobile, his teeth showing white between full black-red lips, yet he was not smiling. The lean, muscular body gracing a close-fitting black jacket and breeches had an alertness.

Spinning on her heel, she headed for the staircase, where she turned and looked back at her abductor. He moved to the fire and shoved a log further into the embers with his booted foot, sending sparks shooting up the blackened chimney.

A steady flow of subdued frustration and anger showed in Alice's flashing blue eyes.

'You will pay for this dearly, Lord Tremain. You have no more regard for a woman and her feelings than that log you have just kicked into the fire. Your vile actions could be expected of a crude ruffian or a criminal of the worst degree, but you, sir,' she said, measuring the length of him with an insolent look and an uplift of her hand, 'are supposed to be a lord of the realm, a gentleman, no less—and now a rightly branded abductor and tormentor of women. I trust I will not be subjected to your lecherous persecutions.'

Ewen's stare was cold and uncompromising, and there was a hard edge to his voice when he spoke. 'Berate me to your heart's content if it satisfies you,' he said irritably, his lips curling over his white teeth, 'but I have never forced my attentions upon a woman when she has made it plain they are not welcome. I have always considered myself to be a gentleman in my dealings with the opposite sex.'

'A sentiment held entirely by you,' Alice mocked.

Ewen's jaw tightened and his features became even harder as he tried to restrain his anger. Never had he met a woman who set him on edge like she did. Her stubborn determination to be as awkward as she possibly could was beginning to aggravate him beyond words. What he could recall of the softer hues of Roberta's gentle nature were far more favourable in his memory and easier to exist with than this tempestuous, venom-spitting female who would test the patience of a saint.

'Your issue is with Lady Marchington, not Roberta,' Alice went on. 'If it is revenge you seek, then punish her. Do not try to get to her through her niece—whose happiest day of her life was yesterday when she became betrothed to Hugh Pemberton. Your villainous plans were ruined when your henchmen blundered heavily and as a result I am the one who must suffer the consequences and torments of this most outrageous farce.'

'For which I have apologised. I can do no more than that.'

'No, I don't suppose you can. Roberta is delicate and gentle to a fault. She would not have survived the ordeal of being kidnapped and dragged into your lair, and if she had she would have despised you forever. She is not wedding Hugh Pemberton against her will. Quite the opposite, in fact. She adores him. To be his wife is what she wants more than anything. Please do not do anything to hurt her. You have only yourself to blame for the way things have turned out. You were gone a long time, with no word to Roberta—'

'That is what the Countess told you,' Ewen interrupted sharply, 'what she wanted Roberta to think, as she disposed of my letters without scruple.'

'Yes—well, I am sorry about that—or perhaps not. Roberta and Viscount Pemberton are well suited. But what was she to think? You lost both her trust and respect. Your absence sent her into the arms of another man. With no knowledge of the letters you wrote to her, she believed that you no longer cared about her.'

'And the Countess—and, I suspect, you also, Miss Frobisher—were instrumental in arranging her betrothal to Lord Pemberton.'

'I have no talent for that sort of intrigue,' she told him, 'but you are right. Lady Marchington was concerned for Roberta's happiness.'

'And what of yourself, Miss Frobisher?' He walked slowly towards her, pinning her with his gaze. 'Were you also concerned for her happiness?'

'What do you mean?'

'Was the occasion of her betrothal not the cause for celebration?'

'Of course it was. The ball was a tremendous success and enjoyed by all.'

'Everyone but you, it would seem. A young woman who wishes her friend well does not leave her betrothal party at its height, nor does she destroy the gown she must have gone to great pains to select for the occasion. Are you really as close to Roberta as you claim to be, Miss Frobisher?'

Alice felt a pang of remorse. She was ashamed of having shown herself so capricious and selfish, and realised that even if she did feel that way she had no right to begrudge Roberta her happiness because of her own failed betrothal, however bitter.

'Is that what you thought—was that how it looked? You couldn't be further from the truth. I have not known Roberta very long, Lord Tremain, but in the time we have been together I have become very fond of her, and she of me. My reason for leaving the festivities early and the destruction of my gown had nothing whatsoever to do with Roberta's betrothal and nor does it have anything to do with you. Mind your own affairs and I will mind mine and concentrate on returning to

London. As it is you and I have been fastened together like a pair of fighting dogs and at present are unable to get away from each other. But when I am gone I shall remain a thorn planted deep in your side which will torment you for years to come.'

Ewen glared at her long and hard before addressing Amir. 'Take the wench to her chamber and keep her from mischief,' he commanded. To Alice, he said, 'I urge you not to venture from your quarters—should you feel so inclined. The Hall is very large and very old and a veritable rabbit warren, a bewildering maze, which can baffle the unwary guest.'

'I won't,' she replied tartly. 'And I am not your guest. I am your prisoner, Lord Tremain, ordered to remain within these walls and forbidden to venture forth until you see fit to allow it. But I am sure that *you* of all people must accept that it is every prisoner's prerogative to attempt to escape his captor.'

Ewen's face hardened. 'For a slave, you mean?'

'Exactly—but that is not how I would have put it. I will try everything within my power to leave this place. I will not be hindered from that purpose.'

Apart from emitting an exasperated sigh, Ewen gave no further argument. The girl made it clear that she would not be easily dissuaded from her course of action. In truth, one might be tempted to have pity on any poor soul who got in her way.

Alice met his hard look with a measuring one. 'I gathered from the conversation you had with Lady Marchington last night that you spent some considerable time in captivity before you became betrothed to Roberta. For reasons of your own you chose to conceal it. Lady Marchington has no intention of tainting the family name. For Roberta to marry a man who was once a slave would be anathema to her. She could not tolerate it. Had you been more open about it you could have avoided any unpleasantness.'

'Unpleasantness? From where I am standing, Miss Frobisher, believe me that is putting it mildly.'

'I expect it is.' She shrugged. 'I wouldn't know.'

'How could you possibly? The only shackles you are familiar with are the ones that keep you fastened to the Countess's skirts, the kind that can be cut free with little effort.'

'You are here now, Lord Tremain. You are living proof that it can be done.'

'It is one thing to sever the chains of slavery, Miss Frobisher. It is quite another to be free.'

Having properly vented her spleen, without another word and with a haughty toss of her head Alice turned from him and headed for the stairs. It had been a long day and she was exhausted. She needed to be alone.

Ready to throw up his hands in despair, grinding an unspoken retort, Ewen watched her go.

He forced his meandering thoughts to a more agreeable subject, his once-esteemed betrothed. By her very nature, Roberta was the very epitome of a genteel young woman whose sweetness and quiet reserve merited his attention. Having spent eight years as an outcast from the world and determined to claim his worth and his place in society once more, he had set about finding himself a wife in Paris, a city where he had spent a good deal of his childhood. Roberta was visiting Paris with her aunt, the Countess of Marchington. They had scarcely got to know one another before he had been summoned to Bordeaux by his brother Simon. He had little memory of the few times they had spent together.

Now he found himself groping for images of her features, her soft eyes and the gentle curve of her mouth and the delicacy of her chin. They shifted in a blur of confusion as he tried to evoke her visage. Her soft smile of acquiescence was all he could recall of her response when he had proposed marriage to her. Strangely, the memory stirred nothing within his breast and nothing whatsoever in his loins.

What had he been thinking when he had arrived in London to claim his betrothed? On discovering that nothing was as he had thought and being completely rebuffed by the Countess, was it for revenge alone that he had sought Roberta's abduction, as Miss Frobisher had suggested?

Cautiously, as if he sought to pluck an irritating barb from his mind, he tested the accuracy of his memory of the previous night when he had stepped into Miss Frobisher's chamber, of the sight of her soft breasts nestling in the cover of her chemise, the peaks erect. His mind betrayed him as his memory expanded to a larger spectrum of visions, of her softly curving form, her glorious wealth of shining black hair, tendrils coiling like serpents down her spine, the stormy, deep blue eyes shaded by long, curling lashes and soft pink lips. She possessed a full-blown beauty, certainly more vivid and lively than that of the pale Roberta. Where Roberta evoked an image of softness and fragility, Alice Frobisher seemed to exude the very essence of vitality and life.

But then he recalled how the set of her jaw had tensed as she berated him, how the headstrong minx had boldly stood her ground before him and spoken her mind, thwarting him, trying his patience like a vindictive young snipe.

Ewen cursed beneath his breath as he realised what those impressions extracted from him— anger, frustration and desire. His awareness of the latter left him both outraged with himself and shaken by its swift encroachment into his life. It ignited his anger into unparalleled fury and had him striding towards the door. Flinging it open, he went out into the swirling snow, slamming it closed behind him.

Amir walked in front of Alice up the wide staircase without making a sound or speaking a word. They gained a landing which opened out on to a long gallery. Alice cast a fleeting glance towards the huge portrait paintings lining the wall. Their stern subjects bore themselves stiffly and formally in their outdated costumes. These were no doubt the ancestors of Lord Tremain's family. At the end of the gallery they turned down another, smaller landing, filing past several closed doors until Amir stopped in front of one and pushed it open, stepping aside as he did so.

'Here you are, lady,' he said, his voice soft and warm and not in the slightest unfriendly. 'You will be most comfortable. I hope you like it. As you see, everything is prepared.'

Alice stepped inside the room, her eyes doing a quick sweep. A large four-poster bed of dark wood took up most of one wall. The tops of the posts were connected by a cornice and from this hung rich blue brocade curtains. The curtains facing the room had been pulled back and tied by a cord. A beautiful down quilt covered the bed, while several pillows had been plumped at its head. A fire blazed in the hearth and everything had been prepared for her comfort—or Roberta's, she remembered bitterly.

'Food will be brought to you and a maid will come to attend you. Hot water will be brought to the room if you wish to bathe. If not, there is fresh water in the ewer. Is there anything I can get you before I leave?'

Alice shook her head. His words, she realised, were a little formal, but nonetheless sincere. 'No, nothing. If I feel so inclined, I shall bathe in the morning.'

Amir nodded. 'Goodnight, then.'

When the door closed, Alice paced the floor. She was bitterly disappointed, boiling with rage and frustration and powerless to do anything about her fate. To be trapped like this just when life seemed to hold such promise, when, with her affair with Philippe behind her, she had been starting to feel some stirrings of hope for the future. Her abduction at the hands of Lord Tremain would blacken her reputation for good. It really was too much to bear.

She could well imagine the state of agitation into which Roberta and Lady Marchington had fallen when she failed to return and she felt deep remorse for causing them such anxiety. She couldn't bear to think of Duncan Forbes and what had happened when she'd failed to turn up for their meeting. What would he do? Would he seek her out at Hislop House or think she wasn't interested in seeking information about her father? It was fortunate that he had mentioned where he was staying.

Alice felt suddenly weary. Her head was heavy and she longed for sleep, yet she suspected there would be no rest for her that night. She sat down on the bed and stared unblinking at the fire as the flames flickered along the wood. The door opened and a maid entered with her dinner. She was young and friendly and she said her name was Lily, but Alice was in no mood for conversation. She declined her offer to have hot water carried up to the room for a bath, but the smell of hot food caused her stomach to rumble, making her realise just how hungry she was.

When she had eaten she donned one of the nightdresses that had been meant for Roberta. She wondered how Roberta would have dealt with the situation had she been the one who had been kidnapped.

Lily left her with a bewildered backward glance. Hicks and Taff had told her what they were about. It was so romantic that Lord Tremain had snatched his love from the arms of another, but the young lady didn't look at all happy about it. Mutiny showed in her countenance and her cheeks were pale. She was a rare sight and anyone could see why she'd taken his lordship's fancy. She was lovely, just lovely, and it wouldn't harm nothing if she were to add a bit of a smile.

Alone at last, getting into bed, Alice gave vent to her misery. She wept, hoping her tears would act as a balm, but they did not. And then the weeping ceased and she longed for rest. If she could sleep she could forget. Sleep did come, though she didn't know when.

She awoke and in those precious moments between sleep and waking she was content, until she recalled what had happened and where she was. She stirred, pushing back one of the bed curtains, and stared at the unfamiliar room. It all came rushing back. It wasn't a dream. It was real.

Turning back the covers, she swung her feet over the side of the bed, shivering as a blast of cold air curled around her feet and crept up her bare legs. During the night the fire had died and with it had gone the room's heat. She thought it was as icy as it was outside. Shivering slightly, she went to the window and pulled back the heavy curtains. It had stopped snowing and the countryside was beautifully dressed in dazzling white. The hills and trees had changed their earthly shapes and now resembled strange sculptures where the snow had been swept by the easterly winds. The sun seemed to offer a bright and impatient challenge to her, as though telling her to get a move on or this time would be wasted. As she stood there mentally going over in her mind everything that had happened to her the day before, she grimaced.

'There has to be a way to get away from here!' she said aloud as she turned away from the window and went over to the ewer of water to wash her face. She began pulling on her clothes. There had to be stables with horses in them. Maybe there was a chance she could saddle one of them and be on her way before anyone realised she had gone. She had never ridden in such deep snow, but she was prepared to try.

Lily came in, carrying a silver tray bearing a jug of hot chocolate and warm pastries. Alice took the tray from her and placed it in front of her at a small table while Lily brought the fire to life. Alice waited for the maid to leave the room and then bolted the food and gulped down the hot chocolate. She then donned her cloak and left the room. Having made a mental note of the route she had taken with Amir the night before, she traversed along the gallery and down the stairs. Apart from the crackling of the fire the hall was quiet and she was thankful that there was no sign of her tormentor.

Chapter Four

Crossing to the door, Alice was relieved when it swung open without a sound and she stepped outside. Her boots sank into the deep snow, but it was not too deep to ride a horse. Her heart beating fast from suspense, keeping close to the house, she proceeded to the back where she knew the stables would be. Here there were signs of activity. Someone had taken the trouble to shovel the snow into great heaps.

Looking around, she saw Hicks and Taff seated side by side upon a low wall some distance from the stable yard. Holding shovels, each watched her approach with a wary eye. Hicks stood up and shuffled uncomfortably as she approached.

'Well, Mr Hicks. What do you have to say for yourself today?'

'What can I say, miss?' Hicks replied nervously.

'Me and Taff here made a terrible mistake and if you've a mind to punish us in some way, we deserve it.'

'Yes, you do. Most severely.'

'I feel a great burden inside me for makin' a right mess of everythin' and if I could I'd take you right back to London and restore you safe and sound in the Countess of Marchington's care.'

Alice considered the man a long moment. Her abductors were simple men and despite their rough treatment of her they looked on her with some respect. It was clear they were truly repentant for what they had done. She sighed heavily. 'Very well, Mr Hicks. You will do that as soon as we are able to travel. Now if you will excuse me,' she said, turning away, 'I'm going for a short walk.'

Hicks opened his mouth to protest, but when she spun her head round and glowered at him, he clamped it shut and sat back down on the wall.

Casually walking away from them while she gave a moment's thought to the details of her forthcoming bolt for freedom, her eyes did a quick sweep of the stables. Two horses had their heads leaning over the half stable doors. Apart from Hicks and Taff there was no sign of a groom or anyone else. If she walked round the back of the stables and entered the yard from another direction, they wouldn't see her.

From within the house, Ewen watched Alice pull the hood of her cloak over her hair and trudge out of sight. The anger and frustration he'd felt last night on finding his plans to bring Roberta to him had been thwarted by his bumbling servants was gone now, alleviated by a night's sleep. In the cold light of day, he realised that Roberta was lost to him now. He waited for a few moments for Alice to reappear. Suddenly he froze, his gaze searching the snowbound landscape. She had gone behind the stables, unaware of the duck pond that lay in her path. Iced over and covered with snow, it would not be visible. Fearing the worst, immediately he was striding to the door.

Ewen's fears were justified. Shaking with a combination of exhilaration and fear, Alice hurried on, uttering a cry of horror when she stepped on to the snow-covered ice and heard it crack beneath her feet. Unable to comprehend what was happening and save herself, to her utter disbelief she felt the ice give way and she sank waist-deep into the icy water. The severe cold took her breath away. Paralysed with fear, afraid that she would freeze to death, she grabbed hold of some tall reeds along the edge of the pond and tried to haul herself out. But with her feet sunk into the mud at the bottom, she was unable to move.

Looking around wildly for help, she realised that the longer she remained in the water, the more she felt as if she would freeze to death. Finding it impossible to move, she was unable to fight against the creeping, growing weakness which froze the blood in her veins. And then a man appeared—Lord Tremain—and he was hurrying towards her. Close on his heels were Hicks and Taff. Coming to a halt on the edge of the pond, he looked down at her. His mouth twitched with barely bridled humour as he arched his brows in mock surprise.

'Well, well, what have we here? Running away, were you, Miss Frobisher? I saw you disappear behind the stables and thought as much. Someone should have warned you about the duck pond.'

'It's too l-late now! So don't stand there grinning like an idiot. H-Help me out.' The last was a desperate plea as she feared at any moment she might pass out with the cold.

Ewen fell to his knees without a pause. He

reached out to her. 'Take my hand,' he ordered. 'We'll soon have you out of there.'

Fortunately his hand was within reach and Alice managed to take hold of it, clinging to it with all her strength. 'D-Don't let me go, I beg you,' she stammered through numb lips. 'I—I'm so cold.'

'I won't. I've got you now.'

As he pulled she began to move. With great effort, and much slipping and sliding, Ewen managed to take hold of her arms and haul her to the bank. Alice's relief was immense, but she could not control her trembling. Lifting her up, without more ado Ewen carried her in his arms to the house.

As soon as he was inside her room he was giving orders to Lily for Alice's comfort. Lily obeyed him willingly, building up the fire and bringing Alice a glass of hot wine, before disappearing to have hot water for a bath brought up. Alice was dazed with relief and a little disorientated. Her hand trembled so much that she could not lift the glass to her mouth, so Ewen took it and held it for her. She opened her mouth like an obedient child.

'You will feel better when you've bathed,' he said softly, drawing her wet hair back from her face. 'At least you are safe now. I don't think we need to call a physician.'

When she had drunk the wine, he removed her sodden cloak and rubbed her cold hands until they lost their blueness and tingled. When Lily reappeared, closely followed by Hicks and Taff hauling ewers of hot water for her bath, he went to his chamber to rid himself of his own wet clothes. When Alice looked for him she was surprised to find him gone. He had left without a whisper. His absence seemed to shout at her and there was within her a desire to have him back again.

Bathed and wrapped in a warm robe, Alice turned her thoughts to her captor. In reality she had no sympathy for the man, whom she considered harsh, sardonic and pitiless—yet he had shown concern and tenderness when he had pulled her out of the pond and carried her to the house. As she knelt before the fire rubbing her wet hair with a towel, she was disquieted. She remembered how it had felt to be held by him, how secure she had felt as he had carried her easily in his arms. Despite her sorry state, she had been almost smothered by his nearness, by the heady smell of him, a clean masculine scent that had shot like tiny darts through her senses and evoked a rush of pleasure that flooded through her. He had been so close he seemed a part of her. To remain calm and quiescent while their bodies touched was without question the most difficult task she had ever had to perform. All the places he had touched still burned as if she had been branded by the heat of his body. In all truthfulness, of stature and face and features she had seen no match and he could be the stuff of any girl's dreams.

Alice mentally shook herself as she realised where her mind was wandering. On a sigh she sat back on her heels, holding the towel in her hands as she gazed into the fire. How could she think of him in that way? After all the indignities she had suffered at his hands, she was not about to soften her attitude towards him. In some embarrassment she drew back from the illusion and averted her eyes to the window. Turning her thoughts to the previous day, she deliberately recalled the abuses to her person until she felt the familiar heat of anger and resentment rise up within her again. Only a faint voice deep within her mind warned her to have a care. This impassioned aversion to the man would take careful tending to survive.

Again she rubbed her hair with the towel, then

froze as she heard a light chuckle behind her. Turning her head, she looked back at the door. Lord Tremain, garbed casually, with his shirt hanging open to the waist, leaned lazily against the doorjamb. Even as she looked his gaze swept over her kneeling form, to her bare feet exposed from beneath her robe and finally rose to meet her accusing stare.

'The door was ajar,' Ewen explained with a shrug. 'I came to see if you are feeling better after your bath.'

'Yes—much better,' Alice replied. 'Although had I not been here I would not have fallen into the pond.'

'What were you thinking of to go wandering off like that? Trying to escape?'

'Yes, I was, if you must know,' she replied, proceeding to rub her hair once more. 'I was planning on taking one of the horses. Unfortunately the duck pond got in my way. It was impossible to detect in the snow.'

'What dreadful poor luck.' He shook his head with mock sympathy.

Alice scowled at him, resenting his effect on her, the masculine assurance of his bearing. But she was conscious of an unwilling excitement, seeing him arrogantly mocking and recklessly attractive. 'I know you must have found the whole incident highly entertaining, but had you not come when you did and pulled me out, I would have frozen to death. Then you would have been charged with my murder.'

Chuckling, Ewen shrugged and crossed the room, peering down at her with a twisted grin. 'But you didn't. Except for the crime of kidnapping, I am innocent of any wrongdoing. For what it's worth I truly am sorry. I have treated you very badly and I apologise.'

Alice was so shocked by the softness of his tone that she couldn't speak.

'Well, I've apologised. I trust you will accept it,' he said sharply.

That was more like it, she thought. She felt on firmer ground when he spoke like that. 'Of course.'

There was a silence which lasted for almost a minute. Ewen studied the top of her head, fascinated by the startling white of her parting, the long silken length of her lashes, the same shade as her hair, which brushed her cheeks, and the delicate curl of her mouth which, even when she was unsmiling and serious as she was now, turned up at each corner. As she leaned close to the fire, his gaze was drawn to her bosom where her robe gaped open to tease him with a brief but tempting view of soft creamy flesh. The effect was disruptive and he became still as his blood began to throb in his veins.

Alice straightened and in some surprise saw his eyes follow her movement, as if reluctant to leave the object of his attention. Her colour heightened. 'I would be obliged if you didn't look at me in that way. What are you doing? Considering a replacement for Roberta? Do you think to add me to your list of conquests?'

Her chilled contempt met him face to face. Leaning towards her, he reached out a finger to flip a damp curl that had strayed from the rest. 'That you replace Roberta never entered my mind—and conquest?' His voice was soft and deeply resonant. 'You mistake me, Miss Frobisher. I do not desire to conquer you. The times remembered and cherished are not taken, or given, but shared. What has happened to you is unfortunate, but while we are together in this house, I would enjoy it if we could call a truce—for you to cooperate.'

Alice, who'd been about to resume drying her

hair with the towel, stopped in mid-motion at the unfamiliar gentleness in his voice and stared at him. Undaunted, he lifted his brows quizzically, a twist of humour about his beautifully moulded lips. In all their short acquaintance, never had he looked more challenging. Uneasiness coursed through her, inexplicable but tangible as she gazed at his proud features. It was as if he had stopped thinking of her as a nuisance and was asking her to do the same and she did not know how to react.

As she gazed into those fathomless silver eyes, some instinct warned her his offer of a truce could make him more dangerous to her than he had been as her foe, yet her mind rejected that notion, for it made no sense. She was suddenly inclined to co-operate. Maybe she could even benefit from some kind of surface friendship. For one thing, despite having slept the whole night, following her dunking in the pond she was mentally exhausted and not up to sparring with him. But the memory of the way he had held her close when he had pulled her out of the water and carried her back to the house, of how it had felt to have him hold her, had nothing to do with her capitulation. *Nothing whatsoever!* she told herself firmly.

'Would it be so very difficult?' he asked more

forcefully, his gaze never leaving hers as he hunkered down beside her.

Pride and desperation were waging a war inside of Alice and her conscience was being assaulted in the fray. She deliberately recalled the abuses of her person and dwelt on them until she felt the familiar heat of resentment. A small voice within her mind warned her to have a care. The impassioned resentment would take careful tending to survive. She accepted what he was telling her, yet still she resisted, trying not to let her vulnerable emotions overrule her intellect.

'What you are asking of me is that I thank my abductor for his leniency, to pretend that all is forgiven and that we are—friends.'

'We don't have to go that far. If you don't believe what I am saying, could you at least pretend you do and agree to call a truce between us for the time we are together? Are you too afraid to try?'

Alice's mind raced as she considered his challenge. As loath as she was to give it weight, stifling the urge to nod, she said cautiously, 'I am not prepared to let you off the hook so easily. What kind of truce do you have in mind? In what way would you like me to cooperate?'

Sitting on the carpet facing her, one arm draped

casually atop his raised knee, he cocked his head to one side. There was a devilish twinkle in his eyes and a smile of the same ilk played about his lips. 'Just to talk without getting angry—'

'You have a temper.'

'My mother is always telling me that my temper and my thoughtlessness are my worst enemies. Light-hearted conversation with a clever and beautiful young woman is a forgotten pleasure to me. So is socialising, going to the theatre, music and dancing, discussing the kind of weather we're experiencing now instead of baking desert heat and constant thirst. If you are not in agreement to a truce, then I shall strive to keep out of your way until such a time when I can return you to London. Until then I shall see that every comfort will be at your disposal.'

Alice hesitated, somewhat taken aback by his reference to her as a clever and beautiful young woman, then she decided he'd meant nothing by it except for a little empty flattery. If she must remain at Mercotte Hall until the roads were safe to travel, then her battered nerves would welcome some time without tension and bickering. There was no harm in what he asked—was there?

'Yes, all right. I will try—but I can't promise anything.'

'Did I hear correctly?' Ewen enquired, unable to believe she had acquiesced so easily. Placing a forefinger beneath her chin, he turned her face to his and considered her closely, a teasing glint in his eyes. 'Are you sure you're not sick, that your time spent in the water has not addled your wits and that I must not call a physician to take a look at you after all?'

Removing his finger from her chin, in a subdued, wistful vein Alice stared into the heart of the fire. 'My wits are not addled. I am perfectly well. I do not ask for the comforts you would have provided Roberta,' she murmured. 'I have made no demands on you except that you send me home. Until such a time we will try to live in peace while we're in this house. Although I know you would prefer to have Roberta with you, neither of us can remedy the mistake that has been made.'

She watched as a burnt-out log fell into the embers. The hearth gave off warmth and she brightened inwardly. The heat touched her cheeks and she felt a comfort and security she had not known for some hours. Surreptitiously she observed Lord

Tremain again as he stretched long, slender fingers towards the flames that flickered ever higher. The faint scars she had observed before caught the light and shone silver. A cold shiver ran down her spine. She realised how little she knew about this man and what he must have been through.

Somewhat relieved by what he interpreted as her acceptance of his suggestion of a truce, and reluctant to end the intimacy of the moment, Ewen rested his back against the leg of a heavy chair. Stretching out his long legs, he crossed his arms over his chest and regarded her, one brow raised in speculative interest. 'Tell me something,' he said as she sat on the carpet and curled her shapely legs beneath her, 'who had you arranged to meet in the park yesterday? If not a beau, then the meeting must have been of some significance for you to venture out in a snow storm.'

The question seemed to discomfit her and, as if stalling for time in which to compose an answer, she drew her legs up against her chest and wrapped her arms around them. Ewen thought she looked incredibly desirable—a charming vision, clad in a dark-blue velvet robe. He also saw that the young beauty was not expert at hiding her feelings and he suspected that tears were not far from her eyes. Her expression was tragic and spoke of an incurable grief.

'Tell me,' he prompted softly.

Inhaling deeply, she continued to look straight ahead. 'The meeting was important,' she uttered quietly. 'Because of what you did I may never know what happened to my father.'

'Your father?'

She nodded. 'I had arranged to meet a man who was to reveal his whereabouts.'

'Why? Is he missing?'

'Until three days ago I believed he was dead.'

'And now?' Ewen murmured, distracted by the firelight glinting on the shining locks of her hair as it cascaded over her shoulders. 'What has changed to make you think he is not?'

Alice turned her head and looked at him squarely, her expression tense. 'My father was to be hanged. He fought at Culloden against King George. He was captured and with other prisoners sent to London where he was put on one of those wretched ships on the Thames.'

'The hulks.'

'Yes. When they came to take him to be executed he threw himself into the river.'

'So he escaped?'

'I don't know. His body was never recovered so it was assumed he was dead. That was what my family believed and they mourned his passing. And then a few days ago I received a letter from a man telling me that he had seen him. He had been with my father on the prison ship and was later pardoned.'

'And do you believe this man to be telling the truth? Do you trust him?'

'I don't know. What can I do? If what he says is true and my father is alive somewhere, then I have to find him. Can you possibly imagine what this is like for me, Lord Tremain? Not knowing for certain that he is alive? If he is, I don't know where to look, where he will be. And because of you I may never know.'

Ewen was contrite. 'I am sorry. But I find it strange. If your father escaped, why did he not contact his family?'

'I don't know that either. I don't know anything.'

'So he fought at Culloden, was captured and taken prisoner. You are young—what? Eighteen—nineteen?'

'You flatter me. I am twenty.'

'You cannot have known him.'

'No. I was born just a few months before

Culloden. I don't remember him. Two of my brothers were killed that day. My mother left Scotland, taking me and my brother William—who was not old enough to fight—to safety in France. After we left, our home was ransacked and burnt by the English.'

Ewen frowned. A thought suddenly occurred to him. 'Your name is Frobisher. Was your father's name Iain of Rosslea?'

'Yes, it was.'

'Then your family were our neighbours. Your father fought with my brother Simon at Culloden.'

Alice's eyes widened with surprise. 'This is indeed a coincidence.'

'I believe I can throw some light on why your father did not seek you out in France.'

'Oh?'

'Everyone believed your mother, along with you and your brother, had perished in the fire.'

'That would explain why he did not look for us. Did your brother survive the battle?'

'He did, thank God. He was wounded, but he was more fortunate than others. A fugitive from the law he, too, sought refuge in France. He had had the foresight to transfer the estate deeds and the title to Edward some months before Prince

Charles went to Scotland to reclaim his father's throne. It caused confusion in the English court at the time, but they accepted that it was legal. My Uncle John, who owns Mercotte Hall and is not of the Jacobite persuasion, whose loyalty to King George was absolute, administered the estate in Scotland until Edward came of age.'

'Where is your brother Simon now?'

'He made his home in Bordeaux with his wife, Henrietta.' A smile quirked his lips. 'He spends his time growing grapes. They have two sons and a daughter. The eldest son, named Edward after our brother, will inherit Mercotte Hall on my uncle's demise.'

'Your uncle never married?'

Ewen nodded. 'His wife died shortly after they were wed. He never remarried so he has no issue. At the time of Culloden, Henrietta was living in a crofter's cottage outside Inverness with her uncle Matthew Brody—who, on marriage to my mother, became my stepfather. They gave Simon refuge after the battle. But this man who says he has information regarding your father—why did he not contact your brother? Why you? And why did he not give you the information when you met?'

'He would have done—for a price. I didn't have

any money at the time, but I told him I would get it and arranged to meet him in the park.'

Ewen saw beyond her words to the truth and recognised the heartless malice and trickery of the man. 'So, this man is a villain. What is his name?'

'Duncan Forbes. Somehow he—he found out I was in London which was why he came to me.'

Ewen could see that she was close to tears. 'It must have come as a shock when he told you your father is alive.'

'Yes, it was.' Her voice dropped to a whisper. 'I can think of nothing else. If Mr Forbes is telling the truth and he is alive, then I have to find him. I must.'

'Yes, you do. I can see that. I can also see you are a woman with opinions.'

'I have a brain in my head to think for myself, if that's what you mean, without elevated principles.'

'I suspect you do yourself an injustice and that you are a very principled young woman.'

'I think for myself and try very hard not to neglect the conventions, but this is a hard world, especially for women—for anyone who does not have a secure place in life.'

Alice fell silent, staring into the fire, thinking of her past and her own insecurities.

'What is it?' Ewen asked.

Alice started and looked at him. 'I'm sorry. I was miles away. Another time. Another life.' She gave him a wan smile. 'I'm all right. It's just that sometimes memories return unbidden and unwanted. It doesn't matter now.'

Ewen didn't question what she said. A secret lurked in her eyes. He was curious. At that moment there was something vulnerable about her. He wanted to ask so many questions, but instinct was telling him to keep quiet and wait. 'And do you have ambitions, Miss Frobisher?'

The look she gave him was open and honest. 'My ambitions are no different from those of any other woman. I suppose that eventually I shall marry and care for my family and help to further my husband's prosperity.'

'Nothing more than that?'

'I don't think there is more than that.'

Ewen watched her closely as she gazed into the glowing embers. He had started out thinking of her as a nuisance. He had ended up listening to her family secrets. He could see her vulnerable side and he found that endearing. She had a way of overturning his plans that was worrying. Worst of all, he was getting to like her. In fact, since their first meeting he had never ceased to be amazed and fascinated by the enticing blend of innocence and boldness he had seen in this young woman. Each trait was wonderfully intriguing and he was never more aware of his growing infatuation than at this present moment.

Alice looked at him closely. For a moment she forgot the accumulated tensions of the last twenty-four hours. She also realised there was something highly comical about having fallen into a duck pond, then sitting on the floor in front of the fire wearing nothing but her robe with a strange man. Suddenly she felt curious to know a hundred different things about him. *What kind of man are you, Ewen Tremain?* she wondered, and realised she had no idea at all. A light blazed briefly in his eyes, then was extinguished. She gave him a speculative look, deeply conscious that his easy, mocking exterior hid the inner man. There was a withheld power to command in him that was as impressive as it was irritating.

'What are you thinking?' he asked. 'You're looking at me as if you're wondering whether I'm...'

She laughed. 'I'm curious about you. Were you really a slave in North Africa?'

A sudden shadow fell across his face. 'I was.' His voice hardened. 'I swore to put it behind me.'

Alice looked at him compassionately. Beneath his cold facade was something dark and savage kept on a tight leash. Something awakened in her, something strange and alien to her nature—longings she had never even felt for Philippe when she had been a girl. Her feelings then had been negligible compared to the feelings this man aroused in her. He glanced up. They held each other's eyes before he looked away.

'I'm sorry. I—shouldn't have asked.' An unexpected emotion made her voice tremble. She glanced at him. He was sideways on and all she could see was his stony profile, which seemed to be deep in thought. She lowered her face. 'Please forget I mentioned it.'

Ewen turned his head and looked at her. 'But you did. Look at me,' he said gently. She obeyed and her eyes glistened with tears. 'You are upset,' he said, astonished. 'Why is that?'

'I—don't know. I—I can't really explain...'

'It's probably better that you shouldn't. I can imagine your bewilderment—the questions you must have put to yourself.'

'It isn't any of my business.'

Ewen did not answer at once. He sat awhile, his head bowed, as if meditating. He hesitated, thinking to refuse this sudden, surprising curiosity. Then he relented. But he could not, would not, tell the whole of it, the part he had closed his mind to—about Etta… He sat up again with the air of a man who has come to a decision.

'It's an old and rather unhappy tale. Ten years ago I was a young lieutenant in the British navy.'

'I am surprised—you being of Scottish descent, and your brother fighting against the King at Culloden, not to mention you spending most of your youth in France.'

'I am still British and the British navy is the most powerful in the world. Being the youngest of three sons and coming to live at Mercotte Hall when I finished my education, I was able to choose what I would do. With the call of the sea throbbing in my veins, believing that a man must choose his own path to glory or eternal damnation—' a bitter smile twisted his lips '—the latter in my case when I was captured by the corsairs—I joined the navy. In those days I was a hot-headed young man and I thought of nothing else.'

'What happened? How did you come to be captured?'

'After being engaged in operations off the west coast of Africa, my ship was returning to England when we were attacked by Barbary corsairs.' He looked at her. 'You have heard of them?'

'Yes—at least only what William told me. I believe they operate freely, attacking ships at will and taking people as slaves from coastal areas all over Europe. Is that what happened to you?'

He nodded. 'We were too weak to put up more than a token resistance. We were captured and taken in chains to the slave markets in Morocco. For almost eight years I could only dream of my home, my family and freedom. I will not offend your ears by going into the details of my captivity, only to say that every indignity known to man was inflicted upon me and my fellow crew members—those who had survived the attack. Some were put to hard labour in the quarries—the less fortunate were sent to the galleys.'

'And you? What did you do?'

'In the early days I was one of the lucky ones. I caught the eye of a pasha and was selected as his personal slave. Then my circumstances changed.' The tone of his voice dropped and trembled with a quiet anger as brutal memories assailed him.

'Something happened. I was condemned to life in the galleys—six to an oar with our ankles chained together. It was considered the next most-severe punishment after execution to be given a life sentence in the galleys. There was practically no hope of escape or rescue.'

'But you escaped. You survived.'

'The ship was caught in a storm off the coast of Spain. It was only thanks to the generosity and humanity of the captain that he ordered one of the under-officers to unlock the chains. After that it was every man for himself. There were only two survivors.'

Silent, wide-eyed with horror, Alice stared at him as if seeing him for the first time. There was no longer any anger in her, only an immense sadness and pity which welled up from the bottom of her heart towards this man whose sufferings must have been great indeed. Alice preferred not to think what agonies he had gone through. A heavy silence replaced Ewen's strangely calm, slow voice in the room, broken only by the sound of the fire in the hearth. A lump in her throat, Alice struggled to find words which were not hurtful, for she sensed in him a raw and quivering sensitivity. She was the one who broke the silence, speaking in a voice that was controlled, but unconsciously tinged with respect.

'The memories of that time must pain you greatly,' she whispered.

Yes, Ewen remembered, for it was *his* blood from *his* back that had soaked into the sand as they had whipped him, and *his* pride and joy and *his* manhood that had seeped into the stinking timbers and bilges of the ship in which he had toiled. As he had bent and strained at the oar, he knew himself to be a man without hope, like the slave he was.

'Amir—your servant? He was with you?'

'Amir is not my servant. His position is a special one. He is with me by choice and will remain as long as he has a mind to. He was born in captivity. He had nowhere else to go. We were chained to the same oar, side by side, for twelve months. We became close—like brothers.'

'How old is he?'

'As to that I cannot say.' He shrugged. 'Twenty-three, twenty-four. I don't think even Amir knows the exact time he was born.'

Alice looked at his serious, proud face, his restless eyes bright in his bronze face. With his hair falling over his brow and his features in repose, he fell silent and his gaze drifted to the fire, which gave Alice a moment to dwell on what he had told her. As she looked at him she felt drawn to him. Yes, he had abducted her by mistake, but he was not her enemy. He never had been. In fact, he made her want to get to know him better, to step beyond the terrible things that had happened to him. But in a vulnerable state herself, where this man was concerned she must proceed with caution.

'You are safe now. No longer a slave of the corsairs.' *But,* she thought as she fell silent, *the consequences lingered on.* 'How full of hate you must have been.'

'Hate keeps a man alive. It makes him strong. I wasn't ready to die.'

'Were you ever afraid?' she asked.

'All the time. Every day. Every night. It's how you survive. Fear keeps you alert, on your guard. It keeps you safe. You think about the moment. That's the only time that matters. Amir is a Muslim. He had his faith. I didn't even have that.' A scowl darkened his brow for a scant second, then his mood changed with the purposefulness of a strong will. He looked at her and placed his hand on her own and smiled. 'There. Does that appease your curiosity, Miss Frobisher?'

Alice was stirred by the depth of passion in his voice. Silence fell once more inside the room. In the hearth a log split asunder and collapsed in a pool of red embers. Lord Tremain sat very still, but it seemed to Alice that his broad shoulders bowed, as though under the force of some strong feeling. For a moment she was tempted to reach out to him, but she was too wary, too much on her guard against men's wiles. His hand still rested on her arm and she moved slightly so that he had to remove it. The warm, strong grip disturbed her, making it more difficult for her to regard him as an enemy who might have ruined any chance she had of finding her father.

'Yes. Thank you for telling me, Lord Tremain. I can understand how difficult it must be for you to talk about it.'

'The truth never is easy—and my name is Ewen. If there is to be any kind of harmony between us, then I prefer not to stand on formality.'

'Yes—and I give you leave to address me as Alice.'

Holding her robe so as not to expose her nakedness, Alice got to her feet. She had a strong feeling that he hadn't told her the half of what had happened to him as a slave. For what reason had he been condemned to life in the galleys? Was it so terrible that he could not bring himself to speak of it?

She waited as he stood up and crossed with measured strides to her. The blue robe flowed in fluid lines about her body, moulding itself against her as if reluctant to be parted, showing the womanly curves of her breasts and the graceful curve of her hips. She looked composed and serene, not in the least like the fiery, angry young woman who had entered the house last night. The memory seared through him. No matter how she provoked him for the time they were together, he vowed he would try not to lose patience with her. He had no right to feel anger or frustration—he had no right to feel anything except guilt and responsibility.

He was determined to do everything in his power to atone for the trouble he had inflicted on her. 'Will you dine with me tonight? I would appreciate it if you would? I could do with the company,' he murmured and his voice was like a gentle caress. His brow arched questioningly, but it seemed more like a plea than an enquiry.

Alice glanced down at her attire and indicated it as she replied, 'I will have to put on some clothes.'

'Then do so,' he urged. 'But dine with me. Will you?'

Alice gazed into those fathomless silver eyes, tempted to refuse his invitation. It seemed a betrayal to thank her kidnapper for his leniency, to pretend that all was forgiven and that they were friends. But it would make life easier for the time she had to remain at the hall if she accepted, despite any misgivings she might have at becoming too well acquainted.

She gave silent assent and a smile slowly spread across Ewen's face, showing his even, white teeth. He looked rakishly towards the dressing gown and her breath held while his eyes boldly appraised her.

'Heedless of your need to attire yourself in more appropriate garb, Alice, I approve most heartily of the way you look now.'

Abruptly, without giving her time to reply, he turned and went to the door. Looking back at her, he said, 'Get some rest before dinner. You are suffering from your fall into the pond and disappointment over your failed meeting with Forbes.

Sleep for a while. Tomorrow, by daylight, everything will look different.'

'You can say that. For me nothing will have changed.'

'I know, but together we will discuss what is to be done.'

A faint hope dawned in Alice. 'You will help me?'

He laughed softly and Alice was taken aback by the way his mirth gave his stern features a tranquil benevolence she had not thought possible before.

'How can I not? It's the least I can do. It's my fault that you didn't meet up with Forbes. Now rest. I look forward to your company at dinner.'

When he left her, Ewen was caught between torment and understanding over what he had seen in Alice's face when she had told him of her failure to meet with Duncan Forbes. Her expression had been agonised when she had told him that her father, whom she believed dead, might be alive.

His guilt was acute. For a hundred reasons it would have been far better if he were alone in the house, but now that she was here he couldn't simply lock her away, have her fed and pretend she wasn't. After the last hour in her company, however, he was sorely tempted to do exactly that, because she was forcing him to recognise and reflect on all the things he had locked away in his mind. When he'd arrived in Spain after his years as a slave, he'd vowed never, ever to look back, to wonder how his life might have been if only things had been different.

Yet now, at the age of thirty, when he was hardened beyond recall by the things he'd done and seen, he thought of Alice Frobisher and succumbed to the temptation to wonder. Had he met someone like her when he was young, would she have been able to save him from himself, to soften his heart? With someone like her in his bed, would he have experienced the same deep and profound feelings he had felt for Etta before she had betrayed him? Would he have found something more lasting than merely mindless pleasure in the beds of all the faceless women since?

Although he was only ten years older than Alice in actual years, he was centuries older than she in experience. Most of that experience had not been the sort she would admire or even approve of—and that had been true even before he was captured by the corsairs. Beside her youth and innocence, Ewen felt terribly old. The fact that he found her incredibly alluring and desirable, even engulfed in her shapeless robe, made him feel like a lecher.

Later, having rested, Alice searched the armoire for something suitable to wear. A short time later Lily entered to find a pile of discarded gowns. Alice finally settled on a violet silk. Pulling it over her petticoats, she settled the yards of fabric around her, then urged Lily to lace her up.

Alice entered the dining room like a warm summer breeze, sweeping in through the open door. Ewen approached her, bearing two glasses of wine. In appreciation of her dazzling beauty he smiled into her radiantly glowing face, his eyes narrowing in masculine predatory appreciation. Her long dark hair was brushed over her shoulders and in the half-light her eyes were dark pools of shadow.

'You're looking extremely lovely tonight, Alice. Take this,' he said, offering her one of the glasses of wine. 'I'd be inclined to say you are in need of some libation.'

'Yes,' she agreed with a valiant smile. 'It has been a fairly eventful two days.'

'Days to savour for years to come.'

'I wouldn't say that,' she replied, taking a sip of wine. 'The sooner I am returned to civilisation and have put all this behind me the better I shall feel.'

Ewen chuckled softly. 'Who knows what will come from our association? I may decide to set aside my feelings for Roberta and leave her to wed her Viscount in order to redeem myself in your eyes.'

Alice stared at him, her eyes wide with astonishment. 'Why on earth would you want to do that? Why should it matter to you what I think?'

His eyes danced as he probed the shining blue depths of hers. 'Considering that I've shocked you out of your wits, I am responsible for your present predicament. I want you to enjoy the evening and limit your protestations by allowing me to attend you for a few rare moments. You'll be rid of me soon enough when the snow melts.'

Alice hoped that would be the case as he escorted her to her chair at the table. 'I wouldn't be so dismissive if I were you. Do not imagine for one minute that I will allow you to dump me on Lady Marchington's doorstep and disappear. You do understand you will have to make your explanations for my abduction to the great lady, don't you? She isn't going to let either of us off the hook lightly. I will be severely reprimanded for agreeing to Roberta's request that I meet with you. She will give chapter and verse. It will be like the Spanish Inquisition all over again and she will not pull the plug on our blood, sweat and tears until she has had her say and we are repentant.'

Seating himself across from her, Ewen grinned. 'I don't expect she will—and I have no intention of dumping you anywhere. I am fully prepared to face the Countess of Marchington. I am not afraid of her.'

'If your encounter with her in my bedchamber was an indication of your relationship, then I believe you. What will you do about Roberta? Will you still pursue her?'

Ewen shook his head, a sadness in his heart, having already decided to let go of his dream of marrying Roberta and abandoning any hope of having a family of his own. 'No. Let her go ahead and marry Pemberton. If that's what she wants, then I will give her my blessing.'

'She'll be relieved to know that. You have no idea how worried she has been. Why did you leave her all that time? Did you really think she would wait for you? Even if Lady Marchington had not withheld the letters you wrote to her, didn't it occur to you how frustrated and rejected she would be feeling?'

Frowning thoughtfully, Ewen looked down, his fingers toying with the stem of his glass. 'My brother died.'

Chapter Five

Alice sat back, staring at him. She hadn't expected him to say that. 'Oh, I see. I'm so sorry…'

'Edward lived in Scotland. At that time my family was my only concern. My mother, who does not enjoy the best of health, had come over from France with her husband—my stepfather. She took his death very badly. He had been ill for some considerable time so it was expected. Nevertheless when it came it was a shock. Edward was unmarried, so I am next in line to inherit the estate.'

'In Scotland?'

He nodded. 'Barradine.'

'But—you have an older brother, shouldn't he…'

'Simon forfeited his right to the title and estate when he took up arms against the King. Besides, he is perfectly happy with his own family in Bordeaux. He will never return to Scotland.'

'If only Roberta had received your letters. Had she known—she would have…'

'What? Waited for me?' He laughed softly, shaking his head. 'It shames me when I think how badly I behaved. Even though I wrote, I should not have stayed away so long.'

'Will you tell her—about the letters?'

He shook his head. 'If the Countess has any decency, she will tell her herself. For myself, I would prefer to let things lie.'

'It was hard for Roberta to keep faith with you. At first she refused to believe you were anything but honourable and defended you loyally. She waited patiently, trustingly for you to come back from wherever it was that you had flown. But then she began to waver, to have misgivings and she became uncertain of her own judgement. And then she met Lord Pemberton.'

'I confess that my pride took a battering when I found out about Pemberton. I could see no further than that. I fear that too long away has made me forgetful of England's courtesies. I was impatient—reckless, even. Still, maybe things have turned out for the best. You say Roberta loves her viscount. He's lucky. We were never that close.'

A little smile touched Alice's lips. 'Please don't

talk like that. If you're not careful, I shall begin feeling sorry for you.'

'Believe me, Alice, feeling sorry for me is the last thing I want to inspire in you.'

'Then—what is it you want to inspire in me?'

'I'll let you know when I've decided.'

Alice laughed. 'That sounds ominous.'

'It was meant to.' Ewen's clear eyes gleamed beneath her pleasure, and he made no effort to limit his own perusal. She looked different when she laughed and for a fraction of a second, he felt it in that rarely used part of his anatomy, his heart, and he was taken by surprise. Her cheeks turned pink and her eyes shone, and her mouth, which was the colour of a rose, was soft, full and stretched over teeth which were white and even. He liked the way she tossed her hair and let out a throaty chuckle that he found incredibly seductive. He wanted to reach out and touch her, a temptation he resisted.

Alice felt herself flushing, for at that moment nothing was more obvious to her than that imperious gaze from across the table, taking in every detail of her face. A most outrageous, devilish smile tempted his lips when his eyes lingered overlong on her mouth.

* * *

It proved to be an especially fine dinner. Mrs Mullen had outdone herself. When they had finished eating, they retired to a sofa set at an angle before the fire. Ewen lifted the lid of an inlaid box of sweetmeats and offered them to her.

'I shouldn't,' she murmured, 'but they look so delicious I am unable to resist. Tell me what it was like at sea,' she asked through the sugary confection.

'There's little of interest to tell. The hours were long, the work often arduous,' he told her obligingly. 'Before becoming a lieutenant, I was taken on as a raw apprentice and had to "learn the ropes". The work was hard, but it did not dissuade me from battling across decks swept by swirling seas, or straddling the yardarms after climbing the masts by the ratlines to secure the sails. It was often done in freezing, gale-force winds and turbulent seas. But when we sailed to Africa the sea was as blue as the sky on a summer's day. It was beautiful, Alice.'

His face became soft and his silver-grey eyes almost transparent. His mouth curled tenderly and Alice realised that what had happened afterwards must have been like a death sentence for him.

'I was ambitious and resolved to succeed,' he went on, 'and one day to take my own command.'

'Until you were captured by the corsairs,' Alice murmured, her eyes watching his face in fascinated attention to every word he uttered.

A pained expression crossed his face and he nodded, falling silent. As she selected another confection and ate slowly, Ewen watched her. At length he said, 'Why did you leave France to come to London? And don't tell me that Paris bored you because I won't believe it,' he said softly.

Alice stopped eating and swallowed the sugary confection. She did not turn her head and look at him. There was silence. The noise of the wind that had risen outside seemed to heighten in the quiet room. After a moment, she said, 'Paris didn't bore me in the least, in fact I do miss my life there— my brother and my friends.'

'Then why did you leave it?'

Abruptly Alice rose and Ewen watched her stroll over to a small table where a chess set was laid out, swaying on her long, shapely legs, the perfection of her body emphasised by her gown.

'I've lived most of my life in France. My education was a mixture of English and French. I—I became betrothed…'

Ewen was surprised to hear this. 'Really? What happened?'

'We—we didn't suit.'

'So—you decided to end it?'

She nodded. 'Something like that.' Her voice trembled. 'It wouldn't have worked.'

'Did the man you were betrothed to end it?'

'No. I did.'

'I see,' Ewen said quietly. His curiosity was roused. Why had she ended it? What had gone wrong? She seemed on edge speaking about it. He decided not to question her further. 'Well, I am surprised.'

'Yes, I'm sure you must be.' She laughed nervously. 'When a betrothal is ended it's usually the other way round. The—man I was expected to marry was an aristocrat—he was not a nice person. I won't hide the fact that when I backed out of the betrothal it created quite a scandal at the time, which was why William thought I would benefit from some time in England to learn some wifely skills—and, hopefully, find someone else to marry. Who better than Lady Marchington to make me into the very essence of an English lady? William's wife is the daughter of Lady Marchington's closest friend. She agreed for me to go to her—and to act as companion to Roberta.' Her lips twisted bitterly. 'I have no doubt that as soon as Roberta weds Viscount Pemberton, Lady Marchington will marry me off to the first available suitor.'

Ewen knitted his black brows, then a ghost of a smile lit up his face as he got up and went to stand beside her, his eyes crinkling ever so slightly. 'Oh dear. I take it you don't approve of that. Once bitten and all that. But come, you are far too serious.'

Hiding her thoughts, Alice turned sideways so that he could see the bold curve of her breasts and, below them, the exquisite moulding of her stomach and softly rounded hips. She stole a look at him from under her eyelashes, wondering what he would say if he knew the real reason why she had ended her betrothal to Philippe. His silver-grey eyes never left her, glimmering and shining and changing with his thoughts. He had long, black silken lashes and his eyebrows were arched, giving him a faintly sardonic air. *Here is a man who reveals nothing of his thoughts and passions, and rules himself like steel.* Ewen Tremain, she knew, would never allow such vulgar displays in himself as Philippe had done.

'I'm sorry. I was distracted by my thoughts.'

'And what is it that burns in your mind? What will you make of the rest of your life?'

'At present, my one desire is to find my father—if what Mr Forbes says is true and he is alive,' she replied quietly. 'I'll not rest until that is done.'

'You do not mention your own desire for freedom,' he pointed out.

A bleak smile curved her lips as she directed her gaze towards her captor. 'You already know my feelings on that subject. Strangely, my freedom has ceased to be the most pressing need in my life. It is only when I think of finding my father that it becomes a goal that has to be reached.'

'Would you like another sweetmeat—a glass of wine, perhaps?'

She gazed at Ewen, suddenly unable to answer his question. She saw again the image of Philippe as he had been, her mind etched sharply with the pain and tawdriness of the outcome of that intense betrothal. It had diminished her in some irreparable way. A strange, bitter smile played on her lips and her eyes swam with tears as the memories crowded in. She remained deep in thought, the whole reason for her being at Mercotte Hall forgotten.

'What is it, Alice? Has something upset you?'

His husky voice broke into her thoughts. She heard his concern. She felt the pressure of his hand on her arm and the world came back. A single tear trailed down her cheek. Slowly she shook her head, ashamed she had exposed her feelings. She allowed him to lead her back to the sofa where he sat close beside her. Then her pride came to her rescue. She was a woman of the Scottish gentry, with a proud and vigorous heritage behind her. She must put what had happened behind her.

Philippe had taught her to expect the worse in men. Philippe had taught her well. What a bad judge of character she had been. Naive and completely innocent, she'd had no idea how convincing he could be. For the short time they had been betrothed he had held her in his power. He'd been charming right up to the moment he'd charmed her into bed, where he'd abused her most cruelly. At first she had accepted what he had done to her stoically as part of her betrothal, but in some strange way she had not allowed those acts he had committed on her person to coat her with their obscenity. She had known that if she did not get away from him, not just him but the life he would force her to live, she would be doomed.

When she'd reneged on their engagement, he had openly maligned her, accused her of being cold and unresponsive and declared to the world he'd be better off without her. Her disgrace had been so total that death itself could not have been worse. Indeed, she hadn't liked what he'd done to her. She'd been repelled. Was she wrong to judge all men by his standards? Particularly Ewen Tremain.

Ewen put his hand to her cheek to brush away her tear. At his touch she froze, almost as if she were afraid, her face turned towards him. He showed her the tear on his fingertip. Her colour rose and he thought she looked very young and desirable. He wondered if she knew it, too. Her face was an uncomprehending mask of carefully held expression. He could not follow her train of thought. He didn't know that for the first time in her life Alice was feeling emotions stir and warm into life.

She met Ewen's gaze and smiled. Here they were, just the two of them, together in this cosy room while the elements ruled outside, in an atmosphere of companionship. 'I apologise. I let my thoughts wander.' The light from the fire revealed the faint lines about his lips and the tiny grooves across his forehead as his brows gathered in the beginnings of another frown. 'I—I was thinking about my father,' she lied and hating herself for doing so. But she could not possibly tell him where her thoughts had led her. 'It hardly seems possible that he has survived at all against the odds.'

'You are caring to be so troubled about what has become of him. You have my word that when we return to London I will do my utmost to assist you in tracking down this Duncan Forbes.'

Looking into his lean face, Alice knew that he would do as he promised. For some strange reason she could not explain, she found her colour mounting. There was still so much of the girl in her at war with the young woman she had become and this man had the knack of bringing it quickly to the surface. Yet despite her earlier resentment towards him, she was very much aware of everything about him—of the long, strong lines of his body, of the skin above his neck linen, tanned and healthy. At close quarters, she saw faint lines of weariness about his face. Silently, reluctantly, she felt drawn towards him.

She tried to change her thoughts, finding her emotions distasteful. She sighed inwardly, striving to control her feelings, suddenly stirred with a terrible unrest. Carelessly his hand brushed hers. His touch stole her breath, its warmth a flame within her blood, and the intensity in his silver eyes held her transfixed. The potency of his gaze was intoxicating, sending shivers spiralling down her spine. It was quite unlike anything she had experienced before.

She felt a sudden stillness envelop them. Vividly aware of the heat of his touch and the spicy scent of his cologne, she was still overwhelmingly conscious of the man facing her. Confused, she looked away. She was irritated by the way in which he had skilfully cut through her superior attitude, the posturing she had assumed to save herself from him. She knew she had asked for it. But the magnetic attraction still remained beneath all the irritation.

Ewen was studying her, his eyes unfathomable, but giving an almost lazy expression to his handsome face that was grossly misleading. Their gazes locked, they were magnetised in the silent communication of sexual attraction. Moistening her lips with the tip of her tongue, Alice was unaware of the sensual invitation of her action.

For a moment she was assailed by the memories

of Philippe. Her flesh went cold. Then a darker fear mingled with her terror. Had Philippe mentally scarred her, left her crippled and unable to respond to a lover's touch? Her mind rebelled. No. Philippe would not triumph.

In a moment too quick for her to consider, Alice found herself leaning towards Ewen. She kissed him lightly on the lips, surprising herself totally. The thought of kissing him had never entered her mind. It seemed like an impulse that came from nowhere.

Ewen was clearly shocked, but he got over it quickly enough and kissed her back enthusiastically. There was nothing tentative about his kiss— he was instantly aflame. Her mouth was warm and sweet and opened under his. Her skin smelled of rose water.

After a moment Alice recollected herself and pulled away from him, gasping. 'Oh dear,' she uttered foolishly. 'I—I don't know what happened...'

Ewen raised a finely drawn eyebrow, giving her a penetrating look. 'You kissed me.'

'I—I didn't mean to. Please—I beg you to forgive me.' Shocked and momentarily ashamed of what she had done, she could feel the hot rush of blood burn her face, then the ice-cold sweat of pain followed it as the degrading memory of the past carved her to the bone. How could she have brought herself to do that? She turned her head away, biting her trembling lip.

Her straightforward admission caught Ewen completely off guard. He was enchanted, delighting in her innocence. She was untouched and unsullied, so inexperienced that she had no conception of how she affected him, which was, of course, part of her charm.

Or was she?

An element of mistrust stirred in the depths of his being. She had been betrothed, a betrothal that she had ended. Why? Why would she do that? For what reason? And just now *she* had kissed *him*, something that no other woman of his acquaintance had done—except one. Etta. What he had had with Etta in the beginning had been perfect, darkly, beautifully perfect. And because it had been so, her act of betrayal had become for him a double profanation. But he was being unfair to Alice. He did not know her well and she was not Etta. And Alice was here, now, young and alluring and so very lovely.

But he could not ignore the *frisson* of unease her kiss had stirred.

'There is nothing to forgive,' he murmured, touching her cheek and turning her face back to his. His arm went around her shoulders, drawing her closer. 'I'm glad you did,' he murmured, and before she could resist he kissed her again.

Alice wanted to break away, but his grip was strong and her will was weak. She felt his free hand steal over her bodice. She stiffened. His large hand closed over her small round breast and he groaned deep in his throat. He caressed her with surprising gentleness and she gave herself up to delicious sensations that she had never experienced with Philippe.

What am I doing? she thought suddenly. *By all intents and purposes I am a respectable young woman and here I am kissing a man and letting him fondle me!* A man she had met just two days ago, a man who had treated her most ill and who she had every reason to keep at arm's length. *What has come over me?* Ewen continued to caress her, his hand becoming bolder. 'Stop,' she cried decisively. Putting up her hands, she pushed him away. So many conflicting emotions swirled inside her, fighting for ascendency. Her thoughts went beyond kissing and caressing. Knowing what *was* beyond that, she was afraid to go any further. 'Stop,' she said again, pushing his hand away.

Ewen released his breath in a halting sigh and straightened. 'Whatever you say,' he said with obvious reluctance.

Ewen's eyes met hers in fearless, half-challenging amusement, saying things Alice dared not think about. She looked away. Shaken to the core of her being, she would not meet his eyes as she smoothed her skirts with trembling hands. 'It was my fault. It was a mistake. I'm acting like a tease, I know. I'm sorry.'

She looked genuinely contrite, but Ewen was having none of it. He reached for her again. 'Don't stop.'

'Please, don't do this,' she whispered. 'If we start again, we won't be able to stop.'

'I'm afraid that if we stop now, we may not be able to start again,' he murmured and his voice was thick with desire.

Alice sensed in him a formidable passion, only just kept under control, and that inflamed her more. He was insistent, powerfully so. He wanted her and he wanted her *now*. She should feel ashamed, but really could anything so lovely, so *right,* be wicked? She enjoyed his touch. After what had happened to her with Philippe she had imagined that she would never want to be close to a man again, but she reminded herself that this wasn't Philippe and things would be different. But then alarm bells began ringing in her head and she pushed him away. Ewen frowned down at her.

'I shouldn't have done that,' she said hurriedly. 'I'm sorry. I don't want you to think I make a habit of this.' She smiled as she apologised and Ewen felt confused—she was saying the words that should have been his.

'I was about to say the same.'

'I don't know what got into me. Only that it seemed the right thing to do at that moment.'

'Do you regret doing it?'

She nodded. 'Yes—yes, I do. For a moment I forgot myself—forgot who you are—what you have done to me.'

'I thought we had overcome that.'

Slowly he lifted his hand and Alice fought the urge to flee as he reached out to touch her cheek. Her whole body trembled beneath his touch and it took all of her resolve to stand quietly while the tips of his fingers caressed the soft curve. He eyed her curiously and she saw the welling and deepening light in his eyes and the long, silken lashes. She saw the thick, defined dark brows and wanted to touch them as one touches a bird's feathers. Then he withdrew his hand, about to slip his arm about her slender waist and draw her towards him.

Immediately she stepped back, twisting round and fleeing, the motion abrupt but not ungraceful. She flew in sudden panic from the room, hearing him call after her, but she ran on, not looking until she was in the safety and refuge of her chamber and the door was closed. Only then did she pause to catch her breath. Whether it was from relief at having escaped her captor, the exertion of her flight, or simple fear, her heart pounded in her breast. With her knees trembling beneath her, she rested her back against the solid-panelled door she hoped would protect her from Ewen Tremain and the new and conflicting emotions he aroused in her.

She suddenly felt, standing there alone and with her heart hammering in her chest, that there was an emptiness in her life that she did not want to admit, like a clock that had stopped ticking. It was as though she had wittingly slammed a door in her own face. But as her mind raced beneath the impact of the evening's events, the fear gnawed at her that Lord Tremain might find his way to her chamber and seek to finish what she had started.

The following day the sun made a rare and brilliant appearance, dispersing with much of the snow. The park and woodlands were turned into a soft and dripping, squelching morass.

Alice was both horrified and mortified by what she had done and shocked more deeply than she knew, which was why, reluctant to face her captor, she kept to her room, ordering her meals to be sent up and listening to the steady drip-drip as the snow melted on the roof.

She forced herself to suffocate all thoughts and feelings for Ewen Tremain after the experience of the previous evening. It was something she preferred to forget. She fervently hoped that he had, but she very much doubted it. Nothing was the same any more, least of all her feelings about herself. She'd been abducted by a man who had treated her friend very badly—an event that would have made an ordinary, decent woman hate her captor and despise everything he represented. Any other moral, respectable twenty-year-old woman would have avoided Ewen Tremain like the plague and tried to escape from his clutches. That was what any decent young woman would have done.

But she was not respectable and that wasn't what she, Alice, had done, she thought with bitter self-revulsion. Instead, she had practically thrown herself at him and, worse, kissed him. With that kiss had come a sense of having released something troubling and dangerous into her life. Her actions had been a sudden overwhelming impulse, heightened in intensity by the knowledge that it shouldn't be happening. She found that her attitude to Ewen Tremain had completely changed. His gentleness and passion towards her when he had returned her kiss had shown her something of the man beneath the worldly, rugged surface and melted her self-engendered resistance.

She was relieved that he did not seek her out. But she would have to face him sometime. The next morning, she had decided. The roads by then should be passable and she was determined she would not remain at Mercotte Hall another day.

The following morning Alice was up and dressed before Lily brought in her breakfast. Though large patches of white remained huddled behind protecting walls and shrubs, the drive was now visible. It was time to leave and she wasted no moment in her haste to do so. The thaw seemed to lift a cloud that had hung over the house since she had arrived. Lily bustled about the bedchamber in high spirits. Her hands flew as she applied the brush enthusiastically to Alice's glistening black locks. In hardly any time at all Alice's hair was dressed in a soft, charming *coiffure* that was swept off her nape and she was ready to meet the man who had turned her life inside out.

Discarding her own cloak and settling another about her shoulders—a luxurious fur-lined garment with a wide hood that had been intended for Roberta—Alice left the chamber.

At the bottom of the stairs she paused to gather her composure. She clutched a hand over her suddenly pounding heart as her eyes sought out her captor. Numbly she stared at one of the servants mopping up a pool of water by the door brought in by careless feet. It was as if she were blind to his presence, for her mind was bound up with the man who stood in front of the hearth staring into the flames.

A tall, slender-hipped and broad-shouldered man, Ewen Tremain was as handsome of physique as he was of face. Attired in black with a white stock at his throat, one black-booted foot resting on the ornate brass fender, he looked every inch the lord he was. His chiselled profile was touched by the warm light of the fire and the growing ache in her breast attested to his handsomeness. It was impossible not to respond to his masculine magnetism.

In an attempt to bolster her self-confidence and regain some of her serenity, Alice let out a slow, steady breath and moved forward, bringing him about to face her as her boot heels tapped against the stone floor. She paused as his eyes, holding a roguish gleam, swept down her. He took in every detail, a curious, questioning quirk lifting his brow as his gaze met hers.

'I realise you intended the cloak for Roberta,' Alice needled deliberately, 'but under the circumstances I am sure she won't mind, since she will soon have a husband to buy her such costly attire.'

Ewen frowned harshly. It disturbed him to be reminded of Roberta, but strangely it was not for the reason Alice might have expected. His feeling of guilt goaded him. It was as if he had turned his back on every commitment he had ever made to Roberta before his absence. When he thought back upon it, she had not mourned his loss for very long at all.

'I wish to leave,' Alice said steadily. 'I am sure the roads are not as bad as they were. I would be grateful if you or one of your servants would escort me back to London. You cannot keep me here any longer.'

'Nor do I wish to,' he murmured. He watched her, his eyes alert above the faintly smiling mouth. He cocked an eye at her, the leaping flames of the fire wavering and setting strange shadows dancing around them. Its light flickered over his thick dark hair, outlining his face. Then a full smile touched his lips.

'You are still cross with me, Alice.'

There was a moment of silence and her agitation faded. A surge of irrepressible excitement rose in her. 'I am not in the least cross with you. What made you think I was?'

'You have been avoiding me.'

Alice glanced at him. His warm, masculine voice brought her senses alive. Blushing, she replied, 'Yes, I have. Please—do not humiliate me more than I am feeling already. I—I am distressed that the wine or—whatever—somehow encouraged me to forget myself, but you have my promise that it won't happen again. I—was not myself and I would appreciate it if you did not mention it again.'

Ewen's brows came together in a troubled frown. 'As you wish—but it is not forgotten. For the life of me, Alice, I can't do that.'

'Please allow me to leave.'

'You are in a hurry.'

Her blush deepened. She did it so often and so quickly that Ewen had to confess—secretly, to himself—that he quite enjoyed bringing the colour to her face.

'Yes. I must.'

He nodded. Ever since she had fled from him after the kiss he had been finding that his thoughts focused almost entirely on the dark-haired beauty. He had almost forgotten the circumstances for bringing her to Mercotte Hall. Or at least it was no longer uppermost in his thoughts. 'Very well. The weather seems to have taken a turn for the better, although I believe more snow is forecast later. I believe the roads are passable. We've more chance of reaching the city on horseback. I've ordered them to be made ready.'

Alice's heart warmed towards him. 'So you did intend to take me back today?'

'I told you I would as soon as conditions improved, didn't I?' Ewen directed a nod towards the door, impatient to begin the journey. 'Shall we go?'

Hurrying after him and pulling on her gloves, Alice swept across the hall. Settling the hood of her cloak over her head, she stepped out on to the top of the steps and looked about. Though the sun was shining brightly, reflecting off the windows and huge mounds of snow, a keen wind chilled the air. Slowly, she descended the steps and walked to where Taff and Hicks were holding the reins of two horses. Ewen followed, having donned his cloak. He drew her to the smaller of the two horses, a chestnut mare. With her large expressive eyes, flowing mane and long, gracefully arched neck, she was of a quality quite appropriate for any lady to ride.

'It may please you to know that I've selected this particular horse for you to ride with care. She is a fit mount, do you not agree?'

'Absolutely,' Alice answered, unable to hide the pleasure she felt when she inspected the mare. She was touched that Ewen had taken the trouble to select such an elegant mount for her purposes. A splendid side-saddle and accoutrements had also been provided. She lifted her gaze to his and murmured with a gentle smile, 'It would seem I am to ride into London in style. I did not expect you to go to so much trouble. Thank you.'

Captivated by the beauty of her gentle smile, Ewen was reluctant to drag his attention away from her. As the horse shifted restlessly, he lifted her effortlessly into the saddle. Taking a moment to adjust her cloak and gown, she took the reins and short whip from Hicks.

'Is there anything you need?' Ewen queried solicitously and, at the shake of her head, questioned further. 'You're warm enough? And comfortable?'

Alice inclined her head again. 'Perfectly, thank you. Shall we go?'

Hoisting himself on to his own horse and gathering the reins, he turned to her as Amir rode up to join them. 'Amir is to accompany us. If you have a need, just call out.'

Ewen lifted his hand in a casual wave of farewell to his two loyal servants and, with a light tap of his heels, nudged his horse into a slow, highstepping gait. He took the lead and headed down the drive. The ground was soft and wet with snow heaped on either side. Wary of occasional slippery patches, Alice rode at a more sedate pace, determined to arrive in London in one piece. She took in deep gulps of the icy breeze that stung her cheeks. She needed its bracing coolness to clear her head and perhaps mend the tattered shreds of her emotions.

The docile mare beneath her splashed along in the deep tracks and with each step threw up splatters of muddied snow until her lower belly and legs were covered. A hushed silence hung over the countryside as they passed along the road. It was as if the whole world held its frosted breath. She gathered her cloak close about her face and huddled in its warmth, aware that Amir was close behind and Ewen held the stallion in check beside the mare. Alice found her tension easing by slow degrees as she began to enjoy the ride. A strange security suffused her, which made her wonder at its source. Could it be the presence of her companion that eased her qualms?

The past two days had chafed hard against her emotions. The short time she had spent with Ewen within the confines of Mercotte Hall had begun an erosion in her defences. His warm and amiable manner was beginning to bring about a change in her, a change which boded ill for her weakening will.

Alice focused her attention more closely upon her captor and, though he seemed at ease, she sensed an anxiety in him that increased the closer they drew to their destination. She pondered on his silence and the attitude he displayed. He seemed quite responsible about her safety and comfort and glanced about often to assure himself of both.

Horse and man seemed like one. It took a firm hand to keep the stallion under control and yet Ewen did it with the ease which could only have come from practised skill. It fascinated Alice how he commanded the huge beast with a light touch on the reins. It almost danced beneath him, as if eager for his weight and companionship. Were he to direct that same gentle touch on a lady, she would be hard pressed to resist a response. Remembering the intimacies they had shared, would she be less susceptible?

It was midday when they reached the outer limits of London and a while later entered into the bustling activity of the city.

'Duncan Forbes. Where can he be found?' Ewen asked suddenly. 'Did he give you any idea?'

'I remember him telling me that he was staying south of the river in Southwark—Bankside, I think, at the Hart Tavern. But how am I going to get there? Lady Marchington watches me like a hawk and, after this, she won't allow me out of the house. Besides, he might have moved on by now.'

'If he has information to exchange for money, he'll not leave. But you don't have to think of looking for him. Leave it to me. Amir and I will go. If he's still there, we will find him.'

Hope stirred within her breast. 'We could go now—before you take me back to Hislop House.'

The startling silver-grey eyes rested on her ironically. 'No, Alice. Don't be ridiculous.'

She controlled a tremor of temper as his powerful frame moved easily in the saddle. 'I'm going with you,' she said, a mutinous thrust to her chin. 'This is *my* business and I insist on speaking to Mr Forbes myself.'

Ewen's face was hard and severe. 'The taverns of Bankside are no place for a respectable young woman.'

Alice met his gaze head on. 'I do not doubt that, but I have made up my mind. I am going, so the sooner we are finished with this discussion and cross the bridge to the other side of the river, the sooner the business will be done.'

It was obvious Ewen was about to refuse again

until he caught the impassioned plea on her face and shrugged. 'I see you're set on it. I doubt you'll give me rest until I consent. You are a stubborn woman, Alice Frobisher.'

A coldness settled over her face. 'So I've been told. I'm going with you, Ewen. This concerns me. If we go now, Lady Marchington will know nothing about it. If she finds out, she will draw and quarter me for sure.'

Bankside, on the south side of the river, was a place of dissipation. They steered their horses carefully through streets swarming with pedestrians, barrow boys and all manner of vehicles. Narrow alleyways where dogs rummaged in heaps of rotting garbage led off into small and dingy courtyards.

The Hart Tavern looked bright and was cleaner than most of the ale houses in this area of Southwark. Ewen called a hovering servant to look after the horses. Inside there was fresh sawdust on the floor and a cheerful fire blazing in the hearth. Several customers were talking over a jug of ale and some slices of bread and cheese and meats. Ewen spoke to the innkeeper, who confirmed that Mr Forbes had a room there. He sent a pot boy to see if he was in, but the boy returned shaking his head.

'He's a regular,' the innkeeper told them. 'He comes and goes.'

'We'll wait,' Ewen said, taking a table in the bow window where they could watch the street.

The innkeeper brought them ale, a jug of wine and some food. Unable to eat anything, Alice sat close to the window and watched every man that came passed. After thirty minutes their patience was rewarded.

'He's here,' Alice uttered a little breathlessly, watching Mr Forbes emerge from the crowd and walk towards the tavern.

Short and stout, Duncan Forbes was unshaven and looked very much the worse for wear. He was restless. He was a learned man, but his life had not been much fun lately. He'd been relying on money from the Frobisher girl in exchange for information about her father, but she'd been snatched from under his nose.

Entering the tavern, he glanced around and saw the aforesaid woman. A startled look entered his eyes before narrowing warily on her companions. 'What's this?' he said, looking at Alice.

Ewen rose, indicating a chair. 'Will you join us,

Mr Forbes?' Forbes sat uneasily in the proffered chair. His eyes flicked from the tall gentleman to his dusky-skinned companion.

'Who are they?' Forbes demanded of Alice.

'They're with me,' Alice replied, her voice soft though fraught with tension. 'Did you think I'd come here alone?'

'I believe you have information regarding the whereabouts of Miss Frobisher's father,' Ewen said, coming straight to the point. 'She arranged to meet with you several days ago, but unfortunately she was detained.'

'I saw,' Forbes growled. 'I was there—didn't think I'd see her again. What do you want?'

'The information, if you please.' Ewen sat back down, his fierce gaze remaining on Forbes.

Forbes's eyes were hard and steady. He weighed his answer carefully. The tension in the room prickled as each watched the other. 'And if I don't? What's it to you?'

'Please tell me what you know,' Alice begged. It was a moment of hopeful anticipation. 'I have the money you asked for. Here. One hundred pounds.' She placed the purse on the table between them.

Forbes reached for the purse, but Ewen snatched it away. 'Tell us what you know about Iain Frobisher first. If you lie, I will hunt you down and you will pay for it with your life. Is it true that he's alive?'

Forbes nodded. 'He was—the last time I saw him.'

'When was that?'

'Eight months back.'

'Where? Where did you see him?'

'Here—in London. Lambeth.'

'Is—is he still here?' Alice asked, hope and excitement lighting her eyes.

Forbes shook his head. 'He left. Said he was going home.'

'Home? What—what did he mean by that? His home now—here in London?'

'Scotland. He said he was going back to Scotland.'

'But—but where has he been? You said you were with him after Culloden. You were brought to London together.'

'I told you we were on the hulks together. He jumped ship when they came to take him to Kennington Common to be hanged. He was shot when he tried to swim away. Everybody thought he was dead—until I met up with him in Lambeth.'

'But—if he didn't die, where did he go? Where has he been living?'

Forbes shrugged. 'He said he was in the river a long time—almost killed him, it did. Someone pulled him out and looked after him. He said he lost his mind for a while.'

'How did he seem? Was he ill?'

'Wasn't good. He hadn't much to say. He just said he wanted to go home.'

Tears welled in Alice's eyes. 'Is this true? Did he not know that his family had managed to get to France?'

'He didn't know he had any family left. He thought his wife and children had died in the fire when the King's soldiers set fire to his home. For a time he stayed away from Scotland—in case he was recognised and arrested—and because he couldn't bear to look at the house where his family had perished.'

'But when you saw my name in the papers, how did you know I was his daughter?'

He shrugged. 'Too much of a coincidence—it was a chance I took.'

'Can you tell me anything else? Where he was living so I can find out more? Who he was with?'

'I'm sorry. I can't tell you any more than I have.'

Alice took the purse from Ewen and handed it to him. 'Thank you, Mr Forbes. I am grateful.'

Not until the Hart Tavern was behind them did Ewen turn his head and look at Alice riding beside him. Staring straight ahead, she was hardly aware of him regarding her. He contemplated the slight tugging of small, white teeth against a bottom lip. He could almost see her mind struggling against a flooding tide of helpless frustration. 'What are you thinking, Alice?'

She looked at him. 'I have much to consider.'

'Did you believe Forbes?'

She closed her eyes and bowed her head as if she prayed intently for it to be true. Ewen's heart went out to her.

'I have to,' she whispered. 'Although what I'm to do now is quite beyond me. I cannot bear to think he might be wandering about Scotland, without family and unable to lay claim to his properties, while I am here worrying about him.' Pulling herself together, she smiled at him. 'Don't worry. I'll think of something.'

* * *

They rode through the slush-covered streets of Piccadilly and finally came to a halt outside Hislop House. As eager as Alice had been to return, she had a deep reluctance to dismount and enter the house where she would have to face Lady Marchington's wrath.

Ewen found himself staring once more at his companion, feeling a sudden anguished need to see her again. It had been his intention to disappear when he'd delivered her safely to the Countess, but that was before she'd kissed him. Memories of the way she had felt in his arms, the heady sweetness of her kiss, had disturbed him deeply. A spirited beauty, she excited him, she shocked him, and while he did not consider himself remotely in love with her, he was in thrall to this beautiful girl.

Perhaps it was because he had suddenly seen the lonely, vulnerable side to her that made him feel so protective of her. Perhaps it was her candour that threw him off balance, maybe the softness of her lips or those fathomless deep blue eyes of hers.

The hardship and tragedy he had suffered at the hands of the corsairs had stunted his emotions.

His relationships with women were about sex. Just the same, he mused as he thought of Alice Frobisher, life could still deliver surprises.

He, who had never needed anyone, found his very soul crying out to feel once more the soft lips of this young woman he barely knew—despite the element of mistrust he had felt when she had kissed him. Even though she bore similarities to Etta. Taking into account the rough handling she had received from the abduction, his own guilt and the sense of responsibility he felt for the ignoble deed, he believed she was a woman who had every reason to despise him. Despite this he was reluctant to be parted from her. On the journey to London he had cast about in his mind desperately for any excuse to keep her with him.

He had come to the conclusion there was only one thing he could do.

Alice smiled down at him as he assisted her to dismount, resting her hands on his arms. 'Well, Ewen, here we are,' she said as he set her on the ground. 'Can you do bowing and scraping?'

'I do many things, Alice,' he said, handing the reins of the two mounts to Amir, 'but bowing and scraping are not among them. I fully expect to feel the sharp end of the Countess's tongue, but I am not afraid of her.'

Taking her arm, he escorted her up the steps, ready to face whatever kind of trouble he might run into.

Chapter Six

Simpson opened the door. On seeing Alice on the doorstep he drew himself up ramrod straight, his eyebrows positively levitating with surprise, his eyes registering relief.

'Miss Frobisher!'

'Yes, it's me, Simpson,' she replied, sweeping into the hall followed by Ewen. 'Is Lady Marchington at home?'

'Indeed she is. She is in the drawing room with Miss Hislop and most relieved they will be to find you delivered safely.'

They followed in the wake of Simpson. He swept open a pair of carved oaken doors and stepped aside to admit them into the drawing room. The two faces that turned to stare at them were beyond Alice's worst imaginings. Roberta jumped up from the sofa with a startled gasp and hurried towards her, and the eyes that Lady Marchington settled on her would have turned a lesser mortal to stone.

Rising from her seat by the hearth, she looked at Lord Tremain with accusation and ire shooting from her eyes as she said scornfully, 'I wondered when you would bring her back. Do you have any notion of the true gravity of the situation? What you did was quite outrageous. I was about to set the constables to finding her.'

'Then I am happy to have saved you the trouble,' Ewen replied in clipped tones, seeing Alice take a position away from the Countess. 'Why the delay? How did you know she was with me?'

'After what Roberta disclosed to me about the letter you sent her, I was convinced she was with you.'

Out of the corner of her eye Alice observed Ewen. Recalling how angry he had been with Lady Marchington when he had last walked from this house, she knew how difficult this was for him. His face was grimly drawn and his eyes were pale and hazardous. He was like an eagle, oppressive, arbitrary and unyielding, his insouciance and engaging charm, which he had shown when she had dined with him, and the concern he had shown for her on the journey to London completely gone.

Uttering a cry of profound relief, Roberta embraced Alice warmly. 'Oh, Alice!' she exclaimed in an agitated, disjointed rush. 'I have been so worried about you. I thought you weren't coming back. And here you are looking as well as ever, except you are a little pale. I pray you have not been treated badly. Where have you been? Was it the note from…?' Her voice tapered off when her gaze went beyond Alice to the tall figure of Lord Tremain across the room. 'Oh—L-Lord Tremain,' she stammered, her cheeks flushing a bright pink. 'I—I… Oh… I didn't expect…'

'Sit down, Roberta,' Lady Marchington ordered sternly. 'You are making a show of yourself.'

Obediently, Roberta did as she was told, perching on the edge of her chair and clutching her hands together in an agitated state.

'You know, Countess,' Ewen said, his expression hawk faced and appearing completely self-possessed, 'I find it amazing that nearly everyone who knows me is half-afraid of me, except a handful of my friends, my family, you, madam, and Miss Frobisher. I can only surmise that courage, recklessness, call it what you will, is present in every one of you. I give you leave to take me to task for what I have done if it will make you feel better.'

Lady Marchington looked at him, her piercing eyes alive with hatred. 'I intend to. What you did, Lord Tremain, was an absolute disgrace. Did it even occur to you that we would be frantic with worry? What did you hope to achieve?'

'Roberta. I saw something that belonged to me and I wanted to take it back.' Ignoring the indomitable lady, he strode to his former betrothed and looked down into her wide, apprehensive eyes. That the Countess hadn't told her about his letters he had no doubt and he had no intention of adding awkwardness to the moment by doing so.

'Roberta, I cannot do more than apologise for my conduct towards you. I ask your pardon if my absence and failure to explain the reason caused you pain. I can only tell you that my brother Edward, who, as you know, lived at Barradine in Scotland, died. My mother was in despair for a while and it was necessary for me to be with her.'

Roberta's expression was soft with compassion. 'Oh—I am so very sorry. I wish you had told me. I would have understood—truly—and I do,' she whispered, still somewhat in awe of this man she had thought would one day be her husband. 'How is your mother now? Well, I hope.'

'She is better and back in France with my stepfather and my uncle. In all sincerity I wish you well on your coming marriage. I pray you will find happiness with Viscount Pemberton.'

The smile Roberta bestowed on him was radiant. She had dreaded this moment for so long that now she had seen him and spoken to him she was relieved he had taken her betrothal so well. 'Thank you. I shall. I know Hugh and I will be happy.'

'You have got off lightly, Lord Tremain,' Lady Marchington remarked coldly. 'Roberta is too soft-hearted for her own good. However, I expected better of you. Your actions were those of a feckless youth—not a man of your standing and experience.'

'I agree absolutely.'

'Am I to believe that your conscience smote you and you have come here to do the right thing and apologise for abducting Miss Frobisher?'

'My conscience has nothing to do with it. For what it's worth I deeply regret what I did. I should have approached you again over the matter of my betrothal to Roberta.'

'It's too late for that. It would have done you no good. Roberta is to wed Viscount Pemberton, so let that be an end to the matter. Where did you take Miss Frobisher and why did you not bring her back earlier.'

'We were at my uncle's house—Mercotte Hall, just north of the city. The weather prevented me from returning her sooner. I give you my word that Miss Frobisher was well taken care of and came to no harm.'

Lady Marchington opened her mouth and when she spoke her voice dripped icicles. 'That may be so, but you have ruined her just the same.'

'Not necessarily.'

'But you have, Lord Tremain. I forbade you to communicate with Roberta, but you defied me. She told me she received a note from you, that Alice agreed to her request to meet you in her stead.' Her eyes slid to Alice and narrowed with displeasure. 'You should not have agreed to it. What were you thinking, you wretched girl? You should have come to me. Your behaviour was reckless and irresponsible. Now you must pay the price.' She looked once more at Lord Tremain. 'By abducting her you have compromised her good name and her reputation. It is most unfortunate

that she was seen and recognised by certain in-
dividuals in the park and being bundled into a
coach. They made great haste to spread the gossip.
It was all over the city within a matter of hours.'

'I am sorry about that. And if anyone can make
a scandal out of a woman being bundled into a
coach, they need their minds examining.'

'Not when that young lady is my ward.' Lady
Marchington gave Alice a withering look. There
was something arrogant and uncompromising in
the set of the girl's head and the light in her eyes.
Even now, when she ought to be mortified by
shame, she stood there and stared back at Lady
Marchington coolly. 'You foolish, foolish girl,'
she uttered with crushing disdain. 'I always felt
you had a tendency to deceit. You do not have the
character and disposition of Roberta. Have you
learned nothing from your time in London? Do
you not understand that you are already skating
on thin ice in society's eyes?' Observing the puzzled look that crossed Lord Tremain's face, she
smiled a chilling, satisfied smile, but she would
not enlighten him as to what she was referring.

When she was reminded of her past, Alice's entire being was engulfed in mortification. It would
appear that Ewen was the only man in London

who did not know of the scandal that had followed her to London. But then, at the time he had been in Scotland, having spent no time at all in London on his return. As far as reading about it in the newspaper, the news had taken up little space and she doubted he would read such trivia anyway.

Her misery increased a thousandfold as she stood stiffly facing Lady Marchington. She knew then why she disliked the older woman so much, for it was in her nature to wound her cruelly. No matter how she had tried to please and obey her when she had come to Hislop House, all her efforts were repulsed and repaid by such words as Lady Marchington had just uttered. The accusation cut her to the heart, especially as she had voiced it before Ewen. She deliberately did not look at Ewen, who was giving her a studied look.

A muscle twitched furiously in Ewen's cheek as his angry eyes took in Lady Marchington. He loathed her at that moment. The injustice of an innocent being so harshly maligned gnawed at every chivalrous inch of his body, although he did wonder what he was about to get himself into.

'This scandal will ruin you absolutely,' Lady Marchington went on mercilessly. 'There are many kinds of persecution that are not readily apparent, such as the whispered conjectures, the gossip and subtle innuendoes that can destroy a reputation and inflict a lifetime of damage. Society has assumed your character must indeed be of the blackest nature and you will summarily be dropped.' With grim satisfaction she observed the hard set of Lord Tremain's jaw. 'You have destroyed any chance of Miss Frobisher making a decent marriage. I congratulate you, Lord Tremain. You have made her into a leper.'

White faced, Alice stared at Lady Marchington. Her disgrace was total, her position irredeemable.

Ewen's eyes had turned positively glacial during this harsh exchange. 'Frankly, Countess, I find that quite ridiculous.'

'Do you indeed.' Lady Marchington seethed, her voice cold and resolute as she met the smouldering anger in Lord Tremain's eyes. They regarded each other across the distance, two fiercely indomitable wills clashing in silence. 'You have subjected Miss Frobisher to a public scandal. What you have done, Lord Tremain, is nothing short of wicked. And now if you think you can ruin my good name by abducting my ward and then disappear from the scene of the crime, you are grievously mistaken.'

Turning then, his jaw set in a hard line, Ewen reached out to take Alice's slender hand in his own. He glanced down at her pale, startled face only once before again fixing his scowl on the Countess. 'I have no intention of doing so,' he said, having no intention of beating about the bush. 'It is my desire to marry Miss Frobisher. I intend to make her my wife.'

His announcement rendered Lady Marchington momentarily speechless. She had certainly not expected him to rescue Alice from a scandal that was greatly of his own making. 'I see. Is it not the custom to ask permission of a young lady's parent—or, in Alice's case, her guardian—before announcing your intentions?'

'I shall notify her brother of what I intend. Do you have any objections, Countess?'

'I agree that it is the only solution that can hold sway over the damage done by you to be adequate enough to protect her.' Of course Lady Marchington had no objection. She was already considering how she could best exploit this situation. This was a providential opportunity to be rid of both Alice and Lord Tremain from her life and she must not waste it.

Unable to believe what Ewen had said, removing her hand from his, Alice was seething with humiliation and struggling to control her temper. It was a difficult moment for her—she hadn't known what to expect. How dare he do this without discussing it with her first? She wanted to maintain an air of aloof disdain, to face Ewen in calm defiance, but her mauled and aching distrust of the future assailed her senses. The suggestion that she marry Ewen Tremain, a man who had treated her appallingly, a man she hardly knew, that she enter into a binding contract that would change her life, something that would determine her entire future, was almost too much to bear.

'No,' she cried, managing to drag her voice through the strangling mortification in her chest. Her glance skidded over Ewen to Lady Marchington. 'I have no wish to marry Lord Tremain. The idea is quite ludicrous.'

Ewen turned his head sharply to Alice and studied her face as if he'd never seen her before. The entire colour had drained from her face and her body was tense. Raising her hand to her mouth, she stepped back from him, as if seeking to be alone so she could think clearly.

Reluctantly she raised her eyes to his and looked at him in desperate appeal. What Ewen saw in their innermost depths—a confusion of anger, pain and fear—almost took his breath.

'Alice, what is it?'

'I cannot believe that you want this. I have certainly not encouraged it.' As soon as the words left her lips she wished she could take them back. Of *course* she had encouraged it. Had *she* not kissed *him*, after all, because she had been unable to help herself?

Ewen's granite features softened and his eyes warmed, as if he understood how confused and humiliated she felt. 'Unconsciously you have encouraged it every time we have been together. Have you any objections to me as a husband?'

'It is not open to discussion,' Lady Marchington stated firmly. 'Lord Tremain has agreed to do right by you, though God knows that if I were a man I would take a horsewhip to him. You have only a little knowledge of the kind of man that he is. No doubt you will find out before too long. Because of what he did, if this is not dealt with in the proper manner—quickly, I might add—you will be subjected to public censure and a scandal that will make us a laughing stock.'

Undeterred, Alice tossed her head in defiance. 'That is no great disappointment to me. My brother will never agree to this.'

Lady Marchington's eyes narrowed with irritation. 'Hold your tongue, Alice. You are severely lacking in respect and discretion when you speak to me. Your brother put you in my charge with instructions that a suitable match be found for you, which has happened sooner than I expected. In my opinion you and Lord Tremain are well suited to each other,' she said on a sour note. 'You will do the right thing. You may be averse to the marriage just now, but I believe that will change when you realise the seriousness of the situation. Of course there is the matter of her dowry to discuss,' she said to Ewen. 'Her brother will make a generous settlement.'

'I don't doubt it,' Ewen replied harshly. 'But dowry or no, I am well able to take care of my own wife.' When his gaze shifted to Alice, however, his granite features softened and his eyes warmed, as if he understood how humiliated she felt. Taking her hand, he marched her to the door.

Lady Marchington gasped at his rudeness. 'How dare you walk out? I demand to know where you are going'

'I wish to speak with Miss Frobisher alone. There will be no one to hinder or influence any decision she might make. It should be done of her own free will without intimidation. The matter of our marriage is entirely between Alice and me, no one else.' He smiled at Alice. 'Come. We will speak of this in private.'

Thankfully the hall was empty. Ewen placed his hands on Alice's shoulders and looked down into her upturned face. 'I realise this must have come as a surprise, Alice, but think about it carefully. I am offering to give you my protection and my name. The Countess is right. I abducted you, and, in doing so, I have compromised your reputation—more than likely beyond repair.'

Alice looked at him for a moment in thoughtful silence, then she said, 'This is all so sudden.' She spoke with measured care, not because she was unsure of herself, but because she felt the need to be cautious. She bowed her head. For a moment she had an odd sentimental thought that by accepting Ewen's loveless proposition she might be cutting herself off from the possibility of someone coming along with a pounding heart who loved her for herself, not because he had compromised her and had no choice but to do right by her. But that wasn't likely to happen. But then, when they had kissed, it was clear they had feelings for one another. Perhaps, in time, love would grow.

'I—I'm surprised Lady Marchington could agree to such a thing. I find it most disconcerting.'

'Do you honestly think I care one whit what that woman may say or think?'

'I will not marry a man whose only reason for proposing is because he has compromised me and is left with little choice. Why, the very idea is so far-fetched, it's ludicrous.'

Ewen lifted his shoulders in a casual shrug. 'I disagree. Actually, I had already decided to suggest that we marry.'

'Oh? When?'

'On our ride to London.'

'But—two days ago you didn't even like me.'

'As a matter of fact, despite my initial anger, I did like you.'

Alice ignored his words and gave him an injured look. 'Forgive me if I appear surprised, but I thought the opposite. I seem to recall you telling Hicks and Taff that they had saddled you with a maddening chit.'

Ewen stepped away from her, rubbing the back of his neck in exasperation. 'That was before I had spent some time in your company. Do not try to examine my heart so closely at this time, Alice. It's a union that would suit us both. We are both alone. Both of Scottish descent. Both our families are in France. At present we cannot say what has happened to your father, but we will pursue that, I promise you, when we get to Scotland.' Alice gazed at him, clinging to the steadfastness he offered. He nodded in reassurance. 'Will you not accept my proposal?'

Alice fought against the logic of his words. She wanted more out of marriage than a union which seemed sensible. 'It is too soon,' she said quietly. 'A week ago we had not even met. By nature I am temperamental—and so are you. We might not suit.'

'Alice, I've never met another woman who is more exasperating.'

'If you find me exasperating, my lord, why bother asking me to be your wife? I may bring you nothing but grief.'

Ewen's mouth twisted in a lopsided smile. 'I'll risk it if you will. What do you say, Alice? Will you be my wife—unless you have preference for another?'

'I have no preference.'

She did not return his smile, but waited for him to continue.

'Would you like it if I were to kneel?' he asked after a moment.

'Please don't,' she said quickly before he did just that. 'You would look ridiculous. I—I'll think about it.'

'I suggest you give me your answer post-haste, for I'll not rest until I know one way or another. I may have known you only days, but one thing I have learned about you is that you are decisive.'

She was also a beautiful young woman, plain spoken, and, he thought, his mother would like her. After all, were their families not neighbours once? Simon, his older brother, had fought beside Alice's father and brothers at Culloden, which must count for something. Alice was straightforward, a woman who could be relied upon, a sensible woman who would look for reliability and dependability in a husband and not necessarily expect more. He could do worse.

'Do you like children, Alice?'

'Yes,' she said, trying to appear composed, while inside she was quaking. 'I have no experience of them, but I hope to have children of my own one day.' She gave him her full attention. 'Lady Marchington has told you my circumstances and that I have a substantial dowry. I am sure you must be wondering if I will make a suitable wife.'

His lips quirked. 'You are a frank speaker,' he exclaimed.

She averted her eyes. 'It's the way I am. Something has to happen,' she said quietly. 'I cannot remain here forever. With Roberta to be married shortly I will have outlived my purpose at Hislop House.'

'You could return to your brother's household in Paris.'

Alice avoided his direct gaze. How could she tell him that she was regarded as a fallen women in the eyes of the community she had left behind?

'I can't do that. It is not an option.'

Placing his finger beneath her chin, Ewen tipped her face up to his. 'Would you care to tell me what the Countess was referring to when she said you were already skating on thin ice? You told me you were betrothed and that when you walked away it caused a scandal. Is there anything else you want to tell me?'

Shrugging his finger away, she shook her head. 'No.'

'There must have been something in your past to warrant her remark.'

'There's nothing, I tell you, except that at the time, suddenly and painfully I learned that when one breaks with convention, one can never crawl back to its comforting shell again. I became cut off from the past and all its connections. At the time the realisation was both chilling and daunting, but I will not, cannot, go back.'

'I must admit to a certain curiosity about your life before you came to London, Alice.'

Something too deeply hidden to have a name stirred in Alice. 'I told you. There's nothing to tell. I was betrothed—I told you about that. I ended it.'

Her voice had become cold and unyielding. She seemed about to crack and splinter like the icebergs Ewen had once seen in the North Sea. The soft, uncertain vulnerability which he had found so appealing had vanished with the speed of the sun behind a storm cloud. Her full, soft mouth was held in a tight line and her eyes had hardened.

'Dear Lord, Alice. What have I said? I swear

you are the most stubborn, controversial female I have ever come across. I know in the beginning my behaviour towards you was disgraceful, but I am prepared to atone for that. I ask you to be my wife, to give you my name and remove you from the strictures the Countess enforces on you, and when I ask you a civil question you act as though I had made some insulting remark. That is hardly good manners, but if you want to keep your past to yourself then that is your affair.'

'I am sorry—truly…'

Ewen watched as the steely hardness slowly left her eyes and her mouth softened. But she was still so serious he wanted to reach out and draw her into his arms, but instinct told him it would be the wrong thing to do. She was still very young and he surmised had been raised in a sheltered household ruled by her brother, yet a moment ago he had seen a hatred and bitterness, along with a soul-destroying disillusionment which no one so young should have to suffer. There was something in her, something secret and contained, some rancour which he had inadvertently stirred and seen flair up malevolently when he had mentioned her past, and yet struggling with it was a strength and a sweetness which showed in the softness of her expression and defenceless vulnerability.

Ewen would say nothing more for now, but he would not let it be.

'There—is nothing, Ewen. But what of your past? Can you in all honesty tell me there is nothing, when you were a slave to be bartered or sold at will, that you want to remain there, that perhaps it is too painful to resurrect?'

Ewen's face tightened and his mouth thinned to an ugly line. 'Yes,' Alice went on, 'I thought as much. I do not ask you to tell me, Ewen. Whatever happened to you at the hands of those barbarians is your affair. I won't ask you to tell me. I don't need to know.'

Alice wondered what he was thinking. She saw the expression on his face change and an odd, almost haunted look pass over it. Then it disappeared, but not before she had felt a swift pang of apprehension.

Ewen nodded and his expression relaxed. 'It would seem that we both have our secrets. It will be a gamble if we agree to embark on a future together—and I mean that without offence.'

There was a tense silence as they sized one another up. Was he really trying to atone for the wrong he had done her in the beginning? Alice wondered. What did he really want from her? Surely it was not just her body since there must be a score of women he knew who would be more than willing to appease his appetite. But what did it matter? His eyes were still on her, his mouth curved in that whimsical, enquiring humour she was beginning to know so well, as though to dare her to accept his proposal of marriage. Why not? his expression said. It was a challenge to be seized.

Alice laughed softly in an attempt to hide her nervousness. 'Why, Ewen, what's this? Why so serious all of a sudden? Are you regretting your hasty pronouncement? Are you having second thoughts about doing the honourable thing and making me your wife?'

Ewen considered her. 'I'm still trying to straighten out my life after my two incompetents brought me the wrong woman. I'm not sure I can handle another surprise.'

The corners of Alice's lips lifted enticingly. 'Are those the words of a coward, my lord?'

In challenging question, the silver-grey eyes fixed their stare upon her and glowed with warmth. 'Have I not a right to be? I certainly felt the sharp edge of your tongue in the beginning. I'm still smarting from it.'

A quiet chuckle escaped Alice as she moved closer to him. 'You portray yourself as an innocent when we both know you deserved it.'

'An arguable statement,' Ewen protested, reaching out and cupping her chin in the palm of his hand. 'But I have to say I never expected you to be such a stimulating diversion.' Taking her small hand between his, he searched her eyes for some hint of denial, but he found none. 'Alice Frobisher, I would be greatly honoured if you would accept my proposal of marriage and become my wife. It would please me if you said yes.'

'You don't speak of love, Ewen.'

'Should I, Alice?'

'No, not if it's not—felt.'

'By whom?'

'Either of us, I suppose.'

Ewen sighed and looked down at her hand he still held. 'We'll manage very well. I am sure of that. There is a strong attraction between us. We both feel it, that I do know. Be assured that I shall do right by you and be a good husband. I protect what is mine. No one shall hurt you and you will want for nothing. I promise.'

'So you are serious,' she whispered in amazement. It was almost as if she were waking from a long sleep, for the full realisation of what he wanted was just now beginning to hasten the beat of her heart. 'You—wouldn't regret our marriage afterwards?'

'I have known you for only a short while, but in that time I have grown to like your company. I will ask nothing of you that you cannot give and if you are not prepared to give it, I am not the man to take it by force. I consider myself a fair and reasonable man, and generous. I am self-indulgent, true, but what I have, so do you. You would be my wife, Alice, and that's all that matters to me,' Ewen declared.

Alice looked at him. This had come before she was ready. Everything he did seemed to take her by surprise. There should be more of a courtship, a period of mutual discovery and delicious anticipation. She wondered if she was giving in too quickly. And yet, the kiss she had given him and his response had been too urgent to be contained for long.

She remembered the pomp that had surrounded the occasion when Philippe had voiced such a question, but for the life of her, she could not recall her heart thumping quite so wildly within her chest as it did after this man's simple but stirring proposal.

She considered what it would mean being married to Ewen Tremain and committing herself to him for the rest of her life. It seemed appropriate for her to make a home with the man who had awakened passion within her, the kind of passion she had never expected to feel. If she did not love him at this time, she certainly desired him, and she could not continue living in the same house as Lady Marchington.

She wanted what would come next as much as she regretted the lost dance of courtship, and by marrying Ewen Tremain she would dispatch Lady Marchington to the shadows, along with the lingering burden of guilt that she had carried with her since leaving Paris. She felt a deep sense of obligation to William, who had worried and suffered so much on her account and fought a duel to the death in her honour. Knowing that he had killed Philippe was an act that had shocked her to the core, overwhelming her with feelings of guilt and shame, for no matter what Philippe had done to her, she had not sought his death.

She sincerely hoped William would approve of

her marrying Ewen. But then the Frobishers and the Tremains had been friends and neighbours for many years before the Battle of Culloden. She suspected William would be happy for her and that she would have had her mother's blessing. She felt a certain amount of guilt about pursuing her own happiness while her father was still missing, but she would carry on searching for him. Nothing would change that.

Slowly she responded with a consenting nod. 'Yes, Ewen,' she whispered. 'I will marry you.' There were tears in her eyes. Tears for the speed of her surrender. Tears for all the other futures there might have been.

'You will be my wife?' he said lightly, watching the changing expressions on her face and reading them correctly.

'Yes.'

'Then we will be married here in London— soon, I think,' he said softly.

Despite her efforts to appear calm, Alice's voice quavered. 'Whatever you think.'

'I will write to your brother. You must let me have his address in France.'

'I doubt William will raise any objections. He will be more than happy with my choice of groom, considering your family's connections to mine in the past.'

Lifting her chin, Ewen settled a gentle kiss upon her lips, as if afraid he'd hurt her with anything more passionate. When he drew back, he explored her face with shining eyes. 'I've been aching to do that ever since you kissed me,' he murmured, and again he lowered his lips to hers, but this time his mouth slanted across hers in a devouring search, quickening her pulse until she felt the stirring of ardour in her woman's body. His tongue slipped between her lips with a provocative boldness, claiming the warm cavern with a possessive voracity that set her senses to flight and awakening a memory of another time with another man.

Immediately she drew away from him and, with a tremulous sigh, said, 'I think we should go back inside and tell Lady Marchington what we've decided, don't you? There is just one thing I need to ask. You said you would take me to Scotland. Is that where we will live?'

'It is. I am Lord Tremain of Barradine. I inherited the title and the property on Edward's demise. What do you say? Does Scotland appeal to you?' He raised an amused brow. 'I sense it might appeal to you following our meeting with Mr Forbes.'

Alice's heart was uplifted and tears suddenly filled her eyes. 'Hopefully it is where I will find my father. I was born there. How could it not? I cannot think of anywhere I would like to live more.'

Later, when Alice had time to reflect on this sudden change to her life, she could not get used to the idea that she was to marry this man, Ewen Tremain, who was as deep and complex as the seas over which he had once sailed. She knew only one thing for certain about him: that she did not know him at all. So much had happened to him in the past, so many things that were locked away inside his mind she could not begin to imagine. They were to be married for one reason only—to safeguard her reputation. If he were to be told the truth, he would hate her.

Would not any man's respect turn to loathing when he learned what the woman in his arms had once been to another?

Not until Ewen had left and Lady Marchington had retired to her room to lie down did Alice and Roberta find the opportunity to discuss the implications of the past few days.

'Naturally your acceptance of Lord Tremain's proposal of marriage has taken me by surprise,' Roberta remarked, making herself comfortable on Alice's bed. 'I did not expect it, to say the least. I blame myself entirely. Had I not asked you to meet him in my stead none of this would have happened. But you don't have to marry him.'

'Yes, I do, Roberta. Besides, I want to—I must.' She drew a breath, rather like a sigh. 'When I agreed to meet him in the park, little did I know I was playing one of the most desperate games of my life. If I lost, I lost everything as a woman in respectable, upper-class society. I did lose, Roberta, for little did I realise I was to be abducted and that there were witnesses eager to report it to all and sundry. Now there is no going back.'

'Please don't tell me you are in love with him. I won't believe you.'

Alice gave a short, wry laugh. 'You would be right not to. It's not like that. Love is the one luxury I cannot afford. I'm no romantic, Roberta. Once bitten, twice shy—isn't that what they say? Ewen has compromised me. He knows that and wants to do the honourable thing. Our marriage will also be one of convenience to us both. There's no sentimental nonsense between us.' Her voice was airy, her manner unconcerned, but Roberta was not convinced and inclined to argue.

'You make it sound like a business arrangement instead of a marriage.'

Alice glanced at her friend steadily, searching for anything that would tell her Roberta was against her marrying the man she had once been betrothed to, but there was no sign, only concern for her friend. 'Once he was an admirer of yours. I hope you don't mind me marrying him.'

'No, of course I don't,' she answered, absently plucking at an embroidered flower on the quilt cover. 'By all means marry him, if that's what you want. But, does he make you happy?'

'I don't need a man to make me happy. I shall chart my own course.'

'Married to Lord Tremain? I don't think so, Alice. A fair-minded and generous man, yes. That I did find out in the short time that I knew him. But he is also arrogant, hard-headed, possessive and dangerous. Have a care in your dealings with him.'

'I will be happy to have an agreement with the man I marry, Roberta. As I said, it will not be a love affair.'

'And will that be enough, do you think, Alice? You are still very young.'

'It will be quite enough,' Alice said steadily, remembering the dinner she had shared with Ewen at Mercotte Hall and the consequence of letting herself get too close to him. She chose not to take his rakish advances too seriously, but that brief, private flirtation had been thrillingly dangerous and had added a zest of excitement to her life that had been decidedly missing before.

'My circumstances do not permit me the luxury of choice,' she went on quietly. 'I am a woman in need of a husband. If Lord Tremain will have me and treat me kindly, then I will marry him. I don't care what his life has been like. What I care about is having a home of my own and children to care for. After that unfortunate affair with Philippe, I had given up on finding someone decent. This is a very good match for me—although perhaps not so much for him. He is to take me to Scotland to live—close to where I was born, where our families were friends. I welcome that.' She looked at her friend and when she next spoke her tone was quiet and pleading. 'Be happy for me, Roberta. Please.'

Roberta smiled and reaching out clasped her

hand. 'I am happy for you, Alice. If this is indeed what you want then I pray you find happiness—and love—together.'

It was two weeks before Ewen called to see her. Had she not received two large bouquets of flowers from him at separate intervals, she would have thought his proposal of marriage had been imagined, but here he was. For a moment she could not speak, she could only hold her breath in anticipation, hoping desperately he was not about to disappoint her with unwelcome news.

'Ewen! You take me by surprise. I did not expect you.'

He was obliged to smile as he looked at her candid gaze, her face suddenly alight with expectation, yet trying so hard to keep the formality of such an occasion.

He banished her suspense by coming straight to the point. 'I apologise for not having visited you sooner, Alice, but I've had pressing matters to attend to before I leave London. The Countess finds my presence irksome at the best of times, so I am sure you will understand why I've kept away. I've had news from your brother,' he said, standing at the side of the heavy, oak desk in the library at Hislop House, where Simpson had directed him. He studied the bright young woman sitting in a chair writing a letter to an acquaintance in France. Putting down the pen, she pushed back the chair and stood up.

'Lady Marchington has written to him and is still awaiting his response. What does he say?'

'That the marriage can go ahead with his blessing. He has graciously given us his permission.' When she did not reply immediately, he raised a finely drawn eyebrow, giving her a penetrating look. 'You do still want to marry me, don't you, Alice?'

After she fully understood what he was saying, Alice's eyes began to sparkle, the blood coursing excitedly through her veins and a wide, spontaneous smile sweeping across her face. 'Yes—yes, of course I do.'

'He also expressed his surprise and delight that you are to wed one of your own kind—a Scot and one of your family's neighbours. He hopes to make my acquaintance in the near future. There is much he remembers of the upheaval in Scotland when both highlanders and lowlanders rose up to follow Prince Charles—his march into England to raise support and the subsequent battle on Culloden Field. But you can't be interested in this kind of talk. It must be detestably boring to a lovely young lady.'

Dark blue eyes, wide with surprise, gazed at him. She tossed back her head with a movement that emphasised the proud swell of her breasts. To his own amused vexation, Ewen's gaze wandered over her slim figure, her fitted vanilla gown with moss-green trimmings revealing the outline of her firm breasts and shapely hips, the folds of material billowing to her dainty, slippered feet. There was colour in her cheeks as she leaned forward, the black shining curls warm against them when she moved her head. At that moment she bore no resemblance to the furious termagant who had tumbled into Mercotte Hall.

'The talk certainly doesn't bore me, Ewen. After all, what happened at Culloden touched both our families with disastrous effects. I have grown up on tales handed down by those who were there and experienced it at first hand. Did you mention to William about my meeting with Mr Forbes and his news about our father?'

'No. It is for you to inform him. I thought you might have done so already.'

Alice sighed and shook her head. 'No, not yet. I will, of course, he has a right to know.'

'But?'

'I thought I would wait until we are in Scotland. If what Mr Forbes told us is true, then my father might be there. I don't wish to raise William's hopes unnecessarily.'

'We'll soon know for certain. If we don't find him in the ruins of your old home, I'll make enquiries in the villages and among the neighbouring gentry. If he is there, with any luck someone will have seen him.'

Alice looked into his lean face, knowing that he would do as he promised. She found herself wishing he would take her into his arms and kiss her passionately as he had done when he'd proposed marriage. She sighed inwardly, striving to control her feelings, suddenly stirred with unease.

'And the Countess? You have said nothing to her?'

Alice's chin lifted. 'No, why should I tell her anything? She has no interest whatsoever in me or my family. Besides, we will soon be married and I will be miles away in Scotland.'

'In the meantime we will prepare for our wedding. Do you have a preference as regards the church?'

'No. I will leave that side of things to Lady Marchington. It will certainly not be a grand society affair. Something small, I think, that will not attract attention. Roberta will help plan it— not forgetting Lady Marchington. We must consult her above all. How soon can we marry, do you think?'

'As soon as it can be arranged. I see no need to wait. You know how things are between the Countess and myself. She will not want me hanging about her house indefinitely.'

'And afterwards? Will we go directly to Scotland?'

'Not immediately. We will spend some time at Mercotte Hall until the weather improves to enable us to travel north.' His features softened and, placing his hands on her shoulders, he looked into the depths of her eyes. 'I would like to whisk you off to the Continent for a couple of months but, like you, I have matters to take care of north of the border. Perhaps next year. We will take the opportunity to stop in Bordeaux so that I can introduce you to my family.'

'I would like that, and afterwards—well—I've

always wanted to go to Italy—Venice and Rome are the places I most want to see.'

'I'll see what I can do.'

'I don't wish to be any trouble.'

'Since when?' he countered, giving her a twinkling glance.

'Since you asked me to be your wife.'

Chapter Seven

Two weeks later, Alice and Ewen were married in a private ceremony at St George's Church in Hanover Square. They both came from Catholic families, but at this time in England, it was a legal requirement to marry in the Church of England. Ewen's faith had suffered over the years and he had no strong views as to where the ceremony took place provided they were wed. But he realised it might matter to Alice and promised a priest would bless their union when they reached Scotland if she so wished and if it could be arranged.

It was a subdued affair, with none of the celebrations that usually accompanied weddings. There were no guests, no bridesmaids apart from Roberta, who presented Alice with a bunch of early snowdrops to carry with her down the aisle.

Standing beside Ewen with Amir looking on, in her wedding gown of blue-and-silver brocaded silk, Alice was oblivious to what was going on around her and yet completely aware of everything that transpired between them. This was not the wedding she had dreamed of—it had a distinct aura of unreality, of strain. She would have loved William and his wife, Anne, to be with her, but it had not been possible.

Without warning, she knew a moment of blind panic. Somewhere in her mind a voice cried that she was making a terrible mistake, committing herself to a man she was deceiving. Ewen thought he was marrying an innocent, a virgin. She should tell him, let him know what she had done before she had come to London, but she couldn't. She was too ashamed. From this point there would be no turning back. She had a sense of being caught up in an implacable destiny, that whatever the future held, she had to endure it for the rest of her life. And what would happen if he ever found out about her past?

But the chill in her heart was only momentary. After all, she had thought about it for a long time and it was the sensible course of action to follow.

As the ceremony was conducted, she felt

dwarfed by Ewen's presence. In muted, trembling tones, she replied to the questions the Reverend presented to her.

Looking down at his bride, Ewen was completely taken aback by the depth of the composure and the delicate, almost supernatural beauty he saw in the expressionless young face that turned to look up at his.

The vows were exchanged binding them together, and Ewen's long fingers clasped hers in an unspoken communication of commitment as firmly but gently he pushed the ring down on her finger, his silver eyes laying siege to hers, as time itself seemed to hold its breath in the church. In fascination Alice observed the play of light on his hand where the silver scars gleamed with a sheen. Her own hand look small within his and she realised with wonder that there it would remain for evermore. Their eyes melded, lost in a world of their own as Ewen lowered his lips to hers and sealed their vows with a kiss.

In too brief a time it was done. As husband and wife there were papers to sign, and as Alice watched Ewen write his name with a flourish, perhaps it was the waking realisation that he was now her husband that made the moment seem so

excitingly strange. When she thought of the circumstances that had brought them to this moment,
how much she had hated him in the beginning,
she could not believe they were wed.

Afterwards there was no hearty repast at Hislop
House. Ewen had made it known to Lady Marchington that he would leave immediately the ceremony was over. Before Alice knew it Ewen was
wrapping a fur-lined cloak about her shoulders
and they were saying farewell.

'Goodbye, Lady Marchington,' Alice said to the
woman who had admitted her into her home, a
home that had not been all that welcoming.

Lady Marchington looked down at her with disdain. 'I trust you will deal well together. You have
an unfortunate propensity to create scandal, Alice.
You are to live in Scotland, which is far enough
away from London to avoid further gossip.'

'I think you have said quite enough, Countess,'
Ewen uttered furiously. 'The trouble you refer to
was of my doing and a scandal has been avoided.'

Lady Marchington stiffened and her eyes
snapped with anger. 'Don't you dare use that tone
on me, Tremain, or I'll—'

'Or you'll what?' Ewen bit back savagely,

drawing Alice close to his side. 'Don't bother to threaten me. I have everything I want now.'

Lady Margaret Hislop, Countess of March-ington, regarded Ewen down the full length of her aristocratic nose, her expression triumphant. Things could not have turned out better. 'You have it because I allow it. Alice's brother entrusted her to my keeping and now I have entrusted her to you. I have fulfilled my obligation.'

'Quite,' Ewen bit back, but he eyed the elderly Countess with thinly veiled amusement. Inclin-ing his head politely, but not low enough to show respect, he said, 'Goodbye, Countess', and turned away.

Roberta was tearful, but wished them well, while Lady Marchington was stony faced and made no attempt to hide the fact that she was impatient to see the back of them.

Ewen led Alice to the door as Amir preceded them. Gusts of wind struck them, billowing their cloaks and snatching their breath with its crisp chill as the door swung open. Amir ran on ahead to open the door of the shiny black-lacquered coach and lowered the folding step while Ewen waited with Alice in the shelter of the portal. The driver was already perched atop his seat, hunched in the folds of his cloak against the buffeting wind and rain that was beginning to fall in great droplets.

Amir motioned for the newlyweds to come, but as they stepped into the open, a blast of wind, heavy with cold rain, struck them in the face. Alice gasped breathlessly and whirled away, finding herself fighting for breath against Ewen's chest. He caught her to him, half-covering her with his cloak. Then reaching down, he swept her up into strong arms and dashed to the coach. Handing her into the snug interior, he immediately followed, taking a place across from her. Quickly Amir folded the step and swung up beside the driver.

The coach drew away from the church heading north out of London. The rocking motion of the conveyance caused the hood of Alice's cloak to fall away and her hair tumbled free of its simple ties, falling around her shoulders in shimmering dark waves.

Ewen looked at his wife. 'This is not what I wanted our wedding day to be like, Alice.'

'No, neither did I, but it's done now. Are we journeying straight to Mercotte Hall?'

'It's a long enough journey on a day such as

this. It will be dark soon. We could stop at an inn if you prefer.'

She shook her head. 'I think I would like to go on.'

Ewen's regard turned full upon her again with all the warmth a man could have for his bride. 'We will have celebrations of our own when we get to Mercotte Hall.'

Alice huddled beneath her cloak, chilled by the crisp air. She accepted the fur rug her husband tucked around her, snuggling gratefully beneath its comfort. She began wondering if all this was a continuing dream. Was she really travelling out of London with a man she hardly knew, having just promised to love, honour and obey him? She began to wonder just how foolhardy she had been to bind herself for life to a stranger. A stranger, moreover, whose past was cloaked in secrecy.

Thinking she seemed very small and quiet in the corner of the coach, Ewen sat beside her. 'Slide over here, Alice, and rest against me,' he urged. 'We might as well be warm together.'

Hesitantly Alice complied and, in a moment, was nestled against his warmth. She could not deny that her comfort rapidly increased. The pleasant heat that seeped through her garments lent her an odd sense of security. His arm curled about her, pressing her closer, and she found no cause to resist. Her head found a niche of its own against his shoulder.

'I had wanted something different,' Ewen confessed against her hair. 'At least something more joyous.'

'It is done now. I am your wife.'

'And the Countess of Marchington relegated to the past.'

'Scotland is far enough away for neither of us to see her again, but…'

'But?' Ewen tipped her head and looked down into her shadowed face.

'My regret is that I won't be there to see Roberta married. I would have liked that.'

'With half of London society looking on,' Ewen said quietly.

'The bond—the vows we have made—is such a fragile thing between us. After all, we scarcely know each other.'

'The vows we exchanged are permanent for me, Alice. We will have all the time in the world to get to know each other at Barradine—or Mercotte Hall, depending on the weather. At least you will have privacy without interference from the Countess.'

Alice met his gaze. 'And what is your intent?' she asked.

Ewen smiled with a gentle charm as he pondered her expression. It was the same expression he had seen on her lovely face when he had asked her to be his wife—apprehension, curiosity and wonder. He gazed into her eyes. He was stunned by the complexity of them. 'Perhaps to keep you captive in my—our chamber for a week or more, to make love to you as I yearn to do. You must be aware of my eagerness for that end.' He looked down at her, a seductive smile curving his lips. 'And I suspect you will raise no objection if the kiss you gave me is an indication of your feelings, Alice. You certainly kissed me with more enthusiasm than is considered proper.'

Alice returned his smile, her eyes aglow. 'And you returned it with equal enthusiasm, my lord.'

'And why not? It's not every day I'm kissed by a beautiful young woman who appeared starved of passion and I was a lonely gentleman only recently arrived in town, where the Countess and others were wont to affix various derogatives to my name because of my treatment of Roberta. If

I returned your kiss, does that make me a lecher? Or is it the fact that you do not like being treated like a woman?'

'Oh, I quite like being treated like a woman,' Alice assured him fervently. 'Especially by you,' she added quietly. Nestling her head once more in the curve of his shoulder, above the noise of the coach wheels she could hear the steady rhythm of his heart beating, the steady rhythm of a man who was very much in charge of his life. But was he as sure of his feelings? She had seen him in moods that could change with startling rapidity. She took advantage of this moment of quiet gentleness from him and gradually relaxed against his body.

Ewen closed his eyes to concentrate on the fresh tender smell of innocent youth that was so much a part of Alice. It was a fragrance he had soon become aware of. He saw her eyelashes flutter and her warm breath caressed the hollow at the base of his neck. It was a place where he was acutely sensitive and he shivered. Alice looked up at him as if she was surprised.

Their gazes met in warm communication and she could not subdue the nervous fluttering in her breast no matter how many times she silently reminded herself that whatever he was going to do to her tonight she had done before. There would be no surprises. His muscular body and fine dark looks helped a little to dampen her fears of what he might do to her. She had no doubt that Ewen Tremain had made love to many women. What was he used to? What would he ask of her? Would he be patient with her? How would he find her? And would she be able to respond to him in any way…would she want to?

In the next few minutes she knew that she would. Taking one look at the slumberous expression in his heavy-lidded eyes, she knew something was in the wind.

'What are you thinking?' she asked.

He smiled, a slow, lazy smile that made her heart leap into her throat. 'I'm thinking about kissing you. Have you any objections to that?'

She swallowed down her nervousness. 'No,' she whispered, looking at his sensuous mouth. 'At least—I don't think so.'

Ewen stroked his hand over her nape. He raised her chin a little more with his hand and touched his mouth to her cheek, trailing a light kiss over the smooth skin. He rubbed his mouth over her trembling lips, tasting their softness, and crushed her closer to him, delicately teasing her lips with his tongue, urging them to part. As before, she sweetly offered him her mouth. The kiss was warm and heady, a leisured meeting of parting lips and questing tongues, the eagerness of one yielding to the bold intrusion of the other. A faint sigh wafted from Alice's lips as his kisses blazed a trail along her throat.

The kissing and caressing had continued until they both noticed they were passing through the gates to Mercotte Hall. Two things hit Alice at once—first, they would be stopping in front of the house at any minute, with servants going about their duties, and, worse, if her reflection in the coach window was even close to accurate, her hair was hopelessly mussed up by her husband's marauding fingers.

'My hair,' she whispered, aghast, reaching up and combing her fingers through the tangled tresses. 'I must look a sight. What *will* people think?'

'What will they think?' Ewen prompted, studying her flushed cheeks and rosy lips.

'I cannot bear to contemplate it,' Alice said, growing increasingly aware of the way Ewen's warm gaze lingered on her lips, which only added to her confusion.

'Worry not, my love,' he said, chuckling softly as the coach came to a halt in front of the house. 'They will rightly assume that you have been well and truly kissed by your husband.'

The velvet softness of his voice was more seductive than any kiss could have been. She smiled and offered her lips to him once more, before the steps were lowered and the door opened to reveal Hicks's grinning features with Taff peering excitedly round his shoulder. They'd been waiting all day to see the newlyweds, hoping some good had come out of their blundering and that the new Lady Tremain would be glowing with happiness.

Stepping to the ground, Alice paused beside Ewen while Hicks ran ahead to open the front door. Mrs Mullen waited with Lily and other servants inside the door and their faces wreathed in smiles momentarily quelled Alice's anxieties. A crackling fire burned in the huge stone hearth, casting a warm glow about the hall. After much well-wishing, Mrs Mullen disappeared into the kitchen to prepare the evening meal.

Ewen divested Alice of her cloak and urged her towards the fire.

'Our rooms have been prepared and an excellent supper awaits us. I hope you're hungry.'

'Not just now,' she replied, still recovering from the devastating kiss and her stomach churning with tension over what she knew would be happening to her later.

Aware of her apprehension, Ewen smiled. 'Some champagne, I think. It will give you an appetite and help calm your nerves.' He turned to Amir. 'Some wine for my beautiful wife, Amir, and a toast to our future.' Seeing Hicks and Taff hovering in the doorway, he went to have a word with them and send them about their work.

Amir, always courtesy and friendliness personified, came to hand Alice a glass of the bubbling wine. He agreed with Lord Tremain's assertion that she was beautiful. Amir liked her, her bearing, and in particular her air of innocence. She would be good for Ewen and hopefully would help him lay to rest the ghost of the beautiful Etta.

'May I say, my lady, you look enchanting,' he said, beaming his angel smile at her.

Alice trusted that smile and, taking the champagne, returned a charming one of her own.

'Thank you, Amir. It's nice of you to say so. But—my lady?' She marvelled at the sound of the address.

Amir laughed, his teeth flashing white in his brown face. 'Yes,' he affirmed. 'Lady Tremain, the most lovely lady of Barradine.'

'Is there one of those for me, Amir?' Ewen interrupted them, coming to stand beside them and placing an arm possessively about Alice's waist.

Amir thrust a glass at him and gave Alice another angelic smile. 'To your health and to your future. You make a handsome couple. You're a lucky man, Ewen,' he declared broadly. 'But then I think you know that. Now I will leave you.'

'Thank you, Amir.' Ewen looked at Alice. 'To our marriage,' he murmured as he lifted his glass.

'May it be nurtured by love—and many children,' Amir added softly before downing his champagne with a toss of his dark head and leaving them alone.

Alice put her glass down. 'I would like to freshen up, Ewen. Am I in the room I was in before?'

'I'm afraid not. We have connecting rooms, which I am sure you will find comfortable.' He beckoned Lily, who was about to disappear into the kitchen. She hurried over to them.

'Did you want me, milord?'

'You may show your mistress to her chambers, Lily. She would like to freshen up before supper.'

'Yes, milord.' Lily bobbed a curtsy. She faced her mistress with a cheery smile. 'Follow me, my lady. There's a warm fire just waiting for you.'

'I'll be in the dining room when you're ready,' Ewen told Alice.

Alice moved across the hall, feeling her husband's gaze following her.

As Ewen watched his wife climb the stairs, he was rather amazed at the lightness of his heart. Where just a short while ago it had seemed dark and empty, now it was light and full of hope.

Lily led the way to the upper floor and to the rooms Alice was to share with her husband. They were comfortable and simply, but elegantly furnished. The walls were hung with cream silk, patterned in peach-coloured flowers. The carpets and velvet curtains were the shade of biscuit. Gentle landscapes hung on the walls, beautiful figurines graced the furniture and an arrangement of deep pink roses in a crystal vase stood on a satinwood chest of drawers.

It was a room to please the senses, a room of sensuality, though she doubted that was deliberate since the house did not belong to Ewen.

Alice marvelled at the preparations that had been made for them. She glanced about her. The small and intimate dining room was aglow with candles and the table had been laid with gleaming silver crockery and freshly cut blooms from Mercotte Hall's extensive hothouses.

She looked at her husband. Like her, he hadn't changed out of his wedding finery. She quietly admired the way his tight-fitting breeches emphasised his long, muscular legs. His white shirt was open at the neck and his black jacket set off his powerful shoulders to wonderful advantage. She prayed that he might find her as pleasing to look at as she found him.

Ewen was studying her as if seeing her for the first time. Not once during the whole day had he commented on her appearance, but now, as his gaze drifted from the top of her shining hair to the hem of her elegant wedding gown, he smiled, a slow, appreciative smile revealing a lightning glimpse of his white teeth. He was momentarily transfixed. Alice's dark hair tumbled over her shoulders and framed her vivid face. She looked like an exotic *ingénue* in her blue-and-silver wedding gown with its low square neckline and fitted bodice that managed to call attention to the tops of her softly rounded breasts and accent her narrow waist before it fell in simple folds to the floor.

She was nervous, he knew that, and yet, he thought he could sense an excitement about her which was unusual. A woman was supposed to be terrified of the experience which lay ahead of her, terrified because she was ignorant of what it entailed, but told to endure it because gentlemen liked it. Even though he had burned to have his way with her ever since she had accepted his proposal, he would be gentle with her. He didn't want to risk alienating her from their marital bed.

Going to her, he took her hand and led her to the table. 'My compliments, Alice. The gown you chose to wear for our wedding is beautiful, but not nearly as beautiful as the woman wearing it.'

The welcome observation warmed her, yet the brightness of his eyes was unnervingly intent, which made her feel as though he were able to pierce through the mystery of her clothes and lay bare her feminine body.

'Thank you, Ewen. I'm glad you think so.'

'Mrs Mullen has prepared quite a spread. Shall we dine? Why are you so nervous?' he asked, feeling her hand tremble within his grasp.

Alice gave a small, forced laugh, saying the first inane words that came into her head. 'Because I've never been married before. I'm not sure how I should behave.'

'I've never been a married man before either, so our pleasure will be learning together.'

Alice looked down at his hand still holding hers, his strong fingers round her small ones. 'But a man knows the—the…I do not wish to disappoint you.'

He laughed softly, releasing her hand and pulling out her chair. When she was seated he lowered his head and with his warm breath caressing her cheek, he said, 'Do you think I would welcome a woman practised in the art of loving into my bed? I love your naivety and your innocence, Alice, but I know it belies all the fire of a sensual woman and it will be my greatest pleasure releasing all that fire.' Walking round the table, he seated himself opposite her.

Aware that her cheeks were as red as a poppy, shyly avoiding Ewen's frankly admiring gaze, Alice complimented the silver bowl of white roses and candelabra in the centre of the table covered with a snowy linen cloth. Only then did she lift her gaze to his and the smile she bestowed on him was so warm, so filled with generosity and unconscious promise, that it took Ewen's breath.

One of the servants poured wine and brought in the food and, having been instructed by Ewen beforehand, left them alone to dine in private.

Ewen lifted his glass in a toast. 'To us, Alice.'

She smiled and sipped her wine. Suddenly overcome, she told herself she wasn't going to cry. She was going to be calm, as composed as he. She began to eat and said what lovely food it was. They ate and sipped their wine and chatted as though tonight was no different to any other night, but they both knew it was.

Later, when Alice had retired, leaving Ewen to finish his port with a promise that he would join her soon, the bed was strewn with innumerable petticoats, hoops and the wedding gown as Lily divested Alice of her finery.

Alice was now wearing a simple nightgown made of fine lawn edged with lace and trimmed with narrow white-satin ribbon. Lily had brushed her heavy hair until it crackled and shone. With a critical eye she gazed at her image mirrored in the glass, wondering what Ewen would make of her. Of medium height and in her opinion too dark to be fashionable in an age which liked its women fair, with long shapely legs, small hips and a tiny waist, her neck long and slender, her heart-shaped face with high cheekbones framed by a mass of black hair, dark blue eyes and arched brows and wide soft mouth, her expression wilful and challenging, she looked more like a Gypsy than a gently reared young lady. She sighed regretfully, thinking of the fair-complexioned girls of her acquaintance in Paris.

Alice tried to restore her confidence by telling herself that Ewen had chosen her even though his hand had been forced. Only he had never told her that he loved her. Perhaps he never would.

She turned from the mirror to smile at Lily, who was carefully putting her clothes away before going on to turn down the bed. She was relieved that the maid was sensitive enough not to employ the indelicate talk usually indulged in on a woman's wedding night. Lily spoke only of the night Alice had been brought to Mercotte Hall by Hicks and Taff and who would have thought it that Lord Tremain and her new mistress would marry as a result of it.

'You look lovely, my lady,' Lily said comfortingly, seeing her anxiety. Like every young bride on her wedding night, it was understandable that she was nervous about what was to happen. 'Everything will be all right.'

'I'm fine, Lily—only a little nervous.'

'Would you like me to put you to bed?'

'No—no, I'll wait.'

Trying desperately to think of other things, Alice gazed into the fire and concentrated on what it would be like when Ewen took her to Barradine. Would she find her father? Please God, she prayed, let what Duncan Forbes had told her be the truth and he was indeed alive and in Scotland.

She was standing by the hearth when Ewen entered. She felt a swift surge of admiration and she smiled a little as he walked towards her with those long, easy strides that always looked both certain and relaxed. Light from the fire flickered across his face, one moment enhancing his handsome features, the next lending dark shadows to them to suggest overpowering wickedness lurking within. He removed his coat and waistcoat, revealing the strong column of his throat. He looked,

Alice thought, as ruggedly virile and elegant in shirtsleeves as informal attire.

Self-conscious in her nightgown, she took a step forward, then stopped, arrested by the spark flaring in those silver-grey eyes as they moved over her body. She felt suffocated by the heat of his perusal, but she waited in silence as his eyes continued to sweep her meagrely clad bosom and her hair resting on her shoulders and spilling down her back. The thick brush of his back lashes veiled his eyes from her, forbidding her visual access into their translucent depths, and though she searched his features, she had no way of knowing what to expect. She could only wonder if this stranger to whom she was married would suddenly turn savage in his quest to fulfil his desires.

Please God, she prayed secretly to herself, not that. Not again. She could not bear it.

Ewen's eyes passed over his bride in a distinctively appreciative caress. 'Would you like a little wine—or some champagne perhaps?' Ewen asked softly.

She shook her head. 'No, thank you, Ewen,' she replied, trying to keep her voice normal. 'I don't want anything.'

Alice felt helpless to counteract his intimate observance of her. The large bedroom was warm, the smell of brandy that Ewen had consumed before coming to her heady and strong. This powerful combination threatened to dull her senses and her wits and she wanted to keep herself sharp and aware of what was happening to her. On the other hand, perhaps it would be more welcome to have all her senses limited and dimmed.

'You're trembling,' Ewen observed.

'I know,' she admitted with a nervous tremor in her voice. 'I can't think why.'

His lips curved in a smile. 'Can't you?' he asked softly.

Alice shook her head, fearful, yet longing for him to take her in his arms.

His long fingers lifted up her face, so that her eyes were full on him. 'I am indeed most fortunate, Alice,' he said huskily. 'I will try not to hurt you. I promise. The pain won't last. It will soon be over.'

Alice suddenly felt lost and hesitant. The sudden, cold truth was that he was talking to her as a virgin, someone to be led into the secrets of the marriage bed gently, when she, who had already been initiated in the union with a man, was less inclined to experience them all over again. She was conscious of a sharp second of nothing except the strange, desolate void of deception that enclosed her, separating her from everything that she had known.

Suddenly he paused and Alice knew it must be her tortured expression and the way she was looking at him with numb paralysis that had brought him to a halt.

'Alice? Is anything the matter?'

'Ewen—I—I want to talk to you,' she said, shrinking at the presumptuously possessive gaze he swept over her, her self-control teetering very close to the edge.

'Talking is not what I have in mind,' he gently mocked. 'Alice, what is this?' he asked with an ominous quietness. 'I am not an ogre ready to force myself on you.' Not having expected to encounter resistance, Ewen was puzzled by her behaviour. He sensed that all was not well with her, that something from the past had asserted itself, and in the hope of finding out what it was, he made a supreme effort to overcome his impatience. 'Why don't you tell me what is wrong?' he asked quietly.

Alice turned from him, clenching her hands by her sides, wishing with all her heart she could confide in him, but because of all that happened between them at the beginning of their relationship—his betrothal to Roberta and his abduction—she still felt an element of mistrust. He had wanted Roberta because she was pure and perfect, whereas she was anything but and she was afraid he would spurn her if he knew the truth. Had he not just told her that he would not welcome a woman practised in loving into his bed? Her eyes burned and her throat ached, but she was determined not to cry. Ewen came up behind her, his fingers closing around her shoulders, feeling a shudder pass through her entire body at his touch.

'Alice,' he asked gently, 'are you afraid of letting me make love to you?'

Shrugging herself out of his grip as if it scorched her flesh, she moved further away from him. 'Please, Ewen, don't touch me. I—I don't want this. Not now.'

Ewen's jaw tensed. Taking her shoulders once more, he turned her round to face him. 'Do you mind telling me what has got into you?'

He released his hold, and when at last she looked up it was as though a mask had dropped over her exquisite face, leaving it remote and expressionless. Her eyes were lifeless and dull, as if something inside her had died. Never had he seen her like this. He was tempted to ignore what she was telling him and draw her into his arms, but a sixth sense warned him not to move too close.

'Forgive me if I appear stupid,' Ewen said, trying to hold on to his patience, to fight his feeling of inadequacy and his inability to break through the invisible barrier she had erected around herself. Raking his fingers through his hair, he began pacing up and down. When he had entered her room he hadn't known what to expect—but rejection? Never. Suddenly he came towards her and stopped, hands on hips.

'I admit to being confused, for whenever I have kissed you, you have raised no objection and returned my kisses with an ardour equal to my own—you even kissed *me* on one occasion, as I recall.' He fell silent, for he remembered that at those times he had been tender, gentle with her. 'Alice, you knew what to expect when you agreed to become my wife.'

She drew a long shuddering breath, drawing from an inner strength the courage she needed for what she was about to ask him. 'Please, Ewen— will you agree to wait—give me time?'

Apart from a tightening of the lines around his

mouth his face was expressionless. 'You do realise that what you ask is highly irregular.'

'Yes.'

'And if I refuse to do as you ask?' His voice was dangerously quiet.

Alice's soft mouth trembled as she stared like an animal wounded unto death into those eyes that rested on her. 'You—you would not force me to submit to you?'

One black brow rose as he gave her a long, cool look. 'I find your choice of word distasteful. When I eventually take my wife to bed, I hope she does not find it necessary to prepare herself mentally before she will let me touch her. I do not expect her to yield or surrender to my will or authority—to subject herself to me as if it is some form of punishment for wrongdoing.'

'All I am asking is that you give me a little time. I—remember you saying that you would ask nothing of me that I cannot give, that if I was not prepared to give it, you are not the man to take it by force.'

Ewen had not expected to have his words quoted back at him. Cursing silently, he turned away in angry frustration. For the first time in his life he found himself confronted by a wall he could not breach. Crossing the room in long swift strides, he opened the door, where he paused and turned back to her. 'Before God, Alice, I will not force you. Either you get into bed with me now, or I shall walk through this door—and it will remain between us until *you* decide to come to *me*. But I will not allow it to remain between us forever.' He regarded her with a terrifying firmness. 'The choice is yours.'

The temptation to give in, to cast herself into his arms, was so powerful to be almost irresistible. Alice needed him so much. Yet fear restrained her on the very point of yielding and it chilled her heart. Naked pain slashed across her face and she looked at him, not knowing what to say. Shame and embarrassment overwhelmed her. She'd really hoped she could put the past behind her, had wanted to, only to behave like a stupid fool. In the end, she lowered her eyes and shook her head. 'I'm sorry, Ewen,' she whispered.

'I see. I would like to say I understand, but I don't. When you decide to be my wife in every sense, you know where I am. But be warned. My patience is not inexhaustible. You cannot evade the issue indefinitely.'

He left her then, closing the door firmly behind

him. That was the moment when Alice knew the true meaning of heartbreak.

In his lonely room, intending to drown himself in drink, Ewen poured himself a generous brandy and tossed the fiery liquid back, immediately pouring himself another, knowing he would get no sleep that night. With the woman—his wife—in the bed next door, the woman he wanted more than any other, he intended getting well and truly foxed to stop himself thinking about her, to keep his mind from dwelling upon the way she had looked today as his bride.

Tossing back another brandy, he threw a virulent look at the closed connecting door. He found it incredible that a man who with cold logic could override his emotions whenever his wished, should find himself in this intolerable situation. This was his wedding night and his wife had denied him her bed—and what was worse was the fact that he had no idea why.

Why was she holding herself from him? Was she not attracted to him? Did she still hold resentment towards him for her kidnap? Or was there a more sinister reason for her reticence to get into bed with him?

* * *

When dawn came to lighten the sky, Alice turned on to her side and stared into the grey light as her thoughts tumbled over each other. Unable to face going downstairs, she breakfasted alone in her room. It soon became obvious to the servants that things weren't as they should be between Lord Tremain and his new wife.

In fact, feelings between Ewen and Alice were strained and tension ran high. At first they tried being amiable to each other, but they were both guarded and it was impossible to sustain empty pleasantries indefinitely.

Ewen found plenty to occupy his time on the estate and he went about the work with single-minded determination and efficiency, but he had withdrawn from Alice as if those tender, happy moments they had shared on their wedding day had never been.

After two weeks the situation had become intolerable. Each avoided the other, and when they did meet, usually at dinner, Ewen was so imperiously polite that Alice wanted to run from the room.

One morning, after taking her early morning

walk, she returned to the house to find Amir carrying a couple of saddlebags across the hall.

'Where are you going with those, Amir?'

'Your husband is going away, my lady.'

'Away? Where?'

Amir's eyes went past her to the library. The door was open. With disbelieving eyes, Alice hurried towards it, coming to a halt a few feet inside the room. Ewen was standing before a large table, sifting through some papers. He'd removed his jacket and rolled up his shirtsleeves. She saw his shoulders stiffen at the sound of her rustling skirts as she moved slowly across the carpet. When he looked up at her, she could almost feel the effort he was exerting to keep his anger under control. His mien was withdrawn, aloof and unbelievably distant.

She felt a pang of longing and a need so strong that she felt faint. He was so splendid, so unbearably handsome, that if he had just smiled at her a little she would have flung herself against him and begged for forgiveness. There was anguish in her blue eyes, but they met his squarely. She searched his granite features, hoping for some sign of softening, of compassion, but he was staring at her with narrowed piercing eyes.

Ewen gazed into her blue eyes and his hands clenched at his sides as he fought to keep his control. The urge to take her into his arms and pretend for just one minute that she was still his beautiful, enchanting bride overwhelmed him. He wanted to hold her and kiss her, to blot out the last two weeks of hell. 'I saw Amir. He told me you are leaving?'

'That is what I intend.'

Alice stared at him with disbelieving eyes. 'Oh, I see,' she said quietly, feeling her heart almost grind to a halt when she looked at his hard, handsome face, seeing that his mercurial mood she had been living with since their marriage had taken a bewildering turn for the worse.

'Am I to go with you?'

'No,' he replied, trying not to notice how ravishing and invigorated she looked after her walk, her cheeks adorably pink and her eyes sparkling. He looked at her with sudden desire mingled with bitterness. The sunlight entering the room bathed her in light. The russet dress she wore had become a garment of flame. She was as beautiful and tragic as sin beneath the folds of her gown, her breasts rising and falling with her emotion. His eyes as he studied the slender form before him, grew clouded. 'You are to remain at Mercotte Hall. No doubt you will find plenty to occupy your time.'

His voice was so cold that Alice lifted her chin in hot indignation. 'You are leaving me here alone? Am I to have no other company? I know no one here. May I ask why you have suddenly decided to go away?'

His face was unyielding and impassive, with no sign of the passionate, sensual side to his nature. 'I would have thought that was obvious.'

Alice's face burned from the cruelty of the remark, and she was swamped with guilt. In silent, helpless protest she stared into his cold eyes, feeling as if something had shattered inside her. He was dismissing her as someone he considered unworthy to be his wife. He wanted to leave her, to be rid of her. She could feel it. And why shouldn't he, something inside her cried accusingly, who could blame him, when he had saddled himself with a wife who had spurned him on their wedding night?

'For the time being you will stay here,' he said, taking his jacket from a chair and thrusting his arms into the sleeves.

Feeling anger at the injustice of it all, Alice

glared at him from two storm-filled eyes. 'You do not command me, Ewen. You are my husband—much as you might have come to regret it—not my master. I do not intend to spend my life living like a nun in some recluse just because I happen to have displeased my husband.'

There was a distinct edge to his voice as he said, 'Displeased is putting it mildly.'

'Might I ask where you are going?'

'Barradine. I intend to leave shortly.'

'I see. Have you forgotten how important it is to me that I find my father? Only by going to Scotland will I find the information I am looking for and now you tell me I am to be left behind. How dare you deny me that! You are being deliberately cruel.'

'Not deliberately. Don't worry. I will make enquiries on your behalf.'

Unable to bear the thought of being left alone at Mercotte Hall while he went off without her to Scotland was a great disappointment. 'Please take me with you. Ewen,' she began, her voice trembling with emotion while she tried to think how to begin to diffuse his wrath. She stretched out her hand in a gesture of mute appeal, then let it fall to her side when her beseeching move got nothing from him but a blast of contempt from his eyes. Her heart thudded in her chest and she could hardly speak. Her mouth was dry and she was desperately afraid, but she tried again. 'Ewen, please listen…'

'Why? Is there something you have to tell me?'

His expectant, bright gaze made her feel worse. Most of all she dreaded the altered expression in his eyes that she knew must follow what she had to tell him, for tell him she must, the whole truth, and she felt ashamed of her reticence now.

Chapter Eight

'I have handled things very badly, and I would like to try to put it right—even though you will think less of me.'

'I'm listening.'

Alice's stomach knotted as fear of what his reaction might be mingled with dread. 'It—it concerns what happened before I came to London.'

'Does it have anything to do with the man you were betrothed to? If so, does it have any bearing on why you turned me from your bed on our wedding night?'

She nodded, wishing she could crawl away somewhere, anywhere, to escape that piercing gaze. At the same time she knew this had to be faced even if the consequences meant disaster. 'I must warn you that it isn't pleasant.'

A muscle jumped in Ewan's cheek. A dreadful

suspicion began to take root in his mind. 'I think you'd better tell me.'

Drawing a long, shuddering breath, she faced up to him squarely, her gaze unblinking and steady, her stance defiant. 'What I have to tell you is that I am not the virtuous woman you thought you married. I am used goods. I was afraid to tell you, afraid of your reaction when you found out, knowing how disappointed and angry you would be. But now it no longer matters what you think. I can't change things. That's what I am. Accept it, Ewen, because that's how it is.'

It took a moment for Ewen to take in the meaning of what she was saying. Then he realised the full significance of her words. His face went white. His mind registered disbelief, it started to shout denial, even while something inside him slowly cracked and began to crumble. He stared at her, his eyes piercing, as though he could see into her soul. She was beautiful, beautiful and desirable. Nothing could be brighter than those eyes, or softer than that skin—those lips, nothing purer than that face or more exquisite than that form—and yet it was all false. Memories of Etta flooded his mind. His mistrust of Alice was proving justified. Anger, humiliation and wild uncertainty all collided into one.

'So at last I have the truth. It—is a problem I had not envisaged.'

'A problem which is not insurmountable.'

'No? It touches the part of a man's life that is sacrosanct—his woman. A man's feelings for his wife are not to be tampered with. It is his life's blood, unshared with any other, private and revered.'

'I was betrothed before, Ewen. I made no secret of that. Had I been widowed, the loss of my virginity would not be a problem.'

'The difference being that you were not widowed, Alice.'

'No, I was not. I never lied to you.'

'Just sparing with the truth.'

His voice was harsh and unforgiving. There was a silence. Alice averted her eyes, never having felt so wretched. She forced herself to look at him, having no trouble reading his expression, and her heart sank. He was disgusted, yet she could not regret telling the truth. Now he knew what she was she could not blame him for his reaction, nor had she expected it to hurt quite so much. 'I am sorry. I should have told you before.'

'Yes, you should. You should have been frank with me. It would have saved a lot of misunderstanding.'

'I know that—and I am sorry to cause you pain. But you must listen. There is more—'

'I have heard quite enough. You are not the virgin bride I thought you were. You are soiled—used… You deliberately deceived me.'

There was so much anguish in his voice that Alice's eyes filled with tears. Such a bitter reaction was too much to be borne. How could he accuse her so brutally? 'Not deliberately. Have pity, Ewen. Listen to me and do not condemn me without hearing the whole of what I have to say—'

Ewen's voice interrupted her brusquely. 'I know only too well. It's evident to me that your betrothed didn't have much difficulty in winning your favours if my own experience and memory of the time you kissed me is any guide.'

'But…' He looked at her and something in his eyes silenced the words on her lips. His face was so closed that it made her think of a wall without windows or doors. She had never felt him so remote from her. She had a fierce desire to sink to her knees before him, to have him hold her, to cry, 'I love you'—for love him she did. She had never been more certain of anything in her life, but something in him stopped her and she waited despairingly for him to speak.

He maintained a cool poise, his face impassive, but there was a pain behind his eyes.

'Will you still go to Scotland?'

He nodded. 'I have to get away—now more than ever.' He couldn't accept what she had told him. Not yet. 'I will send word when I reach Barradine.'

His voice was so cold, his words so commonplace, that her chin came up in consternation. 'Yes, I would appreciate that.' She wanted to tell him not to go, not to leave her. She put her hand to her mouth to stop herself. She'd never be able to respect herself if she begged him. He strode away without another glance at her. She had turned away, unable to bear the sight of him leaving. The door slammed behind him with the cold finality of a death knell.

'He'll come back,' she whispered to herself. 'If I say it often enough maybe I'll believe it.'

With an aching heart she stared in the direction he had gone, empty and destroyed.

With all his attention focused on the journey ahead of him, Ewen was unable to think or feel.

He was, in fact, greatly disturbed by this new-found knowledge of his wife, and therein lay his confusion, because he both wanted and loved Alice. Yes, want her and love her he did and he cursed for his inability to purge her from his heart, for his lack of will and with a fear for a love he was unable to control.

In his fury and ravaged pride, he headed north.

Desolate and alone, Alice wandered through the rooms of Mercotte Hall without purpose. Two weeks after Ewen's departure, feeling the need for air and to get away from the watchful, pitying eyes of the servants, she left the house. The morning air was fresh and cool. She breathed deeply, tasting the freshness. A light breeze lifted her hair as she walked beyond the gardens to the parkland. The tall pines smelled sharply sweet, the ground upon which she walked shaded and soft with bleached needles. Coming to the brow of a hill, she stopped, propping her back against the sturdy trunk of an oak tree, and looked down the sloping pasture.

She had to think—there must be some way to salvage her life from the ruins. She had to find the strength to keep going in spite of everything.

She hadn't given up when she'd been forced to leave France. She wasn't going to give up now. She stared ahead, facing all her demons—what Philippe had done to her, the scandal that ensued, her abduction and Ewen's leaving her.

That was the worst thing of all. That was what she had to meet head-on. She had to find a way to make him come back to her. She shivered, suddenly afraid, her main fear being that now he knew the truth—that she wasn't as pure and innocent as he had believed her to be, that another man had already claimed what Ewen believed was his by right—he would reject her. And why wouldn't he? The knowledge must be anathema to him.

But then, maybe she was judging him too harshly. When he knew the whole truth, maybe he would no longer feel the disgust she had seen in his eyes. At least then, with time to mull things over, there was the possibility that his attitude would become soft with understanding.

But at present that didn't change anything. She was by herself whether she wanted to be or not. If Ewen wouldn't come back to her—and it might be weeks before he sent for her—then she would have to go to him. It was time to take her life in her own hands and she had no time to waste.

Ewen's bitterness would fester the longer they were apart.

From the tops of the trees she watched a flock of birds lift into the sky and fly off beneath a line of white clouds. They were moving on, just like her. Don't look back, what's done is done. Move on. The sun came out and she smiled. Evidence of spring was all around her. It was going to get warmer. It was a good time to travel.

Once her mind was made up, Alice was buoyed up with renewed enthusiasm. She had a goal and all her energy poured into achieving it. She would get ready to leave Mercotte Hall. What would happen when she reached Barradine she had no idea, but once she was ensconced in his house, Ewen couldn't very well ignore her.

Entering the house, her cheeks a delightful pink and her eyes alight with energy from within, her gaze lighted on Amir crossing the hall. She had grown accustomed to Amir's quiet presence in the house, if somewhat strange. Ewen and Amir had a shared bond which was evident when they were together. He had adopted European clothes, but as a Muslim it was not unusual to find him, as now, attired in long brightly coloured silk robes worn over wide pantaloons and soft Moroccan slippers. Alice had found this form of dress strange at first, but she had become accustomed to seeing him drift about the house in such exotic clothes and to smelling the delicate scent of verbena and sandalwood.

Halting in his stride, Amir smiled at her. His black eyes sparkled with customary humour. 'Did you enjoy your walk, my lady?'

'I did, Amir. In fact, you could say I found it—enlightening. I have been doing some thinking,' she said, unfastening her cloak and tossing it over a chair. 'I've decided we shall leave for Barradine tomorrow.'

'But—'

'No buts, Amir,' she chided gently, laughing with happy relief now her mind was made up. 'I will not remain in this house any longer. The weather is conducive for travel so I do not intend wasting time.'

Amir gave her a doubtful look. 'His lordship won't be happy. He gave strict instructions that you were to remain here until he sent word.'

'His lordship can say what he likes,' Alice said with a toss of her head. 'I have decided. Oh, and I would like to get there as soon as possible, which means we will require fresh teams of horses along the way. Of course the coach driver and a groom will accompany us—and Hicks and Taff can travel in another coach with the baggage. They're doing nothing but kicking their heels here so they might as well be employed doing something worthwhile.'

Amir grinned broadly in admiration, his soft lips exposing his strong white teeth. 'Lord Tremain told me you had courage. You are going to need a great deal of it to face him at Barradine. He will be twice as angry at being defied.'

Alice smiled broadly back at him. 'I am quite certain he will be livid. But it will be too late for him to do anything about it by then.'

Alice made the eight-day journey from Mercotte Hall to Barradine in five days—a feat she managed to accomplish by the expedient, if reckless and costly, method of paying large sums to coaching inns to change the team of horses after fifteen miles or so and travelling at first light and not stopping for the night until dark. The only pauses in her headlong journey were to gulp down the occasional meal. As the miles rolled by to the

Scottish borders, Alice listened to the pounding of the horses' hooves taking her closer to Ewen.

She was glad of Amir's company. He sat on top of the coach for most of the journey, but there were times when, eager for someone to talk to, she invited him to join her inside. On one such occasion she managed to draw him on his years as a captive.

'Until I escaped from the oars with Ewen, I never knew anything else,' he told her. 'My mother was a slave girl. When she gave birth to me I was destined to a life of servitude working in the Sultan's palace. I do not know who my father was. I pray to Allah that one day I will know.'

Alice saw a shadow of melancholy pass through his eyes. 'Your faith is important to you, Amir.'

He nodded. 'Prayer is one of the five pillars of Islam. It is the belief of all Muslims that communication with Allah will bring them courage and serves to bring peace to their lives.'

'Your faith must have been strong to withstand the cruel treatment meted out to you by your masters when you were consigned to the galleys— where you met Ewen.'

He nodded. 'My faith in Allah has never wavered. If anything it became stronger. Ewen and I were chained to the same oar for many months.'

'What did you do to make them treat you so cruelly?'

'I tried to run away, but I was caught. After what they did to me before they sent me to the galleys, I tried to make the best of my lot. But then the storm came and that changed everything. I shall be eternally grateful to Ewen. He risked his life to save me when he could have left me to drown. I could not swim, you see. We were the only people to survive.'

'And he brought you with him to England.'

'He has my undying devotion. I serve him as best I can.'

'Ewen does not look on you as a servant, Amir. You are no longer a slave, but a free man, to come and go as you please. Ewen would have it no other way.'

He smiled. 'No, and I am content.'

He spoke softly, in French, and Alice gazed at him in astonishment. 'How do you come to speak French?'

His smile deepened. 'I have always liked learning things and I have known captives from many countries. One, a saintly man from France, taught me the language of that country when I was a child. Your husband taught me the English.'

'I congratulate you for having learned both languages so well, Amir. But tell me. You are deep in my husband's confidence. Something happened that affected him very badly. He will not speak of it, but I know he is troubled. Will you tell me about him, Amir?'

His expression became grave and he shook his head. 'Forgive me, my lady, but I cannot do that. It is not my place.'

'Was a woman involved?' she prompted. 'Did he love her?'

Amir averted his gaze. After moments of much deliberation and soul searching, he said softly, as if he were speaking to himself, 'A woman, yes. Her name was Etta. But I am sorry. I cannot tell you more than that. He has my trust. I will not betray that. The things that happened before he was sent to the galleys he will have to tell you himself. It is very difficult for him, you understand?'

'Yes, I do.' Alice sighed and relaxed into the upholstery, wondering what the girl Etta had done to bring about Ewen's hatred. 'You are a good friend to him, Amir.'

'He is the strongest human being I have ever

known. And the finest. I consider myself fortunate to know such a man.'

Although Alice didn't know it, Ewen was missing her and deeply regretted his hasty decision to leave her and flee to Barradine. What had he been thinking? She filled his thoughts and he knew that, to him, no other woman could outshine her. She had seemed to have great promise, not only being beautiful and refined, but also possessing such spirit and intelligence. However, despite all this, ever since the night they had met when he had burst into her room, there had been things about her that had troubled him—similarities to Etta that had caused him to hold back.

His mind dwelt more and more on the reason why she had rejected him on their wedding night—that she was afraid of what his reaction would be when he discovered she was not the virgin he expected. At first, he had believed it might have something to do with the kidnap. He was relieved that it wasn't, but he was disappointed by the truth. She had told him there was more. He should have listened to her and not walked away. One thing troubled him concerning her betrothal to the Frenchman. It was uncommon for a woman to walk away from the man she was betrothed to. What had happened to make her do that?

In a state of frenetic restlessness, he rode for miles each day, and when he wasn't riding he immersed himself in estate matters. Despite his exertions, he became too exhausted from his internal battle to bother lying to himself any more. When night came he couldn't sleep. He wanted Alice more than he'd ever wanted anything in his life. He needed her and knew that back at Mercotte Hall, she was lying there wanting him, loving him as much as he loved her.

Loved her? Ewen scowled darkly at the thought and then, with a long, derisive sigh, he admitted the truth to himself. He was in love with Alice. A faint smile touched his lips as he remembered how angry she had been when he'd invaded her room on the day they met, looking heartbreakingly young and beautiful. She could enchant, bemuse, amuse and infuriate him more than any other woman had ever been able to do.

Nearing the end of her journey, Alice knew there was no way out of the course of action she had begun. She set her mind against the terrible sense of panic starting inside her. There was a hollow in the pit of her stomach as she looked across at Amir. He was affable and shrewd, and he had a puckish sense of humour which did much to relieve the tension mounting in her as they approached Barradine. But she knew with a rising dread that no one could push Ewen Tremain into any decision not of his own making, and for the first time in her life Alice knew the real meaning of isolation and the icy coldness of its grip.

Barradine stood sturdy and proud in the afternoon sun, exposed against the soft greens of fields and forests. Alice stepped down from the coach. The air was refreshingly crisp, with the hint of pine in the air. After being confined in the coach for a long time, she enjoyed the feel of a gentle wind in her hair as she looked up at the house.

Ewen was seated in the study, seeking distraction in the volumes of bookkeeping generated by his deceased brother's business activities. When he caught himself making the same mathematical errors for the second time and then a third, he tossed aside the books, quickly deciding to leave them for another day. Rising from his desk, he glanced at the clock on the mantel and realised it was much later than he had imagined. Beyond the windows, the sky was already darkening.

His mind turning to his wife, he strolled thoughtfully across the room, leaning with his shoulder against the broad expanse of mullioned glass, knowing that within the local ale houses and villages many a warm bed waited. His hunger grew, but it was not for them out there. His thoughts grew tender as he remembered golden candlelight upon silken flesh, hair curling softly about her shoulders, sweet and gentle arms about his neck and full, pink lips pressed against his, a warm, young body curving into his.

Uttering a curse of exasperation, he rubbed the back of his neck to ease the discomfort. His eyes fell on a coach that had just pulled up in the drive. He frowned, puzzled as to who could be calling at this hour. His gaze became riveted on his wife the instant she stepped from the coach and the sight of her had the devastating impact of a boulder crashing into his chest.

'What in God's name—?'

He turned from the window and with long purposeful strides made his way outside. Alice stood in front of the house, looking about her with interest. She wore a deep blue travelling dress and her hair was drawn back from her face and spilled down her spine. Never had she looked so radiantly beautiful or so serene and never had Ewen been more glad to see anyone in his life.

Looking up at the impressive three-storeyed stone-built edifice, a number of chimney pots smoking over the slick tiles of the roof, and not having seen Ewen emerge from the house, Alice started when a shadow fell across her. Feeling the nearness of him, the strength, the maleness, slowly she turned to face him.

The slight bow he gave her was sufficiently formal to send a chill through Alice's heart, but at the same time acted as a spur, hardening her determination to fight back. His face was so bitter and desolate that her chest filled with remorse. She gazed at the dark, austere beauty, the power and virility stamped in every line of his long body, and her pulse raced with a mixture of excitement and trepidation.

'You do turn up in the most unexpected places, Alice,' Ewen said.

She did not speak at once, considering him closely, thoughtfully, with her lovely dark eyes. Tilting her nose, at length, she said, 'Not unexpected, Ewen. Barradine is my home now, is it not? I hope you don't mind, but I was anxious to come to Scotland—the country where I was born and left when I was no more than a babe in my mother's arms. It was an emotional moment for me when we crossed the border from England.'

Ewen stared at her, all emotion withheld by an iron control. In the long nights and days since he'd left her, he'd rehearsed many speeches to her—from angry lectures to gentle discussions. Now she was here he could not remember one damn word of them. His silver-grey eyes pierced through her—dark, bitter and wary, but not without interest.

Why couldn't he look pleased to see her? Alice asked herself. Why couldn't she at least feel angry? Because she loved him. It was as simple as that. 'I understand if you don't want me here, but please don't send me back,' she murmured inanely.

His granite features were an impenetrable mask and Alice was too nervous to notice anything about his mood except that he was tense. Then his lips turned downward at one corner in the sardonic smile she had come to know so well and feared so much.

'It's a bit late for that,' he answered coolly.

'You're here now.' His eyes sliced to Amir hovering by the coach. 'I thought I told you to wait until you were sent for.'

'Please don't blame Amir,' Alice said quickly in defence of Amir, her black wave of apprehension lifting a little. 'He did his utmost to dissuade me, but I wouldn't listen. I was determined, you see, and he couldn't very well let me travel all this way by myself. How are you, Ewen?' She knew it was an inadequate thing to say, but she had to say something to this cool and distant stranger.

'I am very well,' he assured her drily. 'Remarkably well, in fact, for a man who has been unable to settle since returning to Barradine, who works very hard but fails to achieve what he sets out to do, or been unable to sleep without drinking a strong libation.'

His voice was so frank and unemotional that at first Alice didn't grasp what he was saying. When she did, tears of relief sprang to her eyes. 'I—I came because I wanted to be with you.' Her quiet statement had a simple dignity.

Ewen looked at her straight back and proudly lifted head, and his voice softened. 'Come inside. You must be hungry.'

Alice stood in the grand entrance. It was a cavernous space of dark wooden floors and walls, coats of armour, heraldic crests and mounted animal heads. A young maid smiled as she passed her bearing an armful of clean linen and went up a grand staircase.

Ewen turned to her. Apprehension showed in his eyes. 'There is no escaping my family's presence here. The house is steeped in heritage. Their spirits can be felt in every room. Come and sit down. The rooms I've selected for you have been prepared.'

'You were expecting me then?' Alice queried, eyeing him quizzically.

'Eventually.' He escorted her to the hearth where a fire burned brightly.

His words warmed Alice. So he had intended to send for her after all. Calmly she considered her new home as she stood beside the wide open fireplace where the birch logs sizzled and spluttered beneath the great stone-carved coat of arms.

'How was your journey?' Ewen asked.

'Uneventful, thank goodness, although the condition of the roads worsened considerably the further north we travelled. I was glad of Amir's company. Hicks and Taff are following in another coach with the rest of my baggage. I came on ahead of them so they may not arrive for another couple of days.'

A round-bodied, apple-cheeked woman seemed to appear from nowhere. Dressed in a black woollen dress covered by a white-starched apron, she looked friendly enough.

'Ah, Mrs MacKenzie! Come and meet my wife, Lady Tremain. She thought to surprise me by arriving early. Mrs MacKenzie is the housekeeper at Barradine, Alice. How long has it been, Mrs MacKenzie? Ten years, is it, since Mrs Allott went into retirement?'

'It's going on that way.' The housekeeper faced Alice. 'Welcome to Barradine, my lady,' she said. 'I hope you will be happy living here. It's far from civilisation, mind, so I hope you won't feel lonely, coming from London as you do.'

'Thank you, Mrs MacKenzie. I'm sure I shall find Barradine to my liking. But I only lived in London for a little while. I was born in Scotland—not far from here, in fact, but I spent most of my life in France.'

'My wife was a Frobisher before we wed,' Ewen explained.

Mrs MacKenzie stared at Alice. The colour drained from her face. It was as if she had seen a ghost. 'Frobisher? Would that be the Frobishers of Rosslea, the house not far from here that was burned down by the English in their search for Jacobites after Culloden?'

'The same,' Alice affirmed. 'My husband told me that everyone assumed my mother perished in the fire that destroyed the house, along with me and my brother William, but she managed to escape and we made our way to Ireland. We lived there a short while before going on to France.'

'Saints be praised,' the housekeeper murmured, crossing herself. 'So many died at that time— my own father one of them. As for the house— well, it's a ruin, nothing but rubble. Only the stone walls withstood the flames, which indicates that it was no small blaze. Still, I'm glad to know your mother got away—and so will many others—they were well thought of hereabouts, you see, though it must have been difficult for her with you just a bairn.' Wiping her hands down her apron, she backed away. 'I'll get you some refreshment. You must be hungry after such a long journey.'

'A warm drink would be nice, Mrs MacKenzie,' Alice said, perching rigidly on the edge of the settle set at an angle before the hearth. 'I'll eat later.'

When Mrs Mackenzie had left them, Alice

looked at her husband. 'I would like to see what is left of Rosslea. Is it far from here?'

'Half-an-hour's ride, no more than that. When you're settled we'll ride over. Are you sure you're ready to go there?'

'Yes. I have to see it some time. The sooner the better.'

A strange yearning swept over Ewen as he looked down at his wife's bent head as she sipped the hot chocolate. Although he couldn't determine exactly what he craved, the feeling was nevertheless intense. Part of it, he determined, was a desire to recapture the happiness that had been his on the days before the wedding. Yet whatever plagued him was infinitely more complicated than that. Not for the first time since he had ridden off and left Alice at Mercotte Hall, wearily he sought some practical solution to his mounting problems.

As for the present moment, tired as she was after her journey, it was better for him to postpone any attempt to discuss the matter until the morrow. By then they would have both had time to rest and think things through.

Alice sipped her drink, carefully keeping her attention on the fire until the silence between them began to grow stilted and tense. Whenever her gaze moved to where he stood, she found his piercing silver-grey eyes regarding her. She knew what filled his mind, the questions and explanations that must be talked over before they could move on with their marriage—if they would still have a marriage after she had told him the whole sordid truth.

Nervously she set down her cup and rose to meander about the hall, pretending to admire or inspect a painting here and a tapestry there, yet deliberately seeking an area safe from his regard. There was none. Somehow his quiet indifference stung her more than anger would have. And it frustrated her that until his manner became more approachable, she could not bring up the subject that had driven a wedge between them. She wished he would say something so she could at least defend herself.

'If you wouldn't mind, Ewen, I would like to see my room. I would like to wash and change before dinner.'

'Of course. The rooms I've selected for you overlook the garden. I trust you will find them comfortable.'

'I'm sure I shall.'

Mrs MacKenzie was on hand when he called. 'You may show your mistress to her chambers.'

'Aye, milord. I've already ordered hot water to be sent up.'

The housekeeper led the way to the upper floor. Candles provided the light and cast a softly glowing sheen over the wooden floors and panelled walls.

''Tis the rooms next to Lord Tremain's you'll be having, my lady,' Mrs MacKenzie announced. 'Lovely they are. No one's slept in them for years. Used to be his lordship's mother's rooms before she went to live in France—although she did sleep here when she came over to spend the remaining days with Lord Edward. He occupied your husband's rooms before he died. Poor man. Been poorly for a long time so it came as no surprise.'

They paused before a large panelled door. Mrs MacKenzie pushed it open and stood back to allow Alice to pass through. Alice looked around the room, with its gilded furnishings and its high bed with elaborately embroidered hangings and valances fringed in gold. It was light and airy and everything had been arranged for her comfort. She roused from her daze, realising the kindly housekeep was awaiting her reaction. There was an expectant hope in the rosy-cheeked face and Alice could not deny the gentle-hearted woman.

'This is a lovely room, Mrs MacKenzie,' she murmured with a smile. 'I know I shall be very comfortable.'

'The master's rooms are next door—there's the connecting door,' she said, pointing it out. 'Of course he thought of everything.' She opened another door to reveal a small bathing chamber. 'He was anxious to see you made comfortable.'

In the immaculate dressing room, there were lace-edged linens ready for her *toilette*, a tall mirror and crystal bottles of scented oils and vials of perfume that had been added to the dressing table. Everything was ready for her merest whim or comfort.

'As I said, hot water is being brought up.' The housekeeper cast a frustrated glance at the door. 'I can't think what is keeping the girl. Excuse me. I'll go and see.'

Left alone, Alice stared at the door connecting the two rooms. Going towards it, she turned the knob. It was, for all its ominous presence, locked but she had no doubt at all that the key was on Ewen's side of the door. Stepping away from it, she prayed desperately for the strength and fortitude that would be required to face whatever lay before her should he decide to unlock that door.

Mrs McKenzie came back with a young woman named Tess, who was to serve as personal maid for the new mistress, and Alice was left in her care. A scented bath was prepared and enjoyed. Her skin was gently patted dry, and a light, perfumed oil rubbed into it. Then, in her petticoats, she sat while Tess dressed her dark tresses in an upswept *coiffure*.

Undecided what to wear, Alice held two gowns in front of her, a pink and a blue, surveying them in the long mirror. 'Which one do you think, Tess?'

'I'd say you are spoilt for choice, my lady.'

Alice smiled. 'How very diplomatic, Tess.' She sighed. 'I think I shall wear the pink.'

Her choice was a pink satin trimmed with a deeper pink-satin cording. The bodice fit closely to her tiny waist, the deep neckline bared her bosom, barely rising above the blushing peaks of her breasts.

Considering what had transpired since their wedding night, Alice thought that perhaps it was a poor choice after all and that Ewen might think she was trying to tease him with an extravagant showing of her bosom. With that in mind she considered changing into a more modest gown, but Tess had taken such trouble dressing her hair that she was reluctant to put her to any trouble.

Her dilemma ended when Mrs Mackenzie came to tell her that his lordship was waiting for her in the dining room. Picking up her shawl, she slipped it about her shoulders, purposefully pulling it high over her breasts.

When she stepped into the dining room, Ewen was waiting for her. She felt his gaze glide leisurely over her, taking in every detail of her appearance. Her heart refused to stop its wild thudding. She halted in front of him. Her eyes had to raise slightly to meet the shining glimmer in his.

'I compliment you, Alice. You look lovely.' His hands raised and slowly lifted the shawl away from her shoulders. 'However, since your beauty needs no other adornment and the room is well heated, I prefer the simplicity of the gown.'

He laid her shawl over a chair and Alice saw the glint in his eyes as they dipped downward towards her bosom. It took an extreme effort not to react and shield the bare curves from his perusal.

'Come near the fire, Alice,' he bade gently. 'You're trembling.'

He stood aside, not making any attempt to touch her as Alice neared the hearth. Ewen poured wine into a goblet and handed it to her.

'Here, this will help. Do you find your rooms suitable?'

'They are very nice. My every need seems to have been attended to. Thank you, Ewen.'

'My pleasure.'

One of the servants came in to serve dinner. It was a simple meal of roast lamb, potatoes and vegetables served in the wainscotted dining room. The room was wide and tall, with heavy crimson curtains and leaded windows to three walls. Being winter, a raging fire roared in the massive inglenook hearth that dominated the fourth wall.

Their conversation was wide and varied. They spoke of local matters and Ewen told Alice about the house and the people who had lived there in days gone by. He told her the story of how his brother Simon had ridden to Barradine with his now wife, Henrietta, disguised as a boy, of how she had fooled him into believing she was exactly that until he had come upon her in her bath and discovered to the contrary. Alice was fascinated by the tale and laughed when he told her how his brother had been duped, but all the while they consciously avoided speaking of the thing that was uppermost in both their minds.

Ewen wasn't going to press the issue, at least not yet. But this left him with unlimited frustration. He was disgusted that his absence from his wife had left him throbbing for her like a youth hungering for his first woman. Yet there was little he could do to control either the lust licking at his veins or the disquietingly tender feelings that were prodding at his heart.

'You haven't mentioned your father,' Ewen said when she rose from the table, having stressed her tiredness.

Alice became alert. 'I assumed that you would have told me if you had heard anything.'

'Actually…' Ewen paused for a moment, wondering if he should encourage her. 'When I rode to Rosslea, I spoke to some of the locals in the nearby village. One or two of them have seen an old man wandering in the ruins. No one has spoken to him—they say he goes away, but then he is seen again. One of the villagers who has lived in the village all his life and remembers the Frobishers did say the man could be your father.'

Encouraged by what he told her, Alice felt her courage returning and her hopes surged. 'Do you think it is? Could it possibly be him?'

Ewen shrugged in a casual gesture and went to pour himself a glass of wine. 'I don't know. Don't get your hopes up too much. The man wasn't sure.'

Alice quickly crossed the distance that separated them and Ewen faced her as she laid a hand on his arm. 'But it might have been. How can I not get my hopes up?' Recollecting herself, she quickly dropped her hand. 'How can I learn if it was truly my father who was seen? What did they notice about the man? Was he tall, thin? Dark? Grey?'

Ewen took a sip of the wine. 'The man who was seen spoke to no one and no one described him—apart from the fact that he was elderly and unkempt. I'll make further enquires. Give me time, Alice, and I promise you I shall find out what I can.'

Alice was too impatient to wait. 'I can't believe that he might be here, that he is so close. I want to go Rosslea. Tomorrow we will go and see for ourselves,' she uttered decisively. 'How often has he been sighted?'

'A few times. But there's no knowing when he'll come again—if at all.'

'Don't sound so defeatist, Ewen,' Alice chided sharply. 'I believe he will—I have to believe that and I will wait until he does.'

'Of course you will, but you will wait here until we have something to go on. If word gets round that you are looking for him, there is every possibility that *he'll* find you.'

Alice stared at him in amazement. 'But—if the man is my father, he—doesn't even know that I am alive. He thinks he's alone in the world, that what was left of his family after Culloden perished in the fire. Can you imagine how that will affect him? I want to find him and tell him myself.'

'You must face the fact that that may not be possible. There were hundreds of displaced families after Culloden. The man who's haunting the countryside might not even be your father. You have to prepare yourself for that.'

'Stop it,' Alice exclaimed, her eyes sparking with ire. 'Don't say such things. Have you no heart?'

Ewen's face hardened. 'Heart, Alice? Need *you*, of all people, ask that?'

'I do ask it,' she flared, the matter concerning her father set aside for the moment as their own volatile relationship sprang to the fore. 'Can't you imagine how wretched I felt when you left me at Mercotte Hall? I thought that you had left me for good,' she said, overwhelmed with emotions and the fear that this might have been so.

Ewen stiffened and when he looked at her she could almost feel the effort he was exerting to keep his temper under control. 'What in God's name gave you that idea?'

'I thought I had ruined everything. I thought that when I told you I am not the virgin bride you expected, you couldn't bear to be near me. I couldn't blame you for wishing to be out of my company for a while.'

The very thought that he had made her feel such humiliation made Ewen cringe inside. 'You were quite wrong. I renounced my freedom for you. You belong to me as I belong to you. I do not admit defeat so easily, Alice. For what it's worth, I was already regretting my hasty decision to leave Mercotte Hall before I crossed the border.'

'I am happy to hear it. Running away solves nothing.'

'I fully accepted the depth of my heartlessness

and stupidity and I am not proud of myself. But at the time, when you told me of the close intimacy you had with the man you were betrothed to, I could not accept it. However, I should never have left you alone. But didn't you realise what the enforced abstinence was doing to me? It was both unacceptable and intolerable. I have needs, Alice. I had to do something to quench the fury of not being able to make love to my wife.'

'And these needs you speak of are the kind that you came to Scotland to satisfy? How excruciatingly naive and stupid you must find me,' she retorted scathingly.

Ewen's eyes narrowed dangerously as he fixed her with a piercing stare. 'Are you accusing me of seeking my pleasure elsewhere?'

'What else am I to think?'

'I agree there are numerous beds around here with willing occupants. Do you expect me to live the life of a monk?'

The threatening quality of his behaviour sparked Alice's anger. She suddenly felt weary before this display of selfish rage on the part of her frustrated husband. The only thing he cared about was sating his lust.

'My goodness, you are feeling sorry for yourself, aren't you, Ewen?' she said, her words heavily laden with sarcasm. 'There are other worthier ways of finding forgetfulness for yourself than in the women who will willingly fall into your arms.'

'Don't push me, Alice,' he snapped coldly, his eyes glittering like shards of ice. 'There's been no other woman since I met you. I have been patient. The very sight of you wrenches my insides in a painful knot and begs to release the desire you have aroused in me. There will be no further separation between us, no matter how much you might desire it.'

'But I don't,' she cried.

'Have you given serious thought to what I said before I left?'

'Of course I have. You had a genuine grievance to be angry. I admit that. Ewen, I did not hold myself from you to hurt you. Please don't think that. The fault is entirely mine—I accept that and you can't possibly blame me more than I blame myself. But now you know the truth, there is no reason why we cannot address the issue and remove any obstacles that stand between us.'

Ewen gazed into her pain-shadowed eyes, fighting the simultaneous impulse to shake her for her stubborn refusal to be a proper wife to him and the stronger urge to clasp her to him. She was very lovely, this obstinate young woman he had married. So lovely, in fact, that he would forgive her past indiscretions and the insult of keeping herself from him if tonight she would come to him willingly.

'You think that?'

'Yes. Which is why I am here. You want children—we both do. How are we to manage that if we occupy separate beds?' What she said was calmly, factually put.

'Why, what is this?' One black brow rose in query. 'Are you propositioning me, Alice?'

His bold, glinting smile and the lazy mockery in his eyes almost proved too much for Alice. 'I suppose it does look like that,' she replied, annoyed, when she felt her cheeks flush beneath his penetrating gaze. The pull of his eyes was far worse to resist than the frantic beat of her heart. But only an idiot would have succumbed now. She had dared to challenge him, to let him know how she felt. She must be resolute.

Much less calmly, Ewen said, 'Things are not as they were before we were wed—'

'But we are not as before,' she interrupted. 'We are now man and wife. *In fact*. We are as truly married as any man and woman in the land. There is little sense in shutting your eyes to it.'

'There is more to marriage than a few words spoken in a church.'

'That is true. But what has been said cannot be unsaid. Words were spoken, promises made.'

'What are you saying, Alice? Are you demanding your rights?' When she did not answer, he went on, 'Do you *want* me in your bed?' He so desperately wanted her to say she did.

'I did not come all this way so that things could remain as they are. We have to take life as it is— not as you would wish it. Be we lords and ladies, or lesser mortals, we are married, the two of us, and must accept it. Yes, I have known another before you. Hard facts are best accepted—and can be made softer, I have found. But don't you dare treat me like some despicable baggage. I will not be judged, not by you, not by anyone. You don't know anything, Ewen. You know nothing about my life before I came to England. But we are not children. We know that in matters such as this there are often difficulties, barriers, stumbling blocks. Shy away from it and it becomes more difficult, harder to come together...'

'You make it sound as though we were horses

to be trained to the bit. Spare me more of this. Enough.'

'As you wish,' she said, and with her head held high while her heart was breaking in two, she walked to the door. 'Although I have to ask myself if I married a man or a mouse.' On that note she went out, closing the door none too gently behind her.

Chapter Nine

Ewen glared at the closed door through which his wife had disappeared. Had Alice been standing behind it instead of climbing the stairs—half-convinced that her taunt had hit its mark and that she had not seen the last of her husband that night— she would have felt the heat of that gaze.

Ewen paced up and down, scarcely aware of what he did as he tried to absorb everything that she had said. Vigorous male that he was, and far from under-sexed, his wife's parting taunt and strictures had hit him hard. What right had she to speak to him as she had? It was beyond all bearing that for his own purposes, having forced their estrangement, he should be faced with this ridiculous quandary. The fact that, from one point of view, Alice had the rights of it, made it the more damnable. As she said, the situation would not right itself.

Seizing a glass and pouring himself a drink, he sank into a chair to grapple further with his problem. His love for Alice was at the heart of the matter. He considered himself worldly, but in a wife he had told himself that he could not accept one of well-experienced joys. But now he found himself stricken with one such as that.

He had waited for quite some time before he left the dining room, went upstairs and entered his own bedchamber. His eyes became fixed on the connecting door. His mind dwelt on the image of how Alice would look lying in her bed, her shining wealth of black hair draped over the pillows, her soft, scantily clad body pulsating beneath the covers.

Uttering a sound of disgust, he turned to the great four-poster bed, removing his jacket. Hearing a faint noise from the other side of the door, unable to quash the desire that was pouring through him like liquid fire, he unlocked and opened the connecting door between their suites of rooms to find his wife sitting by the fire—waiting for him. A single candle burned nearby. It was infuriating—she had known her jibe would provoke him and had been so certain he would come.

Unbeknown to Ewen, Alice's heart was beating a tattoo in her breast. She felt her blood pounding in her temples, but, seeing that Ewen remained standing there, looking at her, she finally broke the silence. 'So, Ewen, you came.' She despised herself, for she had set out to seduce the man to whom her heart had gone out, irrevocably and forever. It was his absolutely, whether he wanted it or not.

'You should congratulate yourself, Alice, having got me here,' he ground out coldly.

'I don't. Is it not part of a husband's duty to share his wife's bed? You have taken your time in coming. I had almost given up on you.'

Ewen did not answer that, but walked slowly across the carpet and stood looking down at her. Her nightdress was a flimsy thing and it was clear that she wore nothing beneath it.

'Why are you doing this, Alice? You know the reason why I wanted an estrangement—a temporary estrangement until we can work things out.'

Alice looked up at him, her eyes locking on his. 'I do and, for what it's worth, I cannot say that I blame you. But it could not go on.'

'You are frank—some would say too frank. For myself I prefer it that way.'

'I thought you might,' she allowed, her voice low and a smile flirting on her soft lips. 'I took a chance on it.'

'I am my own man, Alice. I have a will as well as a body.'

'I do know that. Yet you vowed, not so long ago and before witnesses, to love and honour me and keep me. But I do not want to trade words with you. Knowing what I was before, do you think ill of me? Do you think less of me?'

Ewen shook his head. 'No. I would have preferred it to be otherwise, but it is done.' His eyes ran over her scantily clad body. She was very desirable. He burned for what she was offering and he moved closer. As he did so, Alice stood up.

Reaching out, he traced the curve of her jaw gently with the tip of his finger. 'You are very lovely, Alice.' He deeply regretted that she was not a virgin, a bride to be led into the secrets of the marriage bed gently. Having already been initiated in the union with a man, she was less inclined to experience them all over again. He was conscious of a sharp second of nothing except the strange, desolate void of deception that enclosed him.

Suspecting the thoughts going through his mind, impatient for him to hold her, for this first time with her husband to be put behind them so they could move on, Alice said, 'Please consider that I'm not some delicate flower, Ewen. You'll hardly bruise me by holding me close. I assure you I am quite hardy.'

'And inquisitive?'

'And that. I want to know you fully—as a wife knows a husband. Truly, now you know the truth, might it occur to you that I long for what is to come as much as you? I want to please you—if that is acceptable.'

'Indeed it is, my love.'

'Then let me be your lover, replacing all thoughts of any other you might have once cherished.' He became still at her words and a shadow passed before his eyes. It was gone almost as soon as it had appeared, but it made her wonder about Etta.

'Shouldn't you—go and change in your dressing room?' she murmured hesitantly as his face came closer.

One of his eyebrows lifted with quizzical amusement. 'I have no idea. Is that customary, Alice?'

She swallowed audibly. 'I—I don't know.'

'I wouldn't know either.' He grinned. 'This is the first time I've had a wedding night—even if it is somewhat belated—so I am as ignorant as you. What do you think is the correct procedure? Perhaps this.' He moved closer to her and, settling his hands gently on her shoulders, bent his dark head.

Alice felt his warm lips against the curve of her neck, sending tingling sensations down her spine. At her sharp intake of breath, Ewen raised his head and looked at her.

'Does that meet with your approval, Alice?' When she failed to reply he became bolder.

Alice felt his hand slide around her waist, pulling her closer until she felt her chest pressed to his, the imprint of his legs against her own. He again bent his head, his arm tightening as he drew her hair aside and lazily kissed her ear, his other hand slowly brushing up her arm to her shoulder before seeking the side of her breast. His fingers splayed wide in a bold, possessive caress.

Ewen slid his lips across her cheek, his mouth seeking hers, kissing her with slow ardour, his arms moulding her close. Alice kissed him back, helplessly caught up in the stirring sensations his kiss evoked in her, her arms sliding around his neck to hold him clasped to her. The kiss was a leisured meeting of parting lips and questing tongues, the eagerness of one yielding to the bold intrusion of the other. A faint sigh passed Alice's parted lips as his kisses blazed a trail along her throat, brushing past the delicate lace collar and continuing downward until his mouth claimed the soft peak of her breast through the fabric of her nightgown, torching the sensitive pinnacle. She caught her breath at the sudden jolt of pleasure that leapt through her, before he claimed her lips once more.

The kiss seemed to last for an eternity before he broke away with a sigh, leaving her spent and breathless. As if he fought some inner battle on his own, he raised his head and stared down into the encompassing warmth of her deep blue eyes. His own were aflame with fiery passion.

Ewen was overwhelming his wife with his vibrant sexuality, sending palpable signals to her sharpened senses. She could feel them all about her. She was engulfed by something she did not know how to cope with, nor had any understanding of. Suddenly he swung her up into his arms, his mouth still claiming hers as he carried her to the huge bed.

Lost in the kiss, Alice felt her legs gliding down his as he gently lowered her against him until her feet touched the floor. There was no resistance in her. He was her husband and it was quite proper to yield to his caresses, to his kisses, and to anything else he had in mind. His iron-thewed arm slipped about her waist and brought her up against him once more, his mouth slanting across hers with a ravening urgency that would not be denied. The searing lips sent little tremors of delight boring down through her body, flicking every nerve until they were aflame.

'What are you doing?' she gasped when her husband drew back. Her whole body quaked with what he had begun. Lifting her head, she searched his handsome features, silently pleading for him to continue.

The silver-grey eyes delved into hers and he smiled. 'I need a moment to undress, my love. 'Tis only a brief delay,' he murmured huskily. 'I must go slowly lest I cheat you of your wifely pleasure.'

'If my pulse rate is an indication of how I feel, you have not been cheating me.'

'Never have I had a more willing woman,' Ewen

breathed, taking her hand. Lifting it to his lips, he placed a kiss on the back of it and then turned aside.

Alice sat on the bed and watched as he stripped to his breeches, placing his clothes in an untidy heap on a chair. Laughing softly, she got up and went to fold them.

Hands on hips, Ewen watched her with some amusement. 'What are you doing? We have servants to do that.'

'A servant doesn't happen to be present, but your wife is.'

She looked at him. He was naked to the waist. Her heart fluttered and her mouth dried at the sheer beauty of the man—a statue of muscular, olive-skinned perfection brought to life. Slowly her gaze passed down the furred chest and lean waist and moved on to the firm, flat belly with its light tracing of hair. She held her breath when he turned slightly.

At the sight that met her eyes, Alice became still. Unbidden tears filled her eyes and she silenced the horrified gasp that rose in her throat with the back of her hand. Ugly purple scars marred the smooth symmetry of his back, vicious welts that criss-crossed each other like a spider's web. He had been flayed, on more than one occasion it would appear. The raised ridges gave her an understanding of those brief times when she had seen him grimace as if some ache or pain plagued him. Inside her something became tight strung and her heart, which had begun to slow, missed a beat before it quickened again. A sudden surge of compassion rose within her as she thought of the agony he must have suffered during his years of servitude.

Ewen turned back to her. Seeing the shocked expression on her face, he sighed. He should have expected she would react to his scars like this. Taking the hand that covered her mouth, he shook his head slowly. 'I'm sorry, Alice. I should have warned you. They are not an attractive sight, I know. I cannot blame you for your horrified reaction.'

'You—you were whipped.' Her voice was ragged with horror.

'On more than one occasion. It was a regular punishment for anyone who worked the oars.' He smiled a bitter smile. 'They told me I needed discipline.'

Ewen stood quite still as Alice walked round him and touched the worst of the scars gently for, as nothing else ever could, they would remind him of the horror of his captivity. He was scarred for life from it. Was his mind blemished by what had been done to him? She ran the tip of her finger along one that had healed as if to erase it. 'Do they hurt?' she whispered.

'At the time. Not any more.'

'How did you bear it?'

'I had no choice.'

'And Amir? Was he punished, too?'

Ewen nodded. 'He was, though he was little more than a youth at the time. Amir is tough. Like me he survived.' Taking her arm, he drew her round to face him. Holding her face in the palms of his hands, he looked deep into her eyes, burning her with their intensity. 'What I went through, what I endured, is over, Alice. I can't change what happened to me, but I cannot forget either. Many times I thought I would die of what was happening to me. But I am done with coddling my wounds. Now all I want is to reside at Barradine and to live out my life in peace.'

An incredible warmth enveloped Alice's heart as she searched his eyes and found a strange sincerity there. Taking one of his hands, she placed it to her lips, their softness caressing the silver scars that marred them. 'I understand, Ewen. Truly I do. We will live here together and, God willing, raise any children we are blessed with in peace.'

'That is my fondest dream. We are the perfect complement for one another, are we not, and shall manage very well.' The fierce intensity melted away and was replaced with a smouldering desire. 'Speaking of children…'

Her mouth curved in a sublime smile while her eyes grew dark and sultry, burning into his and promising him more than he had ever expected. 'What are we waiting for?'

Taking her face in his hands with infinite gentleness, he kissed her moist lips. Without shame, in her desperation to calm her fears, Alice wrapped her arms around his neck, pressing her body against him.

Since their first meeting Ewen had never ceased to be amazed and fascinated by the enticing blend of innocence and boldness he had seen in Alice. Each trait was wonderfully intriguing and he was never more aware of his infatuation than at that present moment, when they were about to enter the realm of conjugal intimacy. But if she did react to the marital intimacies with fright, he had enough experience with women to be able to handle any problems of that sort.

Warmed and intrigued by her response, he drew a ragged breath. 'It's a mountainous task for me to hold you and remain tender and patient when my hunger for you has brought me to the brink of starvation.' Unable to curb his impatience for her, he released her and peeled off his breeches. Getting into bed, he patted the covers beside him.

The moment Alice had tried not to think about had finally arrived. Slowly, against her will, her thoughts became a sharp disturbance. Without warning she saw Philippe. She knew every detail of his awful presence. He was in the room, corrupt, haunting her like an ugly, bitter memory she didn't want. For a moment she held back. Her stomach clenched into knots and she could have wept with desperation. She felt as if she were being torn in pieces. Her mind pulled her one way and her heart tugged another. Fear coiled in her chest while desire to experience the feelings and emotions Ewen had stirred in her pulsed through her veins and her love for him burned like a steady, glowing fire in the centre of it all.

And she did love him. Very much. She had already admitted that to herself and the admission sent a fierce jolt of pleasure and panic through her. Whatever happened between them this night, she was determined to exorcise Philippe from her mind, to relegate him to the past where he belonged. With that thought in her mind, eager to accept her husband's invitation, Alice pulled her nightdress over her head in one fell swoop and got into bed with him.

For a moment Ewen was stunned at the frank sensuality of the gesture. That a woman could strip herself naked without showing any sign of embarrassment surprised him and confounded his division of women into good and bad. He could only put it down to the fact that whatever her experiences had been before, she was doing what she believed was expected of her. She was, after all, his wife now and it was her right to lie beside him. His desire rose at the sight of her naked body.

Sitting sideways, Alice looked into his eyes on a level with hers. His face was gilded by the candlelight. It was almost too handsome to bear. The perfect profile, the firm, warm mouth and arched brows. Tentatively she put a hand out and touched his face.

Ewen took her hand and pressed it to his cheek, then drew her down to the pillows. Her round breasts gleamed enticingly in the golden candle-light and, becoming still a moment, he drank his fill of their perfection. Gently cupping the soft, scented roundness within his hands, he lowered his head and leisurely caressed them with his mouth, pressing wanton kisses over their warmth. Alice's head fell back as the fires raged in the depths of her body. Ewen raised himself above her and slid warm hands over the rest of her naked body. As if in a trance, Alice lay beyond thought, beyond awareness, unmoving beneath the touch of his hands as he stroked and caressed. She felt desire, unbidden, unexpected, rise up in her. A pulsing heat began to throb in her loins, spreading outward, reaching upward until she thrust out her breasts to luxuriate in the hot, flicking strokes.

Consumed by a pleasure she had never dreamed of, a pleasure that threatened to melt every fibre of her being and leave her naught but a quiver-ing wreck, Alice's shy uncertainty was over-whelmed by the desire to clasp him to her. Her body clutched his, wrapping itself, long slim legs, twining white arms about him. Her mouth wel-comed his, soft and deliciously sweet, her tongue darting out to touch his lips. He crushed her to him, drawing her tongue into his mouth, while desire surged through his bloodstream like wildfire, pounding in his loins. Her glorious hair fell about them both in a way that was undoubtedly erotic.

Ewen could feel it drift like silk across his face and shoulders and he was surprised to find himself in such a position. She had taken over, flowing across his hard body in a way which was exquisitely pleasing but incredible. She was kissing him, caressing him with her tongue, trailing from his lips to his neck and down the eager masculine strength of him to his flat stomach, moving and undulating in a way she should have known nothing about. Evidently, his wife had learned a great deal about kissing.

Taking charge, he rolled her on to her back and his weight was on top of her. For a moment Alice knew a sense of panic as though something was wrong…familiar…wrong…*not again…please, not again…*but this was Ewen, her husband, and she loved him. His penetration when it came was sharp and deep, an agonising desire, a sensation that Alice welcomed, that she wanted to wash away all the pain Philippe had inflicted on her body and her mind.

Their intimacy became a deep pleasure, without pain, without fear, a feeling of submission, absolute delight, leaping desire and deep satisfaction. Her yielding woman's body was eager to submit itself to the languid, stretching, searching joy of his hands and lips. When she moaned it was with a deep, inner joy and a sense of resolution she had never felt before, as if at last, after all she had been through, she understood that what she felt now was the death of what had gone before. She became aware of a driving need to appease a burgeoning, insatiable hunger as her world reeled out of control and ravishing, rapturous splendour burst upon her, as they were forever joined as one, fused by the heat of their loins.

Ewen put his mouth over hers and caught her tumbling climax, miraculously reigniting it and caressing her to a point of such insanity that she had no idea she existed. She became her body alone, and in her body, just that one place as if the rest of her did not exist.

Ewen raced towards his own explosive orgasm. He swelled upward, letting his control shatter and his own reservations shatter with it as he claimed his wife fully and filled her with the urgent desire he'd been keeping so tightly in check since the day of their wedding. It was only when his shuddering release was over and his breath was coming in ragged gasps that he even remembered why he had harboured any reservations at all.

His rock-hard body glistening with sweat, Ewen collapsed on Alice, barely remembering to protect her from his weight with his arms as he lay against her, spent and sated. After a few moments, when he felt the woman beneath him stir, he rolled away and lay still.

He raised his head slowly, searching her face and seeing the crimson blush on her cheeks. 'I imagine this means,' he said quietly, his gaze filled with rugged tenderness, 'that we are truly husband and wife in every sense.'

Alice sighed like a well pampered kitten. 'I shall not call you mouse again,' she murmured. 'Not that I thought you were for a minute.'

'I'm relieved to hear it,' he said softly, his breath warm on her cheek.

Trailing her fingers across his chest, she whispered, 'I meant what I said earlier. That it is best this way—for both of us.'

'It came to this because you made it so!'

As Ewen proceeded to gently trace the outline of her hip, his fingers moving over her slender waist and on to her breast, cupping its fullness, Alice closed her eyes and lay quite still. She was transfixed by a profound pleasure that felt almost holy. It shook her to the very core of her being.

Nothing would ever be the same again. She savoured the memory of what had happened, recalling the details and storing them away. She felt that, deep down, Ewen had been shocked at her abandonment, at her eagerness, at her wanton display. If he had expected a hesitant bride, he had found instead a full-blooded woman ready and eager to enjoy their marital bed together. She felt that when he had entered her had been the moment when she had really lost her virginity. Previously, with Philippe, sexual intercourse had been difficult, hurried and often painful, a pain to be endured, and she had been full of shame and guilt afterwards.

She and Ewen had taken pleasure in one another's bodies. She had been shy, but not embarrassed, uncertain without clumsiness. Ewen had made her feel like a real woman, like his wife. She wanted to savour more, she thought, and she hugged the pleasure she had felt to herself, feeling wanton.

Whatever the circumstances that had driven Ewen into his wife's bed, they were forgotten as he wrapped his arms around her. She was magnificent, exquisitely soft in his arms. From the moment his mouth had touched hers, he'd known they were an oddly combustible combination. What had just passed between them had been the most wildly erotic, satisfying sexual experience of his life. Lying there while she slept in his arms, he marvelled at the intoxicating, primitive sensuality of her. Whatever she'd felt during their coupling had been real and uncontrived. He had no doubt about that. No woman could have feigned those responses, not without a great deal of practice.

Looking at her flushed face resting on his shoulder, gently he pushed her away and got out of bed. He stood looking down at her sleeping form. As she had told him herself, she'd had a great deal of practice.

Alice awoke late in the morning, disappointed not to find Ewen beside her. Getting out of bed, she chafed under Tess's ministrations, who insisted on brushing her hair until it gleamed. Wondering how Ewen might treat her this morning, and as she dressed she felt a mounting tension.

* * *

Entering the dining room, she found him already eating breakfast. He glanced up when she walked in. Pushing back his chair, he strode round the table and pulled her chair out. Uncertain of his mood, Alice seated herself and watched him return to his seat. Her gaze ran over his tall, lithe frame while she tried to ignore the feelings he had roused in her in her bed and how incredibly handsome he looked in a midnight-blue jacket that clung to his broad shoulders and buff trousers that emphasised his long, muscular legs. A single gold stud winked in the folds of the showy neckcloth that contrasted sharply with his bronze features.

'Oh, dear,' she said, helping herself to a knob of butter for her bread. 'You are in a grim mood, I see, Ewen. Have I done something to displease you?'

Ewen's brows snapped together, then he leaned back in his chair and sighed heavily. Reaching up in a gesture of frustration and uncertainty, he massaged the muscles at the back of his neck as if they were tense. Then he dropped his hand. He felt an uneasy pang of guilt for leaving her bed in the early hours.

'Are you angry with me?' she enquired, spreading the butter over her bread. 'Do you regret what happened between us?'

A smile quirked the corners of his mouth. 'If I said I did, what would you say?'

'That your eyes, your body and your very manhood belie your words. You wanted me. Do you think I did not know? Why waste your strength and time denying what is between us?'

She looked across at him, wanting to tell him how she felt, but she was no naive, starry-eyed girl who would blurt out her love after one night of passion. But she was dangerously fascinated by this unexpected vulnerable side of her enigmatic husband.

'Alice,' Ewen said, sounding both rueful and exasperated, 'I want to begin by apologising for the way I treated you last night. I didn't intend to start your time at Barradine by making you feel uncomfortable. As my wife, this is your home as much as it is mine. I am not an ogre.'

Very slightly mollified by his apology, Alice paused in eating her eggs to look across at him. 'Thank you. I accept your apology, but are you apologising for your attitude before we went to bed or what occurred afterwards?'

Unexpectedly, he smiled crookedly and a devilish gleam entered his eyes. 'Both—that is—if you think I need to apologise for what happened between us in bed. I did not hear you complain at the time.'

Caught unawares by the combination of gravity and tenderness in his expression, Alice stared at him in speechless amazement. How could he be so impossibly tender one moment and so cold, withdrawn, and arbitrary the next? she wondered, staring into his mesmerising silver-grey eyes. Her voice was quiet as she voiced the thought running through her mind.

'I wish I understood you, Ewen.'

'What is it you don't understand?'

'How you can be so harsh one minute and almost tender the next.'

'Actually, when you told me you were not the virginal woman I thought I'd married, my pride suffered a blow—richly deserved, you might say, but that is a matter of opinion—and when you challenged me into your bed it suffered another blow,' he admitted quietly.

'Your *pride*?' Alice repeated, gaping at him. 'Now *that* I do not understand.'

She missed the glint of amusement in his eyes, and so it took her a moment before she realised he was ridiculing himself, not her. 'I am an intelligent, experienced man, Alice. I should have approached you regarding which bed we occupy together, not leave it to my wife to broach the matter. Men like to be in charge of such things.'

'Whatever for?' she uttered, puzzled, and then she smiled broadly as she realised what he was saying. 'Really, Ewen! Are you telling me your male ego took a knock?'

'It was more than a knock,' he admitted with a crooked grin. 'And men will go to any lengths to protect their egos.'

'I see. Thank you for telling me.' Looking down at her plate and toying with her food, not wishing to spoil the moment by delving deeper into their sleeping arrangements which was in danger of resurrecting her past, she said, 'Will you take me to Rosslea? In any case it is a fine day and I would like to walk or ride out if I may. I seem to have been confined to the coach for so long that I'm eager to stretch my legs.'

'I was going to suggest it myself.'

Suppressing the urge to shout with relief, she smiled into his eyes. 'Then you will come with me?'

'That depends.'

'On what?'

His brows lifted in a mocking challenge. 'On how well you can ride.'

Impatient to get going, Alice shoved back her chair and stood up. 'I'll have you know I am an accomplished horsewoman—as you will see when I have changed into more suitable clothes.'

The day was pleasant but cold, with frequent gusts of wind that billowed out her skirt of olive green and loosened tendrils of hair about her face. She pressed her mount into a faster pace, keeping up with her companion. Alice was an experienced equestrienne, her expertise drawing her husband's silent admiration.

They rode through the softness of well-watered valleys and gently rolling hills dotted with sheep, fat with their soon-to-be newborn lambs. The sky brooded over them with moody, racing clouds that threw shadows in the dips and rises. A robin rose suddenly from the branches of a skeleton alder, its red breast vivid against the darkness of the valley, flying away at their approach. The horses' hooves were sharp against the crackling bracken and stiff grasses, snapping the air like dry twigs. They climbed higher, Alice's heart stirring almost painfully for it was all so perfect, this place which she was seeing—not for the first time, but she could not remember that other time.

Suddenly Ewen reined his horse to a stop and pointed ahead. Alice stopped to see what he was indicating. She could make out the outline of a ruin which clung to the side of a high hill, a charred, crumbling heap of stones which loomed over the village, its abandoned gardens running down the hill. Some walls stood with big, gaping holes in them and the chimney stacks rose into the sky like giant sentinels.

As they drew closer, an ache for the past and her lost family came to her. A lump rose in her throat when she looked at the empty stables, buildings which had once pulsated with the lives of men and horses alike.

'What are you thinking?' Ewen asked, watching her closely.

'I'm wondering how it must have been for my mother when she was forced to flee her home. The despair, the fear, the wretchedness and the horror would have been overwhelming.'

Her voice trembled slightly as she spoke and Ewen felt the despair for her move in his chest.

'All this time,' she whispered, 'if Mr Forbes

is to be believed, my father has been alive and I didn't know.'

Dismounting, she stood and looked about her. Ewen saw her rigid white face, the long grass licking at her skirt as she walked closer to what had been her home. Her head spun as her eyes darted around the ruin and surrounding tumbled walls and gardens, picking out spots where she might have climbed and played had she been allowed to be raised at Rosslea.

An eerie, haunting silence shrouded the ruins, an unearthly quiet. It struck deep into Alice's heart as she tried to imagine what it must have been like on that terrible night when the English soldiers had burned it down and her grief-stricken mother, mourning the loss of two of her sons at Culloden and her husband a prisoner of the English, had been forced to flee.

'What was it like before the fire? Do you know?'

'I remember riding over to visit on several occasions with Simon. My mother would often visit your mother. In those days it was a large, rambling house—the size of Barradine, turreted and gabled and very fine.'

'That is how I imagined it to be. Now it makes me think of something beautiful after it has been through the throes of death,' Alice murmured as she gazed at the once-noble house, weighted down by a terrible sadness.

She looked around and listened to the sound of the wind as it went sighing and whispering, searching the holes and crevices that had been given over to a past long since gone, and she watched a bird fly out of the ruins and go soaring and searching in a silent sky. She had returned to Rosslea not knowing what to think. All around her secrets seemed to swirl and dart like fireflies, bright and dazzling, unseen, but making their presence felt all the same.

'Where is my father? Where can he be?'

Ewen stood looking at Alice. Pale and fragile as a plucked wind flower, standing defenceless in what had been the great hall of the Frobishers' ancestral home, the lost look that stole over her face drew his pity. It was pity that he felt and a strange urge to protect that he had known when she had been his captive.

To see her anguish dislodged a barrier in his mind. Something dark shifted in his chest, struggling to find its way to the light, tearing and clawing on his past, revealing the stark recollection of what had been done to him. The memory served no purpose to the present and right now this woman was suffering the same desperation he had suffered then.

Deeply affected by what she had seen and the painful images and memories it had evoked, Alice walked towards her husband. 'I have seen enough. Take me home, Ewen.'

In a sad, melancholy mood on reaching Barradine, deeply affected by what she had seen and unable to banish the sad thoughts from her mind, Alice had spent the night alone.

The next morning, roused at daybreak by the twittering of birds outside, Alice dressed and found her way through the corridors to the hall, letting herself out of the front door.

After a restless night worrying about his wife, yet knowing she needed this time alone to ponder on what her journey to Rosslea meant to her, Ewen had respected her privacy. Now, from the window of his room overlooking the garden, he saw her step out on to the terrace and walk slowly towards the river. Wearing her cloak and with her head slightly bent, she appeared to be deep in thought.

Crossing a narrow bridge that spanned the river,

Alice followed the path leading to the low hills and woods. Hearing a footfall, she turned to find Ewen behind her. 'Why, Ewen. I didn't expect to find anyone up and about at this hour.'

'You're up early.'

'I couldn't sleep.'

'Why? Is the bed uncomfortable?' he asked, falling into step beside her and indulging himself with studying minute parts of her. His gaze admiringly caressed a small ear and a pale, creamy nape where curling wisps escaped a braided knot, while her delicate fragrance stirred his senses.

'Not at all.'

'Then why?'

Alice stopped walking. The lane twisted lazily on. A doe with her fawn darted across the path ahead of them and disappeared into the wood on the far side. 'I had a lot on my mind and because there are things we have to talk about and until we do I shall know no peace. You haven't pressed me to tell you about the man I was betrothed to, but I know deep down you are angry and hurt and distrustful. We cannot hide from it. It will always be there, between us, if we don't speak of it now and get it out of the way. You must feel that you have been cheated—I understand that,' she said quietly, seeing his reluctant expression, 'and I am truly sorry.'

Alice was grateful for Ewen's patience, but it was now time for the truth to be told. 'I need to be honest with you. There are things you don't know about me. Bad, terrible things that I need to share with you. I have never told anyone. If talking about it will finally exorcise what happened to me from my mind, from my life, I am ready to try.'

'Tell me, Alice. I am ready to listen. I will not judge you, I promise.'

Chapter Ten

Alice walked on, not speaking for several moments as she considered how best to begin. At length, without looking at Ewen and keeping a steady pace, she said, 'I was just seventeen when I became betrothed to Philippe Duplay—the Comte de St Antoine. Are you acquainted with him?'

Ewen shook his head. 'My time in Paris was brief. I had not been there long when I met Roberta. Shortly afterwards I was summoned to Barradine, which was probably why I heard nothing of the scandal which beset you. Nor did I read the gossip in the newspapers. I had been out of touch with trivial society matters for so long that it held no interest for me. What was he like, Philippe Duplay?'

'Wealthy, handsome, fair, witty—the kind of man girls dream of. He was also arrogant, a roué

and a gamester. In the anxious world of an innocent, I had no idea how I should behave. I had no
feelings to guide me. I had never fallen in love. I
watched other girls' passing infatuations and agonies at balls and picnics with mild amusement.
It never happened to me—until Philippe began
showing an interest in me.'

'How did you feel about him? Were you in love
with him?'

'No—never that. I was flattered by his attentions and did not object when he told me he wanted
to marry me. Our betrothal was approved of by
both our families.' Coming to a halt, she turned
and faced him, her eyes meeting and holding his
gaze so that she could assess his reaction for what
came next. 'He told me about marital duty—and
how it was common practice for a betrothed couple to pre-empt their wedding vows.' Her voice
was devoid of all expression and she held Ewen
frozen into stillness beside her. 'I was not the first
woman to be taken in by a handsome, sweet-talk-
ing man and I will not be the last. Philippe used
me for his own gratification. What he did to me
was obscene and unforgettable. I hated him.'

Ewen's gut knotted. He didn't know which was

stronger, fury or contempt for the perpetrator of such an outrage. 'You were very young.'

'Age does not exonerate me. It was the most shameful time of my life.' Ewen's expression was unreadable. 'I have shocked you,' she said, seeking a reaction, but he was not to be drawn.

'Was there no one to instruct you in marital duties?'

'Don't forget that I was raised by my brother. It isn't the sort of thing a man discusses with his young sister,' Alice said, flushing. 'Somehow I never really understood...I believed I was doing my duty...'

Her voice died away to nothing. High in the sky, a blackbird filled the silence, calling joyously as it soared high. The notes which trilled from it were as sweet and pure as any Ewen had ever heard and he felt the pain of the moment in every part of his body. 'Duty,' he snapped in disgust, turning from her. 'Seduction is what I'd call it.' He turned away in anguish. 'Alice...don't go on...'

'I must.'

Ewen turned slowly back to her and the expression of anguish on his face began to subside. Her simple, toneless monologue—a story of pain and humiliation, a story told without emphasis or she would break, drew him from his own desolation and he felt pity begin to melt his heart. Suddenly he wanted to know—he needed to know—what had happened to her.

'Go on,' he said quietly.

'Philippe's attitude to what he did to me made me feel worthless—cheap and so ashamed of myself. It seems incredible now that I allowed him to do what he did to me, that I submitted to his whims so meekly.' Bright flags of humiliated colour stained her cheeks and tears stung her eyes. 'He promised me the world. But he turned out to be a liar and a bully. I wasn't to know what he was really like.'

'Was he violent, Alice? Did he hit you?'

She nodded. 'Yes,' she answered hoarsely.

'Dear God. Did you tell anyone?'

'No. No one—at least, not then. I was too humiliated. William would have tried to kill him. He—he always hit me where the bruises didn't show.' Alice's voice trembled with emotion as she confessed. In her tortured mind it was almost as though she was back in that time, caught up in a nightmare, when Philippe had demanded things of her which she had thought were strange and did not know the meaning of, but what she now knew would shock Ewen.

'I can't put all the blame on Philippe. I should have known better. I was just a stupid, naive young girl who couldn't handle a relationship like that. I didn't know how to deal with his moods. I was too easily bullied. No other woman would have been so gullible. I should have been strong enough to resist his advances—stood up to him, protected myself.'

Ewen was struggling to contain his fury. The meek and humble girl she spoke of bore no resemblance to the beautiful firebrand who had confronted and fought with him the night he had invaded her bedroom at Hislop House.

'That's all very well, but don't forget you were a young girl of seventeen. That man took advantage of you. He was the one who should have known better, not you!'

Alice made no response to Ewen's wise words.

Ewen was taken aback by what he'd learned. This unassuming young woman had poured out her heart and soul. She had confided her extraordinary and shocking past, and now those awful times, and her suffering, were clearly evident in her face. Her betrothed had taken a young girl and robbed her of all trust and innocence.

'He made me suffer very badly and that was something I cannot shrug off,' Alice whispered. 'He taught me how to be subservient. He taught me the very depths of depravity I did not know the meaning of, things I could not possibly understand, which he told me were quite normal between a husband and wife—things,' she whispered, averting her eyes, 'that I now realise are quite shocking. Philippe also taught me the very depths of hatred. He was a monster. The dark memories remain, of course, along with the firm belief that I will never be like others. Because of the abuse I suffered at his hands, I came to believe a normal life would be denied me. And as long as I live I will never forgive him.'

'At least you found the courage and the good sense to leave him.'

'Yes, I did that. I had to. If I'd married him, I truly believe that, in time, I would have killed myself.'

For a moment, Alice spoke not a word. Instead she turned her head away and walked on.

Walking beside her, Ewen looked at her, deeply moved to see tears flowing down her face. He was a man capable of hatred and cruelty and bloodlust. But he was also capable of compassion, kindness and love. He couldn't imagine the horror of what she had endured, or the kind of courage it must have required to break off the betrothal. Fiercely, he took hold of her and wrapped his arms round her and his love, fierce and incontestable, was undiminished by the knowledge that she had been taken first by another. He felt a surge of reverent admiration for what she had overcome and a humility that was strangely unfamiliar. He also felt a murderous fury for the man who was guilty of nothing short of the brutal rape of an innocent.

'Had I known this I would never have left you to come to Barradine. The magnitude of my error is enormous, but even worse is the knowledge of what you have suffered.' Her pain and vulnerability touched him more deeply than anything else. As her husband it was his part to keep her from harm, not to add to it.

Alice buried her face against his chest. 'He hurt me so much. At least I know I'm safe now. Philippe is long gone. He can't hurt me any more.'

Holding her away from him, Ewen looked at her. There was hurt buried deep. 'How did you end your betrothal?'

'I told him I would not marry him one week before the ceremony. I did not leave him standing at the altar, but anyone would think I had by the reaction of his family and friends. No one knew what he had done to me and they judged me to be in the wrong. Philippe was incensed. He tried to whiten his own hands by saying awful things about me, shameful things. When he made our affair public knowledge and declared to the world I had the morals of a harlot, I was so ashamed and so humiliated I did not deny it. My world fell apart.'

Ewen saw the pain in her eyes as the memories tore at her, and despite his belief that all this had to be said, it took an almost physical effort not to try to ease her hurt with his hands and silence her with his mouth.

'A conflict raged in my mind between shock and anger,' she went on. 'Shock that he had spoken out about me and I was unable to defend myself, and anger that he had done the most terrible thing that could happen to a girl of my station. That was the worst thing of all. It seemed to me that all my innocence had vanished, that I had gone far beyond the bounds of carnal knowledge that had so carefully sheltered me all my life. It seemed there was a terrifying new depth to life I had not noticed before. I was filled with such despair I thought I would never recover.'

'And your brother?' Ewen flared. 'You're his sister, for God's sake. Didn't he stand by you—defend you?'

'William wanted me to marry Philippe. When the gossip started he did nothing to stifle it. He thought I would prefer marriage to disgrace. But I had made up my mind. Besides, the damage was done. Nothing he said could persuade me to marry Philippe. William accused me of behaving with wanton indiscretion. I was too humiliated to argue or protest. It was Anne, William's wife, who told him what Philippe had done to me. She came to my room one day and saw the bruises before I could cover them. Desperate for somebody to confide in, I told her everything.'

'What was your brother's reaction when his wife told him the truth?'

'It affected him deeply. He was quietly incensed. He said very little to me, but on parting he told me that he would take care of everything. I was puzzled by it at the time. I didn't know what he meant, until I received a letter from his wife. She—she told me that William could not ignore what Philippe had done to me, that he should be made to answer for his behaviour. He was duty-bound to defend my honour. Philippe acceded to William's demand for a duel.'

When she fell silent, as though she couldn't go on, Ewen placed his hands on her upper arms and looked down at her. Her face gave an impression of extraordinary resignation and fragility. 'What happened, Alice?' he prompted.

'William is a fine swordsman. He was the victor. Philippe died of his wound,' she whispered. 'I am sure you know that duelling is illegal in France—but it goes on. Philippe's family were ashamed of what Philippe had done and did not want the duel made public. It was hushed up.'

He had allowed Alice to open her heart to him at last, and she had revealed her tragic secret which held a wealth of terrible suffering and shame. 'The man got what he deserved,' Ewen remarked fiercely. Had Alice's brother not taken care of Duplay, he would have been driven to take the first boat to France and called him out himself.

'When I was no longer under the influence of Philippe, I realised that his actions were, in retrospect, exactly what one would expect of an unscrupulous libertine who was bent on seduction.

I became the victim of social prejudice. I had broken all the rules governing polite society. I was soiled and used, unfit company for unsullied young ladies and gullible young heirs. The scandal that ensued left William with no choice but to send me to London.'

'You must not let the emotional scars Duplay left you with ruin your life and destroy your chance to have a warm and happy marriage. You must not give him that much satisfaction. That he wounded you in so many ways makes me furious beyond bearing, but not for one moment am I willing to believe the damage is irreparable. I will do my utmost to eradicate what he did to you. I promise you, Alice.'

Taking her in his arms, he held her close. Actions, not words, would be the only way to make her lower her guard and love him as much as he loved her. A faint, preoccupied smile played about his lips as he contemplated his strategy.

'How do you feel now you have told me?'

She sighed. 'Emotionally exhausted and drained of everything. But I'm glad I told you—that at last you know everything.'

'I can't imagine how you must have felt when you came to Barradine and let me into your bed.

Because of your memories, after all you had endured at the hands of Duplay, you must have been afraid that you would have to experience some understandable revulsion when you were again faced with the intimacy between a man and a woman. I would rather cut off my right arm than harm you in any way. Was it very difficult?'

Alice smiled and confidently shook her head. 'I wanted you and would not allow the shadow of Philippe to destroy that. I did not feel any revulsion at all with you, so there's no need to worry.'

'I'm relieved to hear that.'

'Hearing myself talking about Philippe out loud has made me realise that there is no similarity between the two of you—not at all. Philippe was a selfish, egotistical, sadistic monster, while you wanted to love and protect and provide for me. Even when I defied and infuriated you, you did not physically abuse me.' Tilting her head back, she smiled up at him. 'Thank you for listening. I know it has been difficult for you also. I've had several agonising days to try to think how we could best go on after this—assuming you wanted to—and it seemed to me that talking about it, openly and thoroughly, was the only way.'

Ewen cradled her face between his hands. 'You

must always feel that you can ask or tell me anything without fear or anger from me. I'm not proud
of the way I've treated you. I should never have
left you. I should have listened to what you had
to tell me, but I was so consumed with anger that
another man had taken what I cherished that I
was blind to anything else. I have been beset by
so many torturous imaginings that I have been
transported beyond all endurance. No man should
be made to suffer so.'

Alice listened to him while her heart beat in
chaotic rhythm. 'I didn't mean for you to suffer,
Ewen. Had I known, I would have—'

'What?' he murmured, touching her responsive
lips with his own. 'Relieved my suffering?'

'I could not have done that without you knowing the whole truth.'

'And I was a fool not to listen. You drove me
hard, Alice. You were always so close—yet so
elusive that it became torture for me just to look
at you.'

Fearfully, Alice looked up at him, his achingly
handsome face languid and his silver-grey eyes
dark with passion as his fingers gently traced the
line of her throat. 'Please tell me all is not lost,'
she begged softly.

'I'll do better than that. I will show you,' he murmured, taking her face between his hands.

The sound of his deep, reassuring voice, combined with the feeling of his strong gentle fingers closing around her face, did much to dissolve Alice's misgivings. Her gaze searching his face, she said, 'It would mean a great deal to me, and to our future together, if we could put this behind us.'

'There is nothing I want more,' he murmured, bending his head and placing his lips on hers. They stood together, locked in an embrace which contained not only love and longing, but also a calm peace.

'Love me, Ewen, and show me how to love you—how to please you.'

'Have no fear, my love. I have a thing or two to teach you as regards pleasing me. I trust you will be an avid pupil. But it's a hard thing for me to restrain myself and be tender, when I'm a man starved for so long of your pleasure.'

'Remember that I am no fragile miss. I will remind you that you must please me, too, my lord.'

'And I shall, Alice,' Ewen murmured, looking deep into her eyes. 'And by all that is holy, I shall love you until I die.'

'I like the sound of that,' Alice whispered, tears misting her eyes. 'I love you, Ewen, and I, too, shall love you until I die. But—I have just opened my heart for you. Will you not do the same? Is there not something you have to tell me—about Etta?'

Ewen's eyes narrowed warily. 'Etta? How…?'

'I know you loved someone—when you were a captive. Amir told me when we travelled to Scotland together.'

Anger blazed in Ewen's eyes for a moment, but then he shrugged resignedly. 'He had no right to tell you.'

'He told me nothing else. Only her name. I know that whatever it was that happened hurt you very badly. I think we need each other to heal wounds that are deep, to teach us how to let ourselves love and be loved in return. Will you not tell me?'

'I have never told anyone—only Amir.'

'Was she a slave—like you?' Alice prompted gently.

He nodded, the muscles in his throat worked convulsively. 'Yes,' he answered hoarsely. 'Etta was the Sultan's number-one concubine. She was beautiful—dark haired, like you. She was also as deceitful and wicked and treacherous as sin.'

Alice stared at him. 'What are you saying? That you did not love her?'

He nodded. 'I don't think I ever loved her, but at the time I did not know it. I came to realise that what I had felt for her was something more primitive than love—something ancient and terrible—and ugly. Whatever it was that bound me to her was so powerful that I was in danger of losing my immortal soul.'

'Tell me, so that I can understand.'

'The rules that governed the harem were strictly observed and no one but the Sultan and his eunuchs were allowed into the inner sanctum. The concubines spent the greater part of their lives shut away from the outside world and rarely left this forbidden corner of the palace. Clandestine meetings were made with great risk.'

'A risk you were prepared to take.'

He nodded. 'I was young, angry, a slave—dazzled by her beauty. When the Sultan was away from the palace for some weeks and she took me to her bed, I could not leave her. What she gave me brought fresh meaning to my miserable life and helped me survive the days and nights. I thought she felt the same. But when the Sultan returned she betrayed me, accusing me to his face of panting after her like a dog—even when she spurned me.' Lowering his head, when he next spoke his voice was low and filled with the pain he had felt then. 'My punishment was to be flayed until I became unconscious and consigned to spend what was left of my life at the oars.'

'No,' Alice moaned, wrapping her arms around her and closing her eyes as she tried to blot out the image of her husband being subjected to such demented evil. She stared at him as if seeing him for the first time. There was anger in her for the perpetrators of such a brutal crime and an immense pity which welled up from the bottom of her heart towards this man whose sufferings she at last understood.

A heavy silence replaced Ewen's strangely calm, slow voice, broken only by the sound of the river as it tumbled over the stones on its rocky bed. A lump in her throat, Alice struggled to find words which were neither foolish nor hurtful, for she sensed in Ewen a raw and quivering sensitivity. It was Ewen, however, who first broke the silence, speaking in a voice which was controlled, but tinged with pain.

'During the long, exhausting hours of my captivity, chained to an oar, I chided myself relentlessly for having been tempted by her, for having believed she felt as I felt. Remembering, I hated myself with a hatred and contempt that were absolutely bottomless. Had I resisted her, I would not have been condemned to the galleys.'

'If you look at it another way, Ewen, if she had not betrayed you, you might very well still be in captivity.'

He swallowed audibly. 'Yes, you are right.' Raising his head, he took hold of her shoulders and drew her to his chest, needing to feel the warmth of her, the living flesh of her. Placing his cheek against her hair, he held her close. 'But much has happened since that time. My remembrance of her has become diminished by the passage of time. Only now, since meeting you, am I able to see myself in a whole new different light. Now I have you, Alice. In degrees of love, I have to admit that my feelings for you transcend anything I have felt before. It seems impossible and yet I know it is true, for here I am, totally enamoured with you, my love.'

Ewen's heart was beating so hard Alice could feel it against her own. Raising her face to his, she whispered, 'Kiss me.'

His mouth consumed hers with a hunger that

demanded more, rousing her sensations and persuading her heart to beat in a frantic rhythm.

When they had returned to the house, they immediately sought sanctuary in his bed where his mouth became a living flame as it skimmed over her flesh, his passion gathering in intensity until she was quivering from the pleasure his lips evoked. Alice was enslaved by him and the heat of his mouth laid bare all her senses as her sanity fled and he covered her naked form with his own, crushing his lips over her proffered mouth, fired by a hungry urgency that would not be denied.

There was no holding back. In a mounting, ungovernable surge of fierce, dominant desire, Ewen forced her backwards with his strength, dominating her in the only way he knew. In her heart and mind and resolution she was as strong as he and he knew he would never subdue her will to his, but he could master her body, which suddenly he desperately needed to do.

His hands crushed her to him, his passion flowing through him at the feel of her silken flesh beneath them, becoming sensual and tender at the same time. Her breasts gleamed white in the candlelight, the tiny buds of her nipples a rich rosy pink and hard in the centre. His hands reached for them, knowing she wouldn't deny him, for she was sighing for him now, moaning at the back of her throat which arched with her body better to accommodate his.

He exercised rigid control, touching and kissing her with the skill and expertise of a virtuoso playing a violin. He enjoyed her, making her lose control. She was dazed with it, only half-aware of him and the warm and gentle embrace. He kissed her softly, smoothing her hair back from her unfocused eyes. He was completely in control of her as she floated back from the rapture he had created for her.

Ewen finally took possession of her with a masterful passion which no other woman had ever roused in him. This time it was he who dominated and she who welcomed it. Her body was drawn out in a long stretching of pleasure, willing, eager to receive. They enjoyed one another as men and women do. It was as simple as that with no impediment of emotion or declarations of love and when it was over, Alice sighed and melted into her husband's embrace, unable to believe that she could feel such joyous elation quivering inside.

She was overjoyed that she had been able to

give Ewen what he had desired and sought from her since making her his wife and her only regret was that she had made him wait so long—that she had denied them both the pleasure they were able to give each other. If only she had known it could be like this. Now she did, Ewen would find her an eager, willing wife.

As Ewen held her within his arms, he realised that nothing and no one would ever be able to come between the two of them, that a love like theirs could survive many things and endure the many torments life would throw at them. He knew he would never be strong enough to reject Alice completely. The desire born of pain and hopelessness that had pushed him towards Etta had become a force of habit necessary to his physical well-being, but it seemed a poor sort of emotion compared with the joy he felt just holding Alice in his arms.

It soon became clear to everyone that something important had happened between his lordship and his wife. There was a distinct softening in their attitudes towards each other. Alice positively sparkled, and Ewen no longer went around with a face like an angry bear.

Sometimes the joy of his love for Alice bubbled

up within him until he was giddy with it and, whenever they came together in the intimate rites of love, he felt as eager and excited as an untried youth with his first conquest. Each time she lay in his arms, he marvelled at the overwhelming, all-consuming tenderness and devotion that throbbed in his heart for her.

The lone man who made his way to Barradine was beset with many woes. The battle on Culloden Field had taken place twenty-one years ago, but the memories were still as sharp as glass for Iain Frobisher. Too many people had died that day. Here, more than anywhere else, he felt the memory of that day in the very ground he walked upon, in the landscape all around him, the memory of the ghosts and the earth turned red.

He followed the shepherds' track as he had done many times before. As so often, the ancient landscape brought back memories and at his side walked the ghosts of his family and the men of courage who had stood firm and fought against England's tyranny.

Waiting for the rain to cease so she could ride out, Alice was staring moodily out of an upstairs window when she saw the man moving slowly up the drive in the direction of the house. He was tall and thin and shabbily dressed. He wore a wide-brimmed hat and his head was bent forward so that she could not see his face as, assisted by a long stick, he put one weary foot in front of the other. Close to the house he stopped, lifting his face.

Alice's hand was at her throat, then at her mouth as though to keep in the sound which was surely about to erupt. His resemblance to her brother William was so evident that this man must be a relative—her father.

'Dear God! Let it be!'

Her face was chalk white and her eyes had darkened to a blue that was almost black. Turning from the window, she began to move quickly, hurrying down the stairs and running across the hall to the door. Flinging it open, she stepped out. She felt her heart, usually so steady and strong, lurch with joy. Standing in the doorway she watched the man approach at a steady pace, unaware that she was holding her breath.

'Oh, my goodness!' she gasped.

Surprised by her sudden appearance, the man stopped short. Out of a lined, gaunt face his fading, piercing blue eyes settled on her face. An uncertain smile quivered for a moment on his thin lips, which faded, as if a curtain had been drawn across by some invisible hand and he looked at Alice with sudden disquiet.

'Who are you?' he queried, his voice hoarse.

She stood frozen in place, her eyes roving lovingly over the man as if he were an apparition she was afraid would vanish if she moved. 'I am Alice. I—I think you are Iain Frobisher—my father,' she said, feeling her husband's quiet, supportive presence behind her.

'I am Iain Frobisher—but—Alice? This is impossible,' he muttered. 'I—I thought… How is it that you are here? How can it be…?' His face was fixed in a grim expression as if he were suppressing some profound emotion.

Alice moved to stand in front of him, having to tilt her head back to look at him. He was as tall as Ewen. 'I know you think my mother died in the fire at Rosslea—along with me and my brother William. But she managed to escape—to reach Ireland and then go on to France. She—she thought you were dead…all these years… But I will explain everything later. It is a long story and too complicated to explain here, Father.'

The cherished title was like a tender caress softly soothing him and tears welled up in his tired eyes as he sighed the words. 'Alice. My little Alice.'

He put his arms around his daughter and hugged her hard. 'I thought you were dead.'

Then he began to cry.

Ewen looked away from the outpouring of emotion, giving them time. After a moment he turned and looked at his wife intently as though to assess the effect of this bombshell. When the emotional moment was over and she disengaged herself from her father's arms, he ushered them inside, instructing one of the maidservants to bring refreshments.

'Father, this is wonderful. But where have you been? Until recently we thought you were dead,' Alice said, weeping and laughing all at once. She drew him towards the hearth where a welcoming fire blazed. She was so overcome that she found it difficult to analyse her feelings. 'It is not natural for those who are so close to be strangers to each other.'

Iain was gazing at her with a mixture of delighted and anguished astonishment. His features shone with joy. 'I am dreaming! It is really you!

Good heavens, child, how lovely you have grown! Your mother…'

'Mother died when I was a child.' She squeezed his arm gently when she saw the pain enter his eyes. 'I am sorry. William still lives in France. We will write to him and tell him you are indeed alive. He will want to see you.' Alice told him of Duncan Forbes and he confirmed his account of their meeting in London and that they had indeed been imprisoned together on the hulks on the River Thames. 'When I came to England he saw my name in the papers. He approached me on the chance that I was your daughter.'

'What brought you to Barradine?' Ewen asked.

'I was told you were looking for me so I came. I was a frequent visitor to Barradine in the old days. Simon was a good friend of mine. I am glad he escaped the English after Culloden. I lost two of my sons. Along with other brave men they fought gallantly in defence of the Jacobite cause, but we failed to win the day.' He glanced at his daughter. 'Come and sit by me and let me look at you. I am trying to think what miracle could have brought you here.'

Iain sat in the chair Ewen proffered while Alice, wanting to be as close to this man whose presence had been denied her all her life, chose to sit on a low stool at his knee.

'Alice is my wife,' Ewen informed him. 'I trust this meets with your approval. Had I known where to find you I would have sought your approval. As it was I wrote and asked William.'

'I approve absolutely,' he said, taking his daughter's hand in his own thinly fleshed hands. 'Alice could not have married into a more worthy family. But tell me about your mother and what William is doing in France, Alice. Tell me what I have missed. Had I known you had escaped the fire, that you were in France, I would have come to you. As it was I believed I had no family.'

The refreshments arrived just as Alice began her story. Her father did not utter a word all the time she was speaking, although he stirred restlessly more than once. When she reached the end of her recital, the echo of her words lingered in the hall as Iain drained his cup. Still without speaking, he set it down and remained for a while in contemplation of his clasped hands. Alice respected his silence, stifling her anxiety.

At last he raised his eyelids and looked at her and Alice shivered at the unhappiness in his eyes.

'Your mother—my dear wife, how courageous she was to flee Scotland—how she must have suffered.'

'What happened to you, Father, when you jumped into the River Thames? When they failed to find you—everyone thought you had drowned.'

He sighed, slowly shaking his head. 'I almost did. I don't remember much about it. I remember being shot and hitting my head and going under the water. The next I knew I was being tended by a woman who never left my bedside for the weeks it took me to recover. Her name was Kate Bentley.' A faraway look came into his eyes. 'Many were the times when I prayed for the Lord to take me. I'd heard what had happened to Rosslea—the soldiers taking us to London took great delight in telling me about the fire—that there were no survivors.

'Under Kate's care my strength slowly returned. She told me that her son had pulled me from the water after dark. When I left her I wandered aimlessly—taking work where I could.'

'Why did you not return to Scotland?'

He shrugged. 'The memories hurt. Besides, in the early days I feared that if I showed my face over the border I would be arrested. It wasn't until after my meeting with Duncan Forbes that I decided to head north.'

'But—where do you live?' Alice asked with concern.

He shrugged. 'Nowhere. I sleep where I can find work—or in sheep huts on the moor—wherever there is a place for me to lay my head.'

Tears of immense sadness clogged Alice's throat. 'Oh, Father, that is no kind of life. Now we have found each other you cannot go back to it. I won't let you. Ewen was told by the villagers that a man was often seen at Rosslea. Was that you?'

He nodded. 'Aye.' He looked at her, tenderly tracing the curve of her chin with his finger. 'If only I'd known the fire hadn't claimed you. Our lives would have been so different.'

Alice took his hand and held it against her cheek. 'There was no one to tell you that it hadn't. You weren't to know. But now we have found each other you will stay here with us. Is that not right, Ewen?' she asked, looking beseechingly at her husband.

'I would have it no other way,' he answered, pouring Iain Frobisher a glass of his best brandy.

* * *

It was a promise he reaffirmed to Alice much later that night, as he held her in his arms, his body sated, his spirit quietly joyous.

Alice nestled her face into his shoulder and splayed her fingers over his bare chest in a sleepy exploration that was beginning to have a dramatic effect on the rest of his body. 'I love you,' she whispered, tipping her face up to his and placing a soft kiss on the pulse that was beating a tattoo in his neck. 'I love you for being so kind and understanding to my father, and for offering him a home here with us.'

Ewen decided she could house the whole Frobisher clan at Barradine and that they could stay as long as they liked, if she would continue to look at him as she did now. He told her that with a laughing groan as her hand drifted lower...

One year later

Picturesque and fascinating, Villa Tremain was set within acres of park and beautiful gardens.

Simon Tremain, thickset and greyer in middle age, but still the handsome man who had captured Henrietta's heart in Scotland, had just taken his guests on a grand tour of his vineyard. He was extremely proud of his vineyard—which was a far cry from Scotland and its strife.

The Tremains and the Frobishers, now joined into one, wandered happily back to the house. William Frobisher and his wife, Anne, assisted Iain, William's bone-weary father, to a comfortable chair, while Matthew Brody sat in a chair beside his wife, the Dowager Lady Mary, and sipped from a glass of brandy. Lady Mary was content to have her family all together.

It was into this happy gathering that Simon and Henrietta's offspring burst, having returned flushed and excited from their ride, two boys with shining black hair and blue eyes and a very pretty girl.

The last to enter were Alice and Ewen, with their arms entwined and happy smiles on their faces, for the day bore nothing but blissful family togetherness. Ewen and Alice had journeyed from Barradine with Alice's father to Paris, where they had stayed a few days with William and Anne, before all of them had set off for Bordeaux.

Ewen had invited Amir to accompany them to France, but Amir had no wish to leave Scotland. It was behind the stout walls of Barradine, in the feeling of security and strength which emanated from them, that Amir had found the quiet, peaceful existence of which he was sorely in need. He would be content to await their return at Barradine. Alice suspected there was another reason why Amir was reluctant to leave Barradine—a warmth would appear in his eyes whenever they rested on Tess and Tess did not appear to object to his attention—in fact, she appeared to encourage it. Alice was quietly delighted and hoped that when they returned to Scotland the two of them would have an announcement to make.

Before they had left, Alice had received a letter from Roberta. Amid much pomp and ceremony she had married her Viscount and was living in Kent blissfully happy.

The reunion of the two families and introduction of new members had taken place when they had arrived at Villa Tremain the day before. It had been an emotional moment for Simon and Iain. They had parted company on Culloden Field, neither of them knowing whether the other would live or die.

That night they ate in the courtyard and sat long over the meal until it was dark. It was a joyous time for everyone. They talked desultorily about a variety of things, with much reminiscing and re-membering of family and friends past and present.

Ewen looked to where Matthew and his mother and Iain sat together looking proudly on.

'Did you ever imagine,' he said to Simon, 'that you would see our elders looking so utterly happy? It would seem we've gifted them with new life by bringing the two families together.'

Simon winked knowingly at his brother. 'I think a family soon to be extended if Henrietta's suspicions about Alice are to be believed. Congratulations, Brother. You've done well.'

Ewen grinned. 'I trust I can count on you to keep your silence until my wife decides she wants to make it public. I think an announcement will be made any day now.'

Alice opened the French windows of the room she shared with her husband and stepped outside. The moon shone bright and in the distance she could just make out the pepper-pot towers of a château and the terracotta-coloured roofs of the houses in the little village close by. And there below them were the beautiful landscaped gardens and the sound of clear water running through, and beyond them the ever-present vines.

She smiled as her husband joined her. His arm came around her shoulder, drawing her close as his other hand slipped underneath the large shawl that she had draped round her to mask her pregnancy, which had just begun to protrude beneath the covering of the wrap. He fondly caressed the gentle roundness.

'I think you like it here, my love,' Ewen murmured.

Alice looked up with loving eyes. 'I like it very well. We are fortunate in our families. I never thought it was possible to be so happy. Tomorrow we will tell them about the baby.' Sighing, she leaned back in his arms. 'Our child will be the first of many.'

Ewen laughed, bending his head and nibbling her earlobe. 'One is enough to begin with.'

'And this one—would you be disappointed if we had a girl?'

Turning her round within his arms, he covered her mouth with his in a long, searing kiss. Alice sighed contentedly, nestling against him as his arms folded around her. 'I would love a daughter,' he murmured at last. 'Boy or girl—is fine with me. If I could be given a choice, I'd like to have at least one of each.'

'Not at the same time, surely,' she protested, laughing softly as she traced her fingertip along the firm curve of his jaw. 'I'd like to have a son who looks just like you.'

'Simon's boys certainly look like him,' Ewen mused aloud. 'It would seem there is a strong possibility of that being the case. But then, I think I should like a daughter who looks like you.'

Taking his hand, Alice placed it over their baby. 'Can you feel it?'

'It's becoming more noticeable,' he commented softly. 'I am sure that all is well.'

'And it will be born in Scotland—at Barradine.'

'We will be back long before then.'

'I do love you, Ewen Tremain, and you shall never have cause to doubt it.'

Five months later their child, a fine, healthy boy, was born at Barradine.

Ewen never did doubt his wife's love.

* * * * *